YOUR LOVE IS SWEET

A LIGHT & LOVE SWEET ROMANCE

LEE STRAUSS

COPYRIGHT

GABRIELE HAD DARED her to do this. "Just walk in, sign your name, and play a song for heaven's sake." It was easy for her to say. Eva Baumann's sister didn't understand what it was like to be afraid. What it was like to be invisible. Gabriele oozed confidence, tall and lithe like a runway model, lighting up every room she entered. She was pretty, talented, smart.

And not handicapped.

Eva eyed the graffiti-marred entrance of the Blue Note and watched as other musicians and-patrons strolled into the darkened room. Music pumping from the sound system escaped into the narrow corridor of four-story stone buildings every time the heavy wooden door opened and closed. Eva carefully set down her guitar case and rested her hand over her chest, willing her heartbeat to slow. The muscle pulsed erratically, and her stomach wanted to dry heave.

Eva gripped her cane with white knuckles. She'd learned to master the uneven sidewalks with careful steps, but the cobblestones were still a nemesis, especially in colder months like February. The rubber knob on the tip of her cane had to center on a stone, otherwise she could lose her balance and fall. It was necessary to wait for a break in traffic or to continue to the corner for a walk light before daring to cross the street.

She took a deep breath. She could do this. This was

just an irrational fear—not real. Nothing bad would happen to her in that room. It was filled with people who loved music as much as she did. It was loud and crowded and dark, and no one would expect her to talk. When they called her name, she'd focus on the small stage, blocking out everyone in the room out until she safely stepped up. Then she'd just close her eyes and pretend she was at the street church playing to the people who came for the soup they provided.

She could do this.

A cold wind blew hair across Eva's face and she snapped to attention just as the little green man flashed on to indicate it was safe to walk. She lumbered across with a guitar in her left hand and her cane in her right. The weight of her instrument pulled her shoulders forward, her back arching slightly under her winter jacket. She caught her reflection in a store window and frowned. She looked like a crazy, old lady, not a twenty-year-old girl.

Eva tucked her cane under her left armpit and reached for the door. It swung open sharply, a patron had exited at the same moment, and she was shoved against the wall, nearly losing her balance.

"Excuse me," the guy said. He held the door open, waiting for her to go in. She wanted to turn around and head straight home, but the guy's eyes stayed on her, waiting. The cold air whooshed inside.

It would be impolite not to pass through. "Thank you," she said softly. She leaned on her cane and entered. She'd been to the Blue Note before. Gabriele and her British boyfriend Lennon Smith had dragged her out one night, so she knew what to expect. There was a bar to the right and table seating to the left. A poster on the wall read: "If you want to chat with your pals while the band is playing, take your conversation outside." The air smelled of beer and cigarette smoke clinging to damp wool jackets. At the back of the mid-sized room was a small stage lit by two lights hanging from the ceiling.

Her stomach churned, and once again she questioned herself. Why had she come? What did she have to prove? Why did she care so much what Gabriele thought? She stared back at the door.

"Hello, *ma Cherie*. Would you like to sign your name?"

The gruff yet friendly voice stopped Eva before she could leave. She knew the manager, Herr Maurice Leduc, by reputation, but had never spoken to him before. "I don't know," she answered.

"Well—" His eyes darted to the guitar in her hand. "I just thought since you lugged that thing in with you." He pushed the sign-up sheet closer.

Eva didn't have the heart to deny the man. She took the pen and scribbled her name.

"Wonderful," Herr Leduc said with a sincere grin that filled a round face. "I look forward to hearing you play..." he glanced down at his sheet, "Eva Baumann."

The room consisted of a lot of wood. Tables, chairs, benches and floors—all darkly stained, old wood. Even the ceiling had rough, open wood beams. Eva claimed a nearby empty chair and breathed in and out, long and slow. She was here. She'd done it. Wait until she told Gabriele. Wouldn't she be surprised?

A server arrived, and Eva ordered a cola. The other people who shared the long table gave her sideways glances at her childish drink and cheered each other as they lifted their beer glasses.

Herr Leduc walked on stage and welcomed everyone. He called the first act, a girl with long, golden hair, he introduced as Katja Stoltz.

Eva listened intently, impressed with the girl's talent

and the way she took over the stage like she owned it. That was what Eva needed to do. Own it.

The girl finished her song, and after much-deserved applause, she joined her friends at a table across the room. A guy in his early twenties with a peacock tattoo along one arm stood to give Katja Stoltz a hug. He had messy, dark brown hair and bristles on his face, like he hadn't shaved in a few days. He laughed and high-fived her before sitting and draping the peacock around a thin girl with spiky hair.

A shiver ran up Eva's back. She recognized that guy. Last summer, when she was playing guitar for the homeless, many of them had raised their hands to heaven. The outside metal blinds had been raised, they always were when the church was open, and a group of guys had stopped to watch from across the street. They began to laugh and then threw their arms in the air, mocking the people singing inside.

That was the first time Eva had seen that peacock tattoo, and she'd never forget the laughing face of the handsome guy who went with it.

Her short-lived confidence shriveled at the thought of being the man's next target. Oh, why did she come? She'd leave right now if she thought she could do it without making a scene. The room had filled, and there was no way she could slip out unnoticed with her guitar and her cane.

She sipped her cola and kept her eyes focused on each act as it was called. Every time Herr Leduc stepped to the mic to call a name, Eva's heart filled with nervous dread and emptied with a flush of relief when she didn't hear hers.

"Sebastian Weiss," Herr Leduc said.

The guy with the peacock tattoo hooted, shifted out from behind his table and grabbed his guitar.

So that was his name.

He hopped onto the stage and strapped on a guitar with an over-confidence Eva envied. She wanted him to be terrible so that she could add self-delusion to his other obvious traits of conceit and insensitivity, but unfortunately he wasn't. His voice was smooth and strong, and he had great range.

She also happened to notice the flex in his biceps that poked out of the short sleeves of his dark T-shirt and how his jeans fit nicely on slender hips.

He finished his song and fisted the air like he just won a boxing match. The audience went crazy. Eva couldn't help but join in the applause. Something about Sebastian was electric. His aura and competence, his popularity—she couldn't peel her eyes off him. His arm returned to its position around the girl beside him who hadn't smiled once. Such a contrast to Sebastian who couldn't stop smiling. He seemed quite taken by the pixie girl and kissed her excitedly on the cheek.

"Eva Baumann."

What? Eva had been so busy watching the table of cool people, she hadn't been paying attention.

Herr Leduc's accented German bellowed again. "Eva Baumann."

Eva's heart stopped. Then raced. Her hands broke out into a sweat, and she blinked back the tears welling up behind her eyes, which were opened far too wide. Her head prickled hotly, and she swallowed hard. She could sense the attention of the room, necks craning, everyone searching, waiting for the next act to stand.

Herr Leduc stared at her, and all she could do was shake her head. He gave her a gracious nod and called the next name.

A girl with short, dark hair bounced out of her seat,

and within seconds Eva was forgotten. She took advantage of the swirl of commotion that occurred between acts, grabbing her guitar and cane, and limped to the entrance.

It was a terrible mistake to come, she thought as she hobbled down the crusty street. She kept her head bowed low against the cold, and gripped her guitar case and her cane. If she'd had a third hand, she'd swipe at the bitter tear that slid down her cheek.

ONE YEAR LATER

Sebastian Weiss wrapped the oversized pillow around his ears in a vain effort to block out the pounding on his locked hotel room door. His head throbbed and his mouth felt like sandpaper. He released a slow, low groan. "Go away!"

"Sebastian!" Karl called from the hallway. "The bus is waiting. Get your rear in gear!"

Sebastian tossed the silky pillow across the room and worked the sleep out of his eyes. The bright light that seeped in from the crack in the curtains was like a torch to his eyeballs. He blindly grasped for the hotel phone on the nightstand and somehow managed to punch the numbers for room service.

"Orange juice and coffee. A whole carton of juice and a full carafe of coffee." He'd learned he had to be specific. The first time they'd arrived with a tiny glass and cup of each, and he had to suffer needlessly for another twenty minutes before the service returned with what he needed.

He popped a couple aspirin and downed them with the stale water in a glass by the phone. He gave them two minutes to kick in then stumbled to the shower. The coffee and orange juice would be waiting in the hall when he was finished.

He dug the last clean T-shirt out of his suitcase and

pulled on the jeans he'd worn for the last two days. His room service order waited for him in the hall, and he pushed it inside. He downed the juice in several gulps, breaking once or twice to breathe. This was followed by a swig of coffee; he poured the rest into his travel mug.

At this point in his routine, Sebastian started to feel normal again. Like a computer reboot. He'd come alive on the bus, and by the time they hit the next city, he would be high again—on adrenaline and other things—ramping up for their next concert.

Dirk, their manager, was in the lobby checking out the band when Sebastian arrived. He raised a brow over black plastic-rimmed glasses. "Just in time," he said. "The others are already on the bus."

Sebastian pushed his sunglasses on his face. The brightness of the sun streaming through the windows shot pain to the back of his head. He winced as he exited the hotel and quickly handed his bags over to Florian, the bus driver.

"Next stop, Hamburg!" Florian shouted, and Sebastian winced again as the driver's booming voice made his head feel like someone was trying to rip it off. He climbed on board and took a seat near the front. Karl spotted him and moved up to the empty seat behind him.

"Three more dates, Sebastian, and this tour's over. Time flies."

Sebastian nodded. "I still can't believe we're actually doing this." Touring with his band, Hollow Fellows, had been a dream for so long that he'd lost heart in the pursuit. Funny how things tended to take off once you'd given up the chase.

Karl raked a hand through long, stringy hair. "The gig in Hamburg is being televised! A year ago, I never would've imagined this could happen. But here we are, on our own tour bus, giggin' in front of the cameras. On freakin' TV!" He patted Sebastian on the shoulder. "We're doing it, Seb. We're actually doing it!"

Hollow Fellows' hit song, "What Drives Me," had catapulted up the German radio charts over the past half year surprising everyone. It was the song he'd co-written with Katja Stoltz-Sturm. That was a lucky impromptu decision on his part, agreeing to do the songwriting session with Katja. Both of them were unknowns then. Sebastian rubbed his eyes and sighed. He hadn't written a song since.

Maybe when the tour ended, and he saw Yvonne again... maybe she'd inspire him.

A nagging truth stirred his gut. He wanted to blame life on the road and the alcohol and the ongoing fight he and Yvonne seemed to be engaged in for his writer's block. But he knew the truth.

He chugged back a sip of coffee and shook his head forcing himself to push those old, black memories away. Nothing good could come from dredging that up.

Nothing good.

EVA RAN A FINGER ALONG A THICK, pink scar that zipped up her right leg from just above her knee to the top of her thigh. Normally, she never paid it any attention. It was just a part of who she was, who she had been for the last five years. But now, as she got ready for bed, she stood in front of the mirror and examined it.

It was ugly.

She stopped asking God why this had happened to her long ago. There was no satisfying answer. No answer at all, actually.

The bedroom door flew open and Eva quickly tugged her nightdress down as Gabriele breezed into the room they shared. Gabriele kept promising to move out, but she still hadn't. She had to finish her studies at the university first. Eva felt guilty for wishing her sister gone.

Instead of her usual nightshirt, Gabriele stepped into a tiny little blue and white dress.

"Where are you going?" Eva asked as she watched Gabriele struggle with the zipper at the back.

"Can you get this?"

Eva stood and waited for Gabriele to scoot over to her. It was just faster that way, and Gabriele was always in a hurry. It was a habit they'd formed since the accident. Gabriele always came to Eva.

"Lennon's taking me out for a late dinner. It's our one year anniversary!"

"Already?" Or should she say, *Is that all?* Lennon had been hanging around so much the last few months, he'd become part of the furnishings.

"Yes, and we're going to a really fancy place in the *Altstadt.*" Gabriele floated to the spot in front of the mirror Eva had just vacated and applied hair product to her short bleach-blond hair. Her natural color was the same as Eva's, an ordinary brown, and up until a year ago, just before Lennon, Eva recalled, she wore it long, too.

Gabriele started in on her makeup attacking green eyes (another trait she shared with Eva) with several layers of mascara, and then her full lips with a tube of red. She smacked them together and said with a little squeal, "I think he wants to talk about marriage."

"What? Really?" Yay! Gabriele just got that much closer to leaving home. "That's terrific!"

"Yeah, I'm really nervous." Gabriele selected a pair of white, patent leather stilettos and slipped them on. She spread her arms wide and faced Eva. "What do you think?"

"You're beautiful." It was the truth. Gabriele had a tall, waif-like, fashion model look and the exuberance to go with it. Eva could barely believe they were sisters. Nobody could, really. Apart from their identical green eyes, they were nothing alike.

Eva put on her robe, collected her cane and followed Gabriele out into the living room where their parents joined in with her sister's excitement.

"You look wonderful," their mama said.

Papa sat on the chair facing the TV, and his eyes narrowed as he stared at Gabriele. "Isn't that dress a little short?"

Gabriele laughed. "Oh, Papa. You're so old-fashioned." She bent down and kissed him on the cheek, and Papa's faux frown broke into a smile.

The door ringer buzzed, and Gabriele danced over to let Lennon in. They could hear his footsteps as he made his way to the second floor. He barely had a chance to tap on the door of the flat when Gabriele flung it open.

Lennon wore fashionable jeans and a form-fitting button-down shirt. He wore his dark hair combed back behind his ears, and he had a slight shadow on his chin. He was average height standing eye to eye with Gabriele when she wore high heels. Eva always considered Lennon to be handsome, the only kind of guy that would fit beside her sister, but tonight he was really handsome. And he'd brought her flowers.

Gabriele accepted them, and then they spent long moments taking each other in, their eyes bright with affection. Eva couldn't keep from staring. What must it be like to be in love like that?

"Wow." Lennon shook his head subtly like he couldn't believe his good fortune. "You look gorgeous."

Gabriele blushed and giggled. Papa cleared his throat.

"Herr Baumann," Lennon said, looking up. "Good evening. And to you, too, Frau Baumann."

They engaged in polite banter while Gabriele put her flowers in a vase. Then the pretty couple left, and it was like a vacuum had sucked the sunshine out of the room.

"So, Eva," Papa finally said. "You can do the music for the lunch service on Sunday?"

Eva sighed. "I always do it. Why can't Gabriele?" Her sister was also an accomplished guitar player and a great singer. Unfortunately. For a while, Eva thought she might have one thing that set her apart from the sister who had everything, but soon after Eva started playing the guitar seriously, Gabriele decided she would too, and quickly demonstrated that they had both inherited musical genes from their mother's side.

"Ah, *Schatz,*" Papa started. "You know Gabriele."

That was all he said. Gabriele had made it clear that, though she respected their parents' call into the ministry, she had no interest in the street church. Mama could play the keyboard and sing like an angel, but she spent her time overseeing the kitchen, so the task of providing music had landed on Eva. There were others who could do it, and sometimes Eva asked for help, but the truth was, she didn't really mind. It just bothered her that Gabriele had so much, and yet so little was required of her.

"Okay, I'll do it."

Papa grunted as he lifted himself from his chair. "I'm going to review my sermon notes," he said as he left for his office. Mama had already retreated to her room where she liked to spend the evenings reading. Eva turned on the TV, flipped through the channels, then yelped.

Sebastian Weiss was on TV! She pulled her robe tighter and leaned forward. He was with his band, Hollow Fellows, playing live in Hamburg.

Eva's heart rattled in her chest as the camera zoomed in on Sebastian's face. His eyes were closed and he belted out the words with such emotion and intensity. Then he opened them and stared into the camera. It was like his warm hazel eyes were looking right at her!

She couldn't believe she'd once sat in the same room as him, a year ago at the Blue Note before he was famous. She'd been fascinated with him ever since, nursing a schoolgirl-type crush that only she and God knew about, and she had followed his rise to stardom with dedication.

He lived here, in the *Neustadt* area of Dresden. They were practically neighbors! It'd become a habit for her to stay alert to a possible Sebastian Weiss sighting when he was off tour. She hadn't seen him since that fateful open mic night, though she had spotted the girl he was with once. Eva wondered if they were still together.

Not that it mattered. In real life Eva didn't exist. She was a shadow. An echo.

But in her dreams she was… well, she was Gabriele. And Lennon was Sebastian Weiss.

FALLING TOO DEEPLY

THE HAMBURG GIG WAS A HIT, and Hollow Fellows' first televised concert sent the station's ratings soaring. They partied long into the night afterward, celebrating. Sebastian indulged in one too many beers, but he stayed clear of the women. This was one of the many things he and Yvonne argued over. She was convinced his fame would go to his head and he'd cheat on her. Successful guys were renowned for justifying themselves, rationalizing their behavior—rules didn't apply to them. That was what Yvonne believed, but Sebastian didn't think she was being fair.

He didn't know how to reassure her except to do exactly what he promised and keep clear of the girls. It was a tough job these days. Groupies, usually young, pretty girls, were coming out of the woodwork. Fortunately, the other guys in the band pulled up the slack. Karl, and their drummer Markus had a pretty girl on each arm all night.

Now, after allowing for a late sleep in, they gathered for brunch in the hotel restaurant. They had to request a private room at the back because of those very groupies. There was a collection of them waiting in the hotel lobby ready to pounce.

Sebastian sat across from Karl who sat beside Markus

and Dirk. Florian held his grey head in two hands and moaned.

"One too many last night?" Sebastian chided.

"I didn't drink anything," Florian replied with a dry voice. "Didn't feel good yesterday either."

"You don't look that good," Karl added. "A little green around the gills."

"Guys, I don't think I can drive, and I can't eat." Florian stood to leave, holding an arm around his belly. "I gotta get back to my room."

"Ah man," Markus said. "Do you think he has the flu?"

Karl grunted. "He better not get the rest of us sick."

Dirk had ordered for the band earlier and a small buffet of breakfast and lunch items was wheeled in. Buns, croissants, a collection of meats and cheeses, toast, cereal, fruit and yogurt along with coffee and a selection of juices.

Now that Sebastian's hangover had ebbed a little, his appetite kicked in and he filled his plate.

"Someone else has to drive the bus now," Dirk said after a few bites. "Any takers?"

Karl shook his head. "Not me. I plan on sleeping all the way back to Dresden."

"Sebastian?" Dirk asked.

Sebastian pushed back a wave of panic, plastered a phony smile on his face and shook his head. "I would, but I don't drive."

Dirk scoffed. "You don't drive? You mean you didn't get your license?"

Sebastian shrugged. "Never got around to it."

That wasn't true. His parents had coughed up the money to pay for the expensive lessons, and he had a barely pubescent photo on a German license to prove it.

"Fine," Dirk said. He turned to Markus. "I guess that means you and I have to do it. I'll do the first half."

They finished eating, leaving a big mess in their wake, and snuck out the back way to the lobby to escape the groupies who had yet to leave. This was part of Sebastian's new life he didn't like. He missed being able to walk about freely without photographers snapping photos and girls throwing themselves at him. It was worse when they were on tour. He worried about going home and hoped that the *Neustadt* hadn't changed as much as he had.

Their covert maneuver didn't work this time. The elevator was in the process of slowly returning from the top floor, and they had to wait precious minutes for it to arrive at ground level. Before the doors opened, one of the groupies spotted them. A chorus of calls followed.

"Sebastian!"

"Karl, Markus!"

"Hollow Fellows!"

Before the guys could escape, one of the girls jumped Sebastian and kissed him on the mouth. A flash from a camera blinded him. He knew he'd just gotten photographed in a compromising position and could only hope that Yvonne wouldn't see it. He pushed the girl off him as gently and forcibly as he could. It was bad press to be rude to fans.

He autographed a handful of CDs and one bare, feminine shoulder before the elevator doors opened and Dirk dragged him inside.

Karl laughed out loud. "I love being famous!" Sebastian high-fived him and smiled back. His best friend was having the time of his life. Sebastian just wished he could say the same thing.

He slept on the bus with just a few interruptions when the bus stopped for petrol and bathroom breaks. He found sleeping on the bus easier than sleeping alone in a dark, quiet room. The rumble lulled him to sleep and there was just enough light and motion to keep him from falling too deeply. It was in deep sleep that the bad dreams came.

Sebastian worried about Yvonne. Though she was cute, she wasn't sweet by nature. He didn't mind that. He was just grateful that she had stood by him through all the crap he went through at home when his parents disowned him for pursuing his foolish dream. She was there for him when they weren't. She was his first real girlfriend and he loved her.

He wasn't so sure she loved him in return. Not really. Lately, she'd grown distant, her demeanor cooler than usual.

They often argued, bickered really, not bonafide fighting. It was their way of communicating. Right? They'd fight, but they always made up. He could do this thing as long as she supported him. He'd bring her on the next tour. He'd sleep better if she were by his side.

Sebastian had wanted to bring her this time, but the guys had insisted—no girlfriends. But, he was the leader of this band, right? He would put his foot down next time. Yvonne would be with him snuggling through the long hours on the road. Then fame wouldn't be so bad. The unwanted attention from groupies would wane if they saw he already had a girl on his arm.

It would be okay so long as Yvonne would agree to come. She was fuming mad when he told her she couldn't come on this one. It would be just like her to refuse his offer when he invited her next time. Dig her heels in stubbornly. She was like that. Spiteful, sometimes. He'd have to woo her over again, but he was a pro at that.

It was dark when they pulled into Dresden. Sebastian texted Yvonne. *Home in fifteen. Meet me at my place?*

She was there when the bus dropped him off in front of his building, and he breathed out in relief. The worries he'd had concerning her were unmerited. He dropped his guitar case and suitcase by his feet and swooped her up, twirling her in a circle.

"Oh, I missed you, babe!"

She smiled a rare smile. "Missed you too, Basti."

He kissed her lips, and pressed her thin, little body against his. He was home, and she was here.

Everything would be fine.

SCARS THAT DEFINE

Summer was Eva's favorite season. Not just because it was warm and sunny most of the time, which of course she did like, but because it was *safe*. Or at least, safer. The walkways and cobblestone streets were dry and easy to grip with the rubber tip of her cane. She left the house in the winter only when necessary because of the ice and snow, so summer was a time of freedom for Eva as well. She moved slowly, but she was mobile and she often visited Luther Square to sit on the wooden benches and stare up at the Gothic steeple of the ancient church.

Or, if she felt braver and stronger, she'd walk to the end of *Alaunestrasse* toward the park on the other side of *Bischofsweg*. Crossing the street there was hazardous and she had to walk an extra couple blocks to get to the crosswalk with stoplights, but it was worth it. Especially on a warm, floral-scented day like today.

The park was full of people: families with young children playing on the playground, teens and young adults gathering in groups to smoke and drink beer and colas and laugh, cyclists cutting through them on the bike paths.

Eva wistfully watched one girl pass by on her bike. That used to be her, always on her bike, loving how the wind blew her hair and how her lungs expanded taking in the fresh air. How her leg muscles burned in a way that made her feel strong and athletic.

But that was *before*.

Eva spotted Gabriele and Lennon, the happy soon-to-be-married couple sitting on a blanket with a few of their friends and she watched them from a distance. Gabriele sat cross-legged with her guitar propped over her knees and began to play. Soon a crowd gathered to listen. She feigned embarrassment and put the guitar back in its case.

It was a typical Gabriele move. She was a big tease, and she basked in the praise that followed her "retirement" until she reluctantly agreed to play again. Eva found herself drawing nearer. Despite her desire to avoid being entranced by her sister's charisma, she couldn't help getting caught in her snare. There was something about Gabriele that was magnetic, irresistible.

Lennon watched Gabriele with unabashed admiration as she played. He practically threw himself at her when she finished her next song, kissing her in a way that made Eva blush. Gabriele's laughter rang out as she managed to dislodge herself, and in that moment she spotted Eva staring from outside the circle.

"Eva," she called and lifted the guitar. "Your turn!" She turned to her friends. "My sister is really talented. The true star of the family."

She gushed and waved Eva over. Eva was stunned. Had her sister gone mad? Eva couldn't play in front of these people. She'd melt into a smelly puddle under their watchful, judgmental eyes. She couldn't compete with her sister and Gabriele *knew* this. She just wanted to reaffirm that she was the better, prettier, more talented sister.

Why did Gabriele have to continually embarrass her like this? Eva spun on her heels and limped away. Gabriele had just ruined another perfect day.

"Eva!" Her sister chased after her and grabbed hold of Eva's elbow forcing her to stop. "What's the matter with you?"

Eva glared at her. "You know I can't do that."

"Do what? Play in front of people? You do it all the time at the street church."

"That's different."

"How so?"

"They don't care if you're good. Most of them can't even tell if you're good. It's…"

"Safe?" Gabriele challenged.

"Yeah. It's *safe*. Is there something wrong with that?"

"Eva, I know the accident changed things for you. It changed *you*. But you can't let your scars define you. You still have to live."

Eva blinked back tears and shook her head. "You just don't know what it's like."

"Not personally, no. But I live it every day through you." Her voice softened, "I just want you to be happy. I want you to be fearless, again."

Eva forced a smile. She'd forgive her sister. That was a given. She could never stay angry with Gabriele. "Thanks. I have to go now."

She heard Gabriele huff out her frustration behind her as she turned back to her friends.

I want you to be fearless again.

Eva would like that, too. She just didn't see how that was possible.

Sᴇʙᴀsᴛɪᴀɴ ʜᴀᴅ ᴋɪᴄᴋᴇᴅ out his lazy, noisy, filthy roommates the month the money started rolling in. They protested, but it was Sebastian's name on the lease, so he was the one to call the shots. He actually missed the energy their presence had brought to the place for the first couple of days, but he didn't miss the mess. Now, after being with guys day after day on the road, he was relieved to have the place to himself.

The early morning light woke him gently, but his bladder was a little more demanding. He stretched out his arm for Yvonne, but instead his fingers stroked empty, cool sheets.

He groaned and hefted himself out of bed. Yvonne never stayed. He understood why she had insisted on sneaking away before dawn when his roommates were exhaling their bad morning breath everywhere, but now that he lived alone he just didn't get it. Her roommates certainly wouldn't care if she stayed out all night.

At least he knew she wasn't after his money. Or his fame. At least there was that.

He showered, dressed in lightweight jeans and a muscle shirt and headed for the kitchen. A cursory look told him what he already knew. He didn't have any food. Or coffee.

He tugged on his cap and slipped on a pair of wide-lens aviators and headed out. Dresdeners didn't normally rank people one over the other, so there was a good chance he could accomplish his goal of finding breakfast without being mauled. He walked past headbangers and stoners, young pregnant women and women pushing strollers. Well-dressed folks mingled among those who pretty much wore the same thing every day. All he had to do was keep his head down.

There was a good café and bakery run by ol' Maurice's new lady friend. He stepped inside and breathed in the rich aromatic scent. Fortunately, the place wasn't very busy at the moment.

Frau Beck was at the counter when Sebastian reached it. He was in the habit of keeping his cap and glasses on now, and he refrained from removing them when he ordered.

"Coffee, black and strong. Two brötchen with ham and butter cheese, please."

"Certainly," Frau Beck said with a smile. "And you can remove your sunglasses, young man. I already know who you are." She smiled conspiratorially. "I won't tell."

Sebastian pulled them off, hoping his eyes weren't too bloodshot and awful. "Thank you. I appreciate it."

"Are you in town for long?" Frau Beck poured his coffee, placed it on the tray and took out the pre-prepared buns.

Sebastian took the coffee and sipped it even though he'd yet to pay. "Um, not very long. Our next tour starts in two weeks."

"I hope you're enjoying your success."

Sebastian nodded. He would try. "Do you still keep in touch with Katja?" he asked.

Frau Beck rang up his order and he handed her the cash.

"Yes," she said. "She's quite happy with her life in Berlin now. And with being a new bride as you know."

That was right. The last time Sebastian saw Frau Beck was at Katja and Micah's wedding.

"Thank you, Frau Beck. It's good to see you again." Sebastian picked up his tray, searched for an empty table and sat with his back to the door. He put his sunglasses back on as a precaution and wolfed down his breakfast.

His phone buzzed in his pocket and he reached for it, hoping the text was from Yvonne. It wasn't. Dirk was calling a meeting in one hour. Seriously? They couldn't have one freaking day off?

He tipped back his coffee mug until every last drop dribbled into his mouth. Then, after taking a quick glance over his shoulder to ensure he hadn't been spotted, he slipped back outside into the sunlight. The bright sky and hot weather legitimized his use of a cap and glasses, but even so, he kept his shoulders hunched and his chin down.

To get to Dirk's flat, Sebastian had to walk past the street church. His mind was full of so much junk he'd forgotten to cross to the other side of the road like he usually did. On most days he believed in some kind of higher power, but he didn't like religion. Religion caused nothing but trouble in the world as far as he was concerned. But, here he was, right in front of the street church, the metal blinds opened wide. The people inside were preparing for a soup line. He could smell the savory aroma escaping from the propped-open door.

A girl sat on a low stool plucking strings on a guitar. Something made him stop to listen. She wasn't plugged in, so he had to strain to hear her play, and he conceded that she was pretty good. An older lady entered the room and the girl looked up from under her sheath of straight, brown hair.

Sebastian stroked his chin, thinking. He'd seen this girl before, but he couldn't remember where. He'd probably just bumped into her in the grocery store one time. He pulled down his cap, shoved his fists deep into his pockets and kept walking. Didn't matter. It wasn't like their paths would ever cross again.

He hurried to meet the guys at Karl's new flat. He and Markus had each moved to flats on a nicer street with more square meters and higher price tags. Evicting his roommates was enough of a step up for Sebastian. He liked his Neustadt neighborhood and his unassuming apartment building. Yvonne had pleaded with him to make a change when the other guys were doing it, but he didn't see the point. Maybe if she'd agree to move in with him once and for all, he'd consider it.

He pushed the buzzer and Karl let him in. He and Karl went way back, as far as kindergarten. He was like the brother Sebastian never had, and they fought and annoyed each other like real siblings.

"Hey," Sebastian said. He went straight to the fridge and grabbed a beer. "What's the big emergency?"

"Yeah, help yourself, man," Karl said.

Sebastian sat and put his feet up on the coffee table. "Always do."

Dirk and Markus were already there and they nodded at Sebastian. Dirk ran a finger over his iPad. "Okay, our schedule's getting really full."

"Let's just get to it," Sebastian said. They spent so much time together, no one expected or delivered pleasantries.

"Lots of interview requests, mostly magazines so I can fill those in, but there's a radio spot tomorrow morning. Sebastian you're on for that, eight o'clock."

"Why Sebastian?" Karl challenged. "What's wrong with me? Or Markus?"

Sebastian picked at the label on his bottle. "Yeah, let Karl do it." He didn't like to get up before noon anyway.

Dirk shook his head. "They specifically asked for you, Seb. Like it or not, guys, Sebastian is the lead singer and therefore the face of the band. We gotta give the people what they want."

Dirk looked down at his notes as if the matter was clear and settled, but Sebastian could feel the tension roll off Karl. Sebastian couldn't help how the chips had fallen. Yeah, they'd started off as a duo, but somehow Sebastian had taken the lead in the eyes of the public.

"Photo shoot in two days. Make sure you're sober. There'll be a stylist to help, but arrive in something close to what you want to wear. Shower and shampoo, too, please."

"Where is it?" Sebastian asked.

Dirk gave the address and Karl shot Sebastian a glance. "I'll drive. You can catch a ride. Just don't be late."

Yes, sir.

Dirk scratched his balding head. "We need a new CD. I hope you guys are writing."

Sebastian puffed. "It's not like we've had a lot of free time." It was an excuse, and he knew it, but he needed an excuse.

"Hey, find the time. I've booked the studio for October, so you've got two and a half months to pull twelve songs together. We've been pushing your debut for a year now. We need something new."

Sebastian slugged back the rest of his beer. He remembered when this had been fun. That had lasted about three months. Now the pressure was starting to weigh heavily.

"Next tour starts in two weeks. Dates in Nuremberg, Munich, Salzburg and Zurich."

"I'm bringing Yvonne," Sebastian said. He hadn't even asked her, but he would as soon as this meeting ended. Two weeks would be enough time for her to get her shifts covered at the bookstore where she worked.

Karl leaned forward, elbows on knees and eyed Sebastian. "No girlfriends."

"Why not?"

"Because it would make the rest of us uncomfortable."

"Then don't behave like animals."

"Yeah, and what about you two? You think we want to watch you go at it all the time?"

"We're not like that, and you know it. I promise we'll be civil in your company."

"No."

Sebastian looked at Dirk and Markus for support. "If you guys want to bring someone, I don't mind."

Markus shrugged boney shoulders.

Dirk sighed. "Look, it doesn't matter to me, but if one of us is uncomfortable with it, then we have to respect that."

"What if I'm uncomfortable? I'm uncomfortable living with pigs who do nothing but get stoned and sleep all day."

Karl stood and bore down on Sebastian. "Are you calling me a pig?"

Sebastian sprang to his feet in response. "Maybe I am."

Two seconds later, Dirk had wedged himself between them. "I think we need to take five. We can't have our band break down in the first year, okay? Let's not become another stupid statistic."

WEIGHTLESS, BREATHLESS

Nerve explosions went off in her hip—it felt like dry bone against bone—and Eva bit her lip to fight back against the pain. After five years, she should have known better than to walk so far, at least without popping a pain reliever before leaving. By the time Eva made it back from the park and up the one flight of steps to the flat over the soup kitchen, she felt faint.

Her mother was stuffing dirty laundry into the machine in the compact kitchen and when she saw Eva, her smile flattened. "Is everything all right? You're sweating." Mrs. Baumann retrieved a clean cloth from a drawer, ran it under cold water and moved quickly to her daughter to pat her forehead.

Eva pulled back. "Mama, I'm fine." She hated when her mother treated her like a baby. She escaped into the WC and hung her cane on the hook her papa had fastened to the wall for that purpose. The room was small enough that she could maneuver where she needed to go without the help of the cane. In fact, in these tight quarters, her cane proved to be more harm than help. To accommodate her, bath rugs were always removed from the floor and hung over the edge of the tub otherwise she could trip and fall. They knew this because it had happened once, and

Eva still had a small white scar on her forehead at her hair-line where she'd hit it on one of the towel racks.

Her hands shook as she twisted the cap off the pill jar and shimmied one into her palm. The water from the tap was warm, and she nearly choked on it as she slugged the pill back. A rack of coughing ensued, resulting in the pounding of her mother's fist on the door.

"Eva?"

"I'm okay." Eva splashed cool water on her face. "The water just went down the wrong way." She waited until she heard her mother's slipper-covered feet pad away on the wood floors before reaching for her cane and heading to her room where she eased onto her bed, relieved to finally be lying down.

Breathe through the pain.

It met her in varying degrees depending on the type of excursion, which was why she didn't make too many. And there was always a nice dollop of emotional pain to go with it, as if the physical pain wasn't enough.

Her medication kicked in after a while, and she dozed a little. When her eyes fluttered back to consciousness, her gaze rested on her guitar in its stand in the corner. She hobbled to the chair beside it and cradled it on her lap. It was a Duncan Africa, handmade by local craftsmen in Uganda, and it played beautifully. After the accident, when it became apparent that she would never drive, her parents had bought her this guitar. Gabriele got driving lessons.

It was a consolation prize of sorts, but now Eva couldn't imagine living without it. Plus, its origins reminded her that there were people in the world who had a harder go of it than she did.

Thought I came to wet my lips
Maybe cool my feet

But you pushed me from behind

Eva hadn't written in a long time and suddenly it was like the pen in her hand couldn't write down the ideas fast enough. She was interrupted by a knock on the door and her mother's head poked in.

"Mama, I'm busy."

"Annette's here. I thought you'd like to see her."

Annette was Eva's ginger-haired friend from *before*. She really didn't have any friends from *after*, except for the regulars that came to the soup kitchen twice a week, if you could call them friends. Eva used to have a lot of friends, but they gradually faded away as Eva withdrew from life and they continued on with theirs. Annette had been the one exception, stubbornly holding on to whatever thread of friendship was left between them.

"Hey, Eva."

"Hi. Come on in."

Annette sat on the bed, getting comfortable against Eva's big pillow like she'd done a million times. Her gaze moved from Eva's guitar to the pen in her hand. "Are you writing a song?"

Great deduction. "Yeah."

"Can I hear it?"

"It's too soon. I haven't even finished it. But when it's done for sure."

Annette twisted the end of her ponytail around her index finger. "So, what's new?"

"Gabriele and Lennon are getting married."

Annette's face lit up and she squealed. "That's fantastic. They are such a cute couple!"

"It is. And I know."

"When?"

"Soon. Lennon's in a big hurry." Eva grinned. "I think

Gabriele's holding out on him. We're good Christian girls, you know."

"Nothing wrong with being a good Christian girl."

"Not at all. Gabriele is almost finished at the university, so the wedding is after that."

"Oh, it's so romantic. And Lennon is so cute. I love his British accent."

"His German is hilarious. Good thing she is majoring in English. Who knows? They might move to England."

Annette sighed. "Such an adventure. So, what about you?"

Eva blinked. "What do you mean?"

"Any cute boys?"

"At the soup kitchen?"

Annette frowned. "Eva, when are you coming to university?"

Annette was in her first year. Eva had opted to take time off. She'd been behind in her studies since her accident and pleaded that she needed to catch up. Only, she hadn't been catching up.

"I don't know," she hedged and placed down her pen.

Annette sprung off the bed and went to stare out the window. There was a commotion going on outside, not unusual for *Alaunstrasse*. Eva was so used to bouts of shouting and hollering and music of every style blaring randomly, she never bothered to look anymore.

"Oh my gosh, Eva."

"What is it?"

"I think that's… it is! It's Sebastian Weiss!"

Eva sat the Duncan Africa back in its stand, grabbed her cane and moved faster than she'd thought possible until she stood beside Annette at the window.

He wore a cap and glasses, but it was clearly him. He was walking right by their building! Someone had recognized him, and he stopped in front of the Italian restaurant across the street to sign autographs. Her heart palpitated. He was so close! If he just tilted his head up a little, he'd spot them staring down at him from her second-floor window.

Eva took a step back. She'd be mortified if he caught her looking.

Annette startled her by calling out, "Sebastian!" Then she squealed and waved her hand like a crazy person. Eva's jaw dropped. Was Sebastian Weiss looking up at her bedroom window?

"He waved at me, Eva! Sebastian Weiss waved at me!"

Eva leaned forward a little to peek. Sebastian had moved on, his back now toward her. She sighed. She'd missed out again.

NOW I AM DROWNING

THE LAST WEEK was so busy with interviews, photo shoots and band rehearsals, Sebastian barely had time to think. He did manage to get in one good fight with Yvonne, however. She was curled up on his sofa, thin arms crossed over her small chest. When she pouted like that she looked like a pixie, almost childlike. Sebastian exhaled hard as he sat beside her. He laid his palm on her thigh. "I hate being away from you, baby. I just want you with me."

She twisted her neck and glared. "You seriously want me to drop everything and follow you around the country like one of your groupies?"

"Not like a groupie. Jeez, Yvonne. Like my girlfriend. Besides, last time you were mad because I didn't ask you to go."

Yvonne's lips tightened and she stared back across the room. "I was just mad you didn't ask. So thanks for asking, but I can't just leave my job."

"I'm making enough money for both of us. Why don't you move in with me?" Sebastian ran a finger along Yvonne's cheek. "I'll take care of you."

She pulled back. "You don't get it. I don't need taking care of."

Sebastian's phone buzzed in his pocket, a reminder that his band rehearsal was about to start. Yvonne unfolded her arms as she stood and draped her purse over her shoulder. A sadness brewed in his chest. He was losing her and he didn't know why. Worse, he didn't know how to stop it.

He stood and faced her. If she were closer he'd have to duck to look in her eyes. She'd have to stand on her tiptoes to kiss him. But she was already headed toward the door. "Can we continue this later?" he asked. "I'll drop by your place after rehearsal."

Yvonne shook her head subtly. "I'm going to bed early tonight."

"Then tomorrow?"

"Yeah, sure." She left without kissing him good-bye. She never used to leave without kissing him good-bye. His lungs felt like they were collapsing and he held his breath. He and Yvonne were in trouble and he didn't know how to fix it. He had to find a way. He didn't want to lose her.

Dirk had found the band an empty warehouse to rehearse in on a rundown street in an area that was part of the industrial district. Most of the surrounding buildings were abandoned, windowless brick structures that had eroded away over time. This one was different. Someone had spent the time and money to keep it functional. The fact that it sat among the other empty buildings meant they didn't have to worry about being too loud. And tonight, Sebastian wanted it loud.

Karl boomed out loud riffs on his Fender bass guitar, his slender fingers running up and down the fret board.

Markus banged on the drums, running fills as he tuned the skins. Sebastian tuned his Gibson electric, turning the amp up.

A song had been running through his mind for some time now. A quick email to Katja, and he'd gained permission to rock up one of her songs and add a bridge. The angst it expressed was exactly how he was feeling right now.

"This is a cover," he said into the mic. "See if you can keep up."

Sebastian introduced a new guitar riff that'd come to him in a dream. Markus kicked in with the kick drum, while Karl plucked out a complementary bass line. The band was familiar with the lyrics and only needed a few prompts when Sebastian introduced the bridge. He didn't hold back, tilting his head back with his meanest guitar face and bellowing the new lines.

I'll take the long way around
Sling shot around what I thought
was the darkest side of the moon
Coming round took so long
Sun light nearly stole my eyes

"Love that version, man," Markus said when it ended. "We should record it."

Karl shrugged. "Dirk wants us to do originals."

"We can do one cover," Sebastian said. "Besides, I wrote the bridge, so it's a co-write."

"Fine," Karl huffed. "You have any ideas for a new song? We should write something of our own."

"Do you have any ideas?" Sebastian shot back. Why was he the one who always had to come up with a start?

Karl unstrapped his guitar. "You know what, Seb? This

funk you're in? Let me know when you're over it." He left the rehearsal without looking back.

"That went well," Markus said. "Should I be looking for a new gig?"

"No man," Sebastian said. He unstrapped his guitar and laid it in the case. "We'll work it out. It's just a lot is going on at once."

Sebastian killed the lights and locked up. "Hey, Markus. Can I catch a ride home?" He could take transit, but that would mean facing the public, which was always a crap shoot. Chances were he'd get home without issue, but there was always a chance he'd get mobbed by fans.

Markus dropped him off in front of his building. He hesitated at his front door. He wasn't ready to face his empty flat. He didn't want to be alone right now. He wanted Yvonne. He knew she blew him off when she said she was tired. But she was just angry. She'd have cooled off by now. He needed to apologize for assuming she'd drop everything and follow him. If he did that, she'd snuggle under his arm and kiss him. Maybe she'd ask him to stay the night. He swiftly walked the four blocks to her building.

He stopped at the corner when he spotted her leaving her building. She wore shorts and a light summer sweater. Her short pink hair was spiked up on top. Someone followed out from behind her and at first Sebastian thought it was another tenant. But the guy stopped and gripped her hand. Sebastian's heart dropped. There was no mistaking who it was. He'd recognize that tall, thin form and mess of dark hair anywhere. What was Yvonne doing with Karl?

Karl lifted Yvonne off her feet and kissed her. A bomb went off in Sebastian's heart. His legs moved without his bidding, and within seconds he tugged his girlfriend out of his best friend's arms and right hooked him in the face.

DO SOMETHING

Eva spent a couple days stewing over what Gabriele had said, but hid her bitterness by keeping a soft expression and smiling at appropriate times. Gabriele was a whirlwind of joy, more than enough to compensate for Eva's lack of happiness.

At least she thought she was pulling it off.

"Seriously, Eva! You need to snap out of this blue mood you're in. You're raining on my parade."

"What? I'm not doing anything to you."

"Kind of my point. I'm about to get married and you are supposed to be happy for me."

"I am happy for you."

"If that were true, you'd be asking how you could help. You'd be interested in the details. Instead, you hole away in this room like everyone has a life but you."

Everyone did have a life but her.

"Mama and Papa baby you, but that doesn't mean I'm going to. So make some decisions, Eva. *Do* something."

She hated Gabriele in that moment. Because the truth hurt. She *had* let her accident define her. She focused more on what she couldn't do than what she could. She worried about what people thought and that if she looked slow and stupid. She saw herself ten years from now, still living with her parents, working in the soup kitchen, and with no boyfriend or husband or children to show for it.

If that happened it would be her fault.

What *did* she want to do? Her eyes landed on her guitar and she knew. She wanted to play at the Blue Note. It wasn't a big decision like what to study at university, but it was a start. And she was afraid of it, so it was the first step to facing her fears. Open mic night was tonight. The fact that she kept track of that proved she should do this. She limped to her chair and began to play her latest song, and imagining herself performing it in front of a crowd.

She'd talked herself in and out of it a hundred times throughout the day, but at eight o'clock that evening she arrived at the Blue Note and signed her name. She sat in an empty chair near the door and held on to her guitar like her life depended on it. Maybe it did. The room around her buzzed with energy. The chatter of the patrons, clinking of beer and wine glasses, money being exchanged, energy of anticipation filling the place as each artist was called and performed. Eva felt strangely distant from the commotion, like she was a caterpillar in a transparent cocoon. The membrane squeezed her, taunting her. She wasn't one of *them*. She was alone and invisible.

Herr Leduc called her name, and it was like a clanging bell. Her body froze, prickling with nerves and she swallowed dryly.

"Eva Baumann?" the pub manager called again. His eyes were on her face, and she subtly shook her head.

He called the next name and she shrunk further, growing smaller and more insignificant, the membrane squeezing the air out of her lungs. She felt dizzy and feared she faint. The magnitude of another humiliation caused her to take a huge breath, and she mentally tore out of the cocoon. Not so gracefully, she lumbered out, gripping her cane and guitar, head down, her long, straight hair sheathing her face.

Eva cried throughout the night, but put on a happy face the next morning. She asked Gabriele if she could help with the wedding plans, and Gabriele smiled. "So glad you asked, Eva. I have a million things to do, including studying for my exams."

Eva checked the website of Hollow Fellows like she did every day. They were still in *Neustadt* apparently. Sebastian didn't update the site, their manager did, and the latest entry was two days ago—an update on their interview schedule and new photos from a recent photo shoot. Eva kept her eye out for him when her mother sent her to the bakery for buns in the morning, but she suspected he slept in late.

She went back to the Blue Note on the next open mic night. Sebastian never seemed to be there anymore. He was too famous to show up at that venue now, she supposed. She signed up to sing again.

And again she shook her head no. She refused the next two times as well, and she knew it was becoming a bit of a running joke with the regulars. But she didn't care. She'd shown up. She'd celebrate that small victory.

Maybe if she invited Annette to come along with her, it'd give her a sense of accountability. She'd be there to push her to perform. It was the very reason she hadn't told her friend and invited her before, but Eva knew that if she wanted to make it to the next step in her personal journey, this was something she had to face and conquer.

Annette was more than happy to attend with Eva. She gripped Eva's hand as they sat at a small table together.

"I can't believe you've been coming here all this time. Alone!"

"I've never played. I always chicken out at the last minute."

"But you came, and that's something. And tonight you will play."

Eva's heart thrummed in her chest. Her breaths were short and tight and she hoped she wouldn't hyperventilate.

Annette ordered them each a beer. "I think you need this, Eva. You don't want to dehydrate, and it'll help calm your nerves."

Eva sipped her beer and concentrated on breathing. In. Out. Herr Leduc sighed before calling her name, his gentle eyes landing on her once again.

"Go, Eva," Annette said, pushing gently on her back. "You're going to do great!"

Eva stood and Herr Leduc smiled. He gave her an encouraging wave and somehow Eva managed to limp through the crowded, dimly lit room, guitar and cane in hand, without tripping.

The stage lights blinded her and she was glad she couldn't really see anyone. She rested her cane against a stool, strapped on her guitar and stood in front of the mic. The crowd quieted, and she sensed the people's anxiety. Would they feel embarrassed for her? She hoped not.

She closed her eyes and took a breath. She could do this.

ACHINGLY BEAUTIFUL

"SEBASTIAN, WAIT!" Yvonne's tinny voice called out to him, and he heard the clopping of her shoes in quick succession as she ran after him on the sidewalk. He didn't stop or turn to look at her. She made him sick.

Sebastian rubbed a hand roughly across his face. His head throbbed as if he were the one who'd been hit. The pain shooting up his arm testified that Karl had indeed been the recipient of the punch.

He struggled to process the information he'd gained in the last two minutes. His girlfriend was cheating on him with his best friend. How incredibly cliché!

Yvonne grabbed his arm, and he tugged it back sharply, eying her with a blistering glare of disbelief and disgust. "You and Karl?"

"It's not what it looks like."

"What was it then? That wasn't a kiss between friends. You said you were too tired to be with me. Clearly, you lied."

"I'm sorry, Basti."

Sebastian stopped to consider her. Tears ran down her face, and he struggled to remember if he'd ever seen her cry in the six years they'd been together.

"Why?" he asked simply.

"I don't know. It was stupid. I was feeling bored, and I

was angry that you put your career before us. You're gone all the time."

"Karl is gone as much as I am." Was she acting out to get back at him?

"I know. I said I'm sorry. Please, Basti." Yvonne clasped his hand and Sebastian stared at it for a moment before pulling it free.

"I never cheated on you, Yvonne. Not once. And I could've. On tour? Girls are throwing themselves at me all the time. But I didn't."

Yvonne sniffled. "What can I do to make this better?"

"How long have you been sneaking around?"

"Basti…"

"Tell me the truth."

Yvonne stared at the sidewalk, and then glanced back at her building where Karl leaned against the door, his hand covering one eye as he watched them with the other.

"Two months," she whispered.

Two months? That was before their last tour even started. The whole time Sebastian was on the road, staying loyal, Yvonne had already started something with Karl. *Karl* was the one who'd hooked up with groupies. This was why he had been so adamant that she not come along with him on their next tour.

"We're over."

"Basti, no!"

Sebastian stared at her small fist on his arm, and he grimaced. Yvonne's grip loosened and she shrank back under his steely glare.

He didn't care that he left Yvonne sobbing in public. He was glad she felt some pain. Hopefully, it equaled the scorching burn inflaming his shredded heart.

He walked briskly around the block, keeping his eyes averted when he passed anyone, thankful for the dark of night. He really didn't feel like going home. What he needed was a good strong drink.

How could Karl do this to him? They'd been friends since they were eleven years old. They'd shared dreams about starting a band and making it big one day. They were inseparable in those days.

Then, when Sebastian was seventeen, he'd met Yvonne. She was in his advanced math class. It wasn't love at first sight, or anything. She didn't actually talk much, but she was a good listener. She was there when his dad kicked him out of the house. She was the one who knew some guys who were looking for a roommate, and she helped him find a place to live.

They just kind of happened. He was grateful for everything she'd done for him and he eventually fell in love with her. Karl watched the whole thing unfold, and the closer Sebastian got to Yvonne, the testier Karl got with him. He and Karl argued over her; Karl said Yvonne was like their Yoko Ono, bad for the band. They didn't talk to each other for three days after that fight, and then Karl admitted to being jealous. He showed up the next day with a new girl-friend on his arm, and all was forgotten.

At least, that was what Sebastian had believed.

What a mess. Dirk expected them to write music for their next CD and Sebastian couldn't even picture being in the same room with Karl right now. Or ever.

A door opened ahead of him and Sebastian heard the sound of applause. He looked up, surprised to find the sound was coming from the Blue Note. Somehow he'd found his way back to a place of comfort and familiarity. Maurice sold good beer, too.

He slipped inside, grabbed an open stool at the bar and ordered a drink. He pulled his cap low, keeping to the shadows of the darkened room. He took a moment to catch his breath, and wrap up the pain and anger to a manageable size. When his drink arrived, he gulped it back. He ordered another, determined to put Karl and Yvonne out of his mind. They weren't worth his time. He wasn't worth it. She definitely wasn't worth it.

Maybe if he drank enough, he'd believe it by morning.

Maurice was on the stage calling the next act, and Sebastian watched with interest as a slender girl with shoulder-length brown hair and a limp made her way to the stage. It was awkward to watch her maneuver up the lone step, cane in one hand and guitar in the other. She managed to sort it all out and Sebastian caught his breath when she faced the audience. It was the girl from the soup kitchen. Now he remembered where he'd seen her. It was here. Maurice had called her name, but she refused to go on. He'd had a good laugh at her expense.

Looked like she finally found her courage. He worried that she might have stage fright, that she might not be any good. A lot of the acts weren't. For some reason, he found that he really wanted her to be good.

She plucked the strings of her guitar, and her skill was immediately evident. It wasn't a simple picking pattern and Sebastian focused on her fingers, taking in the sophisticated melody. She opened her mouth and her voice filled the room. The song was magnetic. The lyrics, haunting. The way the light glowed around the girl made her look ethereal and angelic.

By the time the song ended, Sebastian Weiss was enthralled. Who was this girl?

Thought I came to wet my lips
Maybe cool my feet
But you pushed me from behind
Thought I came to our safe place
By the riverside
Now I'm swimming
For a moment it feels so good
I am floating free
But the current and these clothes are against me
Body weakens, mind races I am far at sea
Nobody hears me
Now I fight to find the surface
Will my lungs explode
Heavy water pushing down on me
Your hand reaches in rescue
Then melts away
Now I am drowning
Now I'm weightless, now I'm breathless
Now you have your way
Feel the water flowing through my veins
This liquid embrace, this consummation
You are the water I breathe

Eva didn't open her eyes once. Even after her last strum, she kept them close. The silence that settled on the room terrified her until dramatically, it erupted with the sound of clapping and cheering, at which point, Eva's eyes sprung open.

She couldn't make out faces but she could make out bodies. One by one they stood until the whole room was standing.

Her hand clasped her mouth and she blinked back tears. *A standing ovation?*

"So beautiful, *ma Cherie*," Herr Leduc said as he approached, surprising her by giving her a quick bear hug. "I will assist you back to your table if you don't mind. The crowd is wild for you and may not give you the space you need."

She nodded and smiled. She didn't mind.

"Excuse us," Herr Leduc said loudly, "talented lady coming through!"

Annette gave her an excited squeeze before Eva finally collapsed into her chair. Her nerves shot off as she became aware of all the stares. Out of habit, she allowed a wall of hair to cover her face.

"None of that, Eva!" Annette said. She reached over and pushed Eva's hair behind her ear. "You were amazing! You must stay in the moment and enjoy it!"

Herr Leduc called the next act and gradually the room quieted and refocused their attention to the guy on the stage. "Well, that's a tough act to follow," he said lightly.

After being somewhat blinded by the stage lights, Eva's eyes adjusted once again to the darkness. Candlelight flickered, casting a warm glow on Annette's face. Eva was so glad she'd invited her friend to come along. Otherwise she wouldn't have done it.

She basked in the euphoria, feeling stronger than she had in months. Years even. Then her gaze landed on a figure sitting at the bar. The man's eyes bore into hers and she quickly looked away. Her heart hit the floor, bounced and ricocheted off the ceiling. She knew that face. She dared to look back and the guy's gaze hadn't shifted. He was *watching* her. *Sebastian Weiss* was watching her. He'd seen her *play*.

"Are you all right?" Annette asked. "You look spooked." Then she turned to find what had captured Eva's attention.

Annette swiveled back to Eva, her eyes wide with excitement. "No way!"

"Oh my heart, Annette. He's coming over."

Sebastian Weiss slid into the seat next to Eva and she felt like dying. Perhaps she could slip out of sight under the table? He leaned in so close she could smell his soap. Her hands trembled and she hid them on her lap.

"That was fantastic," Sebastian said in a low voice. He leaned in close, his breath tickled her ear and she nearly melted. "The song, your voice—really hit me." He pounded his chest over his heart. "Right here. Did you write that?"

Eva nodded. She felt light-headed, like she was floating from the ceiling watching someone else have a conversation with Sebastian Weiss. Well, it would be a conversation if she could actually say something.

To Eva's surprise, he said, "I saw you the other day."

She dared a glance at him. When? She was sure he hadn't seen her when Annette waved at him from her window.

"In that soup kitchen," he offered. "You were playing guitar."

Oh man, if she could just move her tongue. Form at least one word.

"I'd like to see you again," he said. Eva couldn't hide her startled look and he quickly added. "To talk music."

The act on the stage ended, so they were forced to

break from the awkward chat and applaud. Annette shouted at Sebastian now that the room had grown loud. "I love your music!"

He smiled. "Thanks."

"And," Annette continued, "Eva would love to talk music."

"Eva," Sebastian mused. "I should officially introduce myself. I'm Sebastian Weiss." He held out a hand.

Eva swallowed dryly and allowed him to shake hers. His hand was warm and strong. She mustered up the ability to form her own name. "Eva Baumann."

"A pleasure to meet you," Sebastian said.

"And I'm Annette Vogel." Annette could barely conceal her celebrity crush. A squeal escaped along with the handshake.

Other patrons began to notice the guy who'd joined their table and before too long, someone recognized him.

"That's Sebastian Weiss!" Within minutes of this declaration, the table was swarmed with people wanting his autograph. Eva was pressed against the table and her cane that had been hanging on the back of her chair fell to the floor.

Sebastian whispered in her ear. "I have to go before this gets crazy. Can I come see you sometime? At the soup kitchen?"

Eva could only nod. Sebastian's closeness turned her into a helpless mute. Her eyes stayed trained on his back until he disappeared and the crowd with him.

Annette laughed out loud. "What a night!" Then she cocked a brow and wiggled it at Eva. "I think he has a thing for you."

THE PULL HERE BENEATH

SEBASTIAN BROKE into a jog to ditch his fans. Fortunately, they were a group of girls in heels and not fit for racing across cobblestone streets. He zigzagged through a narrow lane and down an alley in the opposite direction of his building until he was certain he'd lost them. Then he circled back, keeping his head down and fists ready. Just in case.

His pace slowed until he reached his building, and headed up the stairs. He flicked the switch and lit up the flat. It was an untidy mess with dirty dishes scattered about and sofa cushions out of place.

Sebastian collapsed on the couch, stretching out with his hands folded over his chest like a corpse in a coffin. He closed his eyes and thought about the girl and the song. At moments, the image of Yvonne kissing Karl would pop into his mind, and he'd shake his head. Focus on the girl and the song. The girl and the song.

Most people had paintings and photographs hanging on the wall: he had guitars. Some were vintage collectibles, including a 1957 Gibson Gold-Top and one Fender Stratocaster which was once owned by Clapton, but most were just recent impulse buys from the corner music store. He also had a Baroque violin, the chin piece worn by a million hours of practice as a kid. He hadn't touched it since Hollow Fellows took off.

He'd set up a mini studio in the corner. Two flat-screen monitors and an audio/midi interface sat on a dusty desk. Long black cords twisted around two condenser microphones in metal gooseneck stands. He liked to work on ideas and get them down when inspiration struck, no matter the time of day. It was something that hadn't happened for him in a good long while.

Sebastian needed noise. He searched the room for the remote, finding it under a cushion and turned on the TV projector. He fell into a chair and let out a long hard breath, working to focus on the program.

Normally, he liked being alone—he hardly ever was—but tonight the solitude mocked him. He no longer had the comfort of knowing his relationships extended beyond these doors. If he couldn't trust his girlfriend and best buddy—correction, *ex* girlfriend and *ex* best buddy—then who could he trust?

His fame had grown, but his world had shrunk. He hadn't called his parents in years. He commented on his sister's Facebook status once in a while, but that was the extent of that relationship. His band was his family, and now that was gone too.

A dark cloak of depression settled on him as he stretched out once again on his couch. He wished he would've turned out the lights, but he was too weary to get up and shut them off. Instead, he placed a cushion over his face.

He was alone. He didn't even have a pet. Not a good idea when you're only home half the year in spurts.

The image of Yvonne and Karl passionately kissing in front of her building burned stubbornly at the back of his mind. How could they do this to him??

Now that he thought about it, he could recognize the signs that something had been amiss. Yvonne had been pulling away for some time, and Karl rarely held Sebastian's gaze. Right. Now it was freaking obvious. They'd both played him, and Sebastian was the fool. Now he wished he'd blackened Karl's other eye.

The TV program was nonsense that got on his nerves and he clicked the remote to turn it off.

"The Water Song" from Eva Baumann ran through Sebastian's head, tugging him out of slippery despair before he slid too deep. He hummed the haunting melody over and over again. So achingly beautiful.

He had to meet up with this girl. He had to get to know the person who could write a song like that. She wasn't conventionally beautiful like the groupies who wore too much makeup, or like Yvonne, whose Goth edge caught attention, but she was cute in her own way.

Too bad about the limp and the cane. He wondered what happened to her? Was it a birth defect? Had she been born with a withered leg?

Whatever it was, it hadn't affected her pipes. The girl could sing. And she seemed to like him, even if it was directed at Sebastian Weiss the icon and not Sebastian the guy around the corner. It wasn't the first time he used his fame to his advantage. Just flash his winning smile, turn on the charm, flex his tattoo. Worked every time. If he could get her to sing for him, just for him, that might soothe the angst that ate away at the core of his being. He hummed her tune like a lullaby and let the emotional weariness overtake him. He fell into a deep sleep and surprisingly never had any nightmares.

Sebastian awoke the next morning feeling discombobulated. This wasn't an unusual experience. For a fleeting moment his mind raced to remember what hotel he was in, then his eyes registered the familiar surroundings of his living room. Why didn't he sleep in his bed?

Then he remembered Yvonne and Karl's betrayal. An avalanche of anger built up from the day before swooshed down and pooled in his gut. He reached for his phone on the end table where he'd tossed it the night before. He'd turned it off when he entered the Blue Note and had forgotten to turn it back on. Nine text messages. Eight from Yvonne, which he deleted, and one from Dirk who'd called a meeting for that afternoon and wanted the band there.

Sebastian groaned. He'd hoped for at least one day off. One day to not have to look at Karl's ugly mug. He texted back that he was sick and couldn't make it and turned off his phone. He removed his clothing and was about to crawl into bed when he heard pounding at the door. What now?

"Who is it?"

"It's me, Yvonne."

No. He really didn't want to see her yet.

Yvonne didn't relent. "Please, Sebastian. Can we just talk for a minute?" The handle quivered as a key was inserted—he'd given her a copy—and Yvonne pushed the door open. Sebastian huffed and realized he was standing there in just boxers. He cursed and stormed back to his bedroom, frustrated that Yvonne had followed him. He ignored her and shuffled into jeans and a button-down shirt.

Her voice was barely more than a whisper. "Can't you give me one more chance?"

Sebastian looked at her then. Her red-rimmed eyes and hollow cheeks. Short and spiky pink hair with dark roots. Her thin, waifish body. He waited for his emotions to kick in. Something that resembled affection, some residue of the love he'd had for her just yesterday, but he felt numb. "I don't think I can."

She stiffened and a hardened look crossed her face. "So, you're just going to throw away six years."

He snorted. "I didn't throw them away. You did."

Someone else was pounding on the door before Sebastian could even get his buttons done up. How were people getting in the building without buzzing? Yvonne had a key, which he needed to get back, but whoever was on the other side of that door must've slipped in behind another tenant.

He opened it to Dirk and Markus.

"I said I was sick."

"Which is why we brought the meeting to you," Dirk said. He pushed his glasses up as he took in Yvonne. "Hi, Yvonne." Then back to Sebastian, "Karl is on his way." He lowered his voice. "He was less than excited. He said you two had a falling out?"

Sebastian huffed. "You could say that."

Dirk nodded to Yvonne, his face registering that maybe something was wrong. "Sorry to intrude."

The tension in the room was thick. It was Yvonne's fault. She was the cheat.

"She was just leaving," Sebastian said, holding out an open palm. "My key?"

Yvonne dug into her purse and handed it over slowly, her eyes hard, and lips in a firm, thin, line. She let the key fall to the wood floor, where it landed with a clink and slid under the couch. Then she turned sharply and slammed the door on her way out.

"Whoa," Markus said from his position on one of the low-lying living room chairs. His feet were crossed at the ankles and rested lazily on the coffee table. "Did you guys just break up?"

Sebastian lowered himself to the floor to reach under

the couch for the key. "Yup." His fingers wrapped around it and he shoved it into his pocket.

"Wow," Markus continued. "You two were together, like, forever."

Dirk frowned and took a seat on the couch opposite Markus. "So *that's* the sickness. What happened?"

Sebastian moved to the kitchen and gulped orange juice from the carton before answering. "Ask Karl."

"Ask me what?" Karl entered through the unlocked door and stood there sheepishly. His dark hair hung over the black eye that had formed there.

Sebastian scowled. "Your girlfriend just left."

Dirk and Markus's gazed moved back and forth between them. "Whose girlfriend?" Dirk asked. "What's going on?"

Sebastian pointed at Karl. "Him and Yvonne. That's what's going on."

Markus gawked. "You hooked up with Seb's girl?"

"It was stupid," Karl said. "I know. But it's over. I'm sorry."

Sebastian shook his head. "You think you can fix this with a lame apology?"

"What else do you want from me, man?"

"I want you out of the band."

Dirk's wide eyes cut back and forth between them, his cheeks puffing out like a squirrel's. "Hold up, Sebastian. Let's just calm down here."

"What? You can't expect me to keep playing with him?"

Dirk's fingers tapped nervously along the top of his tablet. "I know. It... sucks. But, you'll need to work it out somehow."

Sebastian thrust his shoulders back. "I'm not working anything out. Either he goes or I go."

Dirk broke into a sweat, which caused his glasses to slip down his nose. "Well, his name is on the record contract. So is yours. Unfortunately, neither of you can quit."

Sebastian stepped into his shoes and headed for the door. "Yeah. Watch me."

IT WAS a lot easier having a celebrity crush from a distance. Having Sebastian Weiss sit right next to her and whisper in her ear almost blew her circuits. Eva was sure he'd been drinking too much and that she'd never see him again. Still, the high of it along with her performance kept her from falling asleep until dawn. In fact, she floated along in a happy daze for a couple days afterward.

"You seem especially chipper," her mama noted at breakfast. "Is there something we should know about?"

Her papa eyed her over the newspaper he read each morning, bushy eyebrows taut with curiosity.

"I already told you," Eva said, keeping her eyes averted, spreading marmalade on her toast. "I finally had the courage to sing at the open mic night." She couldn't tell them about Sebastian, but the way they kept eyeing her it was like they already knew. "What?"

"Nothing," her mama said quickly. "We're happy that you're happy. Are you going to play there again?"

Papa added, "Maybe we can come see you next time."

Eva's smile flattened. As much as she loved her parents, she didn't want them there. She wasn't sure why. It wasn't like she was embarrassed of them. If anything, she was the one who brought the unwanted glances their way. But what if Sebastian came again? What if he talked to her? She didn't think her parents would approve. Not that they wouldn't like him as a person. But he wasn't the kind of boy they'd like to see with their daughter.

Which was an absurd thought anyway. Sebastian Weiss wouldn't be interested in someone like her. He liked her *song*, not *her*. It'd been three days since she'd played, since he promised to come see her, and he hadn't shown. She was foolish to entertain fantasies of any kind that included Sebastian Weiss.

"*Schatzi*." Mama lay a hand on her arm. "Are you okay? Did we upset you?"

Eva snapped out of her reverie and forced a smile. "I'm fine. Just a little tired."

"You're not feeling unwell, are you?" Papa asked.

"No, I'm fine." A familiar annoyance rose in her chest. She was twenty-one years old now, but she felt like her parents couldn't stop seeing her as their crippled teenager.

"Good." He pushed his glasses up on his nose and snapped his paper. "We're serving lunch today, so there's lots of work to do."

Eva knew this, of course. Her world was small, revolving around the house church that existed one floor below her. She sighed. Would she ever break free from this neighborhood? Do something different with her life? Live on her own? Travel? Go to university?

That would be up to her.

The thought of branching out in any way both excited her and scared the pants off her. And as usual, fear won out. It was safer for her to stay here with her parents. She wasn't ready to live on her own. What would she do?

What if she fell?

She reached for her cane that hung on the back of her chair and then carefully carried her dishes to the sink. She stopped at the WC to brush her teeth before lumbering back to her room. She'd turned her laptop on when she awoke, like she did every morning, and the page for Hollow Fellows was still up. She refreshed it, but there was nothing new. She found it a little strange since the band's webpage generally had daily updates. She clicked on one of their music videos and indulged in her morning dose of Sebastian Weiss. She caught her reflection in the dresser mirror—cane in one hand, the computer mouse in the other, unbrushed hair and a frown. This silly crush she harbored was pathetic. She was pathetic.

Eva pressed the laptop lid closed and moved to her bed to lay down. She was tired, but not the kind of weariness that came from a lack of sleep. She was crashing from her three-day high, like a plane whose propellers suddenly quit, and it was a long, hard fall.

Who was she to think she would ever be truly happy? And what did true happiness look like anyway? Eva huffed. It looked like Gabriele.

She stretched and groaned and bemoaned the fact that she couldn't lie in bed forever. Her papa would be knocking on the door if she wasn't ready to head downstairs soon. She sighed long and hard again before rousing herself to dress for the day.

Eva stared wistfully at her Duncan Africa, wishing she could carry it downstairs herself. She had a second guitar in the church, a community instrument left there for anyone to play. It was all right, but it didn't resonate the same way. She always had to ask Gabriele or one of her parents to carry it up and down for her when she left for the Blue Note.

She could already smell the soup her mama had prepared halfway down the circular cement stairwell. Even though Eva enjoyed cooking, she was too slow in the tight quarters of the soup kitchen. Mama had other volunteers from the church who helped. Providing music was Eva's most useful contribution.

Papa had raised the outdoor blinds and unlocked the front door, and the tables were already filled with the hungry. Papa welcomed them all with a sincere smile, and then opened with a prayer. Eva played a worship song and a few of the patrons lifted their hands. Her gaze wandered to the window and her heart stopped. Her hands plucked the strings of her guitar and her mouth moved, but her brain had disengaged. Sebastian Weiss stood across the street, one arm folded across his chest and the other on his chin.

She remembered when he stood in that same spot over a year ago, waving his hands in the air, mocking. He wasn't mocking now. His eyes seemed to lock on hers. Could he see her through the glass?

Then his hand moved from his face, and he waved his fingers.

He could see her! She quickly looked away.

Papa cleared his voice. "Is something wrong?"

Eva blushed. She'd stopped the song midstream without explanation. "No, I'm sorry." She began again, cautiously glancing through the hair she allowed to fall in front of her face and out the window. Sebastian Weiss was gone and a strange disappointment wrapped around her collection of flustered emotions.

Eva could barely concentrate during Papa's short pre-meal message from the Bible. Her mind was fixated on Sebastian Weiss. She pictured him standing across the street, the way he leaned back slightly, with his weight on one leg. He stared at her through the window, stroking his chin beneath beautiful lips that had so recently whispered hotly in her ear. This time, in her imagination, he hooked a finger calling her outside to meet him. With perfect grace and without her cane she hurried to meet him.

Then what?

She ran her hand against the back of her neck as if she could sweep away the heat that her fantasy brought on.

Oh, mercy. She had a debilitating crush. An embarrassing infatuation. She really had to pull herself together. Her obsession with Sebastian Weiss and Hollow Fellows couldn't be healthy. At best it was extremely immature.

She engaged in light conversation with the patrons in an effort to clear her head.

"Nice weather," she said to one of the regulars.

He huffed a gruff reply. "Too hot."

"Well, it's July," she said. "Not long ago we were complaining it was too cold."

When the lunch rush ended, Eva pushed the rolling tray full of dirty dishes to the kitchen and returned with a wet cloth to wipe the tables. Her back was to the door as she hobbled from table to table. That was why she didn't see him enter.

"I'm sorry young man," she heard her papa say, "but lunch is over. I can get you a bun if you like."

"I'm not here for the food."

Eva stiffened, her spine like a cold copper pipe. Chills shot up to the base of her neck. She didn't have to turn around to know who the voice belonged to.

She swiveled slowly. The sight of Sebastian Weiss standing in the middle of their small house church made her knees give out, and she lowered herself onto the nearest chair. She wasn't imagining it this time. He was really there, in the flesh.

Her brain couldn't compute. Sebastian Weiss belonged on stage and on TV. A crack in the universe had erroneously delivered him here.

Papa's eyes, looking larger through the thick lenses he pushed up on his face, darted from Sebastian to Eva and back. His thin lips drew downward. "What are you here for then?"

Eva's pulse surged, and she found it hard to swallow.

Sebastian pointed at Eva. "For her."

Papa stared at the large tattoo on Sebastian's arm, then to the earrings in his ears, and a soft growl escaped from his throat.

"It's all right, Papa," she said, her voice barely audible. "He just wants to ask me about a song I sang at open mic night."

Papa bore down on their visitor. "What did you say your name was?"

"Sebastian Weiss."

Papa's eyes moved back to Eva, his bushy brows jumping. Then he grunted again. "Never heard of you."

Eva knew that wasn't true. Everyone in their small flat was aware of her fascination with Sebastian Weiss and his band, and they often teased her for it. Papa's thick brows furrowed deeper but thankfully he turned back to the kitchen and left them alone.

Sebastian slipped into the seat across from Eva. "He's scary."

She nodded feeling like a pixie had suddenly stitched her lips together. Her papa may be scary, but he wasn't the one who terrified her now.

PRETEND I'M NOT HERE

THE GIRL, Eva, looked like a frightened rabbit shrinking into herself on the other side of the table. She hid behind a swath of brown hair. Sebastian wondered if he'd made a mistake in coming. He liked her sound, but it wasn't worth getting taken out by her old man.

"I suppose I should've called first," Sebastian said, "but I didn't have your number."

Eva blinked.

"I thought maybe you could play me your song again?" Most musicians jumped at the chance to showcase their music to Sebastian with the hope that he could somehow pull strings to help them break into the industry. He had a collection of CDs that hopeful artists had shoved into his hands on tour. They stalked him in the lobby and ran after him as he climbed on the tour bus. They were almost as bad as the groupies.

The girl's eyes popped even wider than they already were, if possible, at his request and he thought she was going to say no.

Finally, she spoke. "I guess."

She didn't ask if he wanted to record it or perform it and she didn't have that eager, puppy dog expression like any other singer would have. It was like the thought hadn't crossed her mind. He waited for her to retrieve her guitar, but then she didn't move. Her eyes darted to the guitar sitting on the stand across the room as she rubbed her right thigh.

Right. Her gimpy leg. Was she self-conscious? Maybe she didn't want him to watch her struggle across the room.

He waved toward the instrument. "Do you want me to get it?"

Eva stared back and nodded.

Sebastian sprinted across the small room and back and carefully handed her the guitar. She propped it across her lap, her knees peeking out from the hem of a light-colored skirt. "This isn't mine," she said. "I have a Duncan Africa upstairs."

"Really?" Sebastian said. "I've heard good things about them, but never played one."

"It's amazing. The warm tone and resonance… I'm sure you'd love it."

She smiled a little, like talking about guitars relaxed her, and Sebastian smiled back. She strummed and picked at the strings, and he recalled the melody.

She looked up from under long eyelashes free of mascara. "I'm kind of nervous. You're *you*, and you're so close."

Her eyes were green and they sparkled when she spoke of him and something tweaked. Sebastian surprised himself by thinking that the girl was pretty. Not just cute, but *pretty*, in a very wholesome, natural way.

"Just close your eyes and pretend I'm not here. Pretend you're at the Blue Note."

"Okay." She closed her eyes and a few seconds later began to sing. Her voice was clear as crystal and pure. No showcasing, no showing off. Just straight, honest, beautiful vocals. The lyrics moved him as strongly as the night he'd first heard them, but today, sitting this close to Eva

Baumann, he couldn't take his eyes off her soft, moist lips.

Idiot. He was glad she had her eyes closed. He could only imagine the blush that would spread across her face if she could read his mind right now.

She strummed the last note and opened her eyes. Sebastian broke into applause, filling the room with the sound of his appreciation.

"Do you realize how good you are?" Her face flattened with surprise and Sebastian believed that she truly didn't. He inhaled in shock, not used to seeing true humility.

"Thank you," she said. Her eyes flickered to movement over his shoulder and Sebastian turned in time to see Herr Baumann about to leave. The large man nodded at Eva, but narrowed his eyes when his gaze landed on Sebastian.

Her father was bristly, but Sebastian liked how he so obviously cared for his daughter. The man didn't have to worry about Sebastian. Sure, Eva was sweet and pretty, but he wasn't interested in her in a physical way. Despite her alluring lips, she wasn't his type, and besides his breakup with Yvonne still stung too much.

Eva sat statue still, waiting for his next move. Sebastian understood his current popularity could be intimidating. He searched for a way to break the ice. "Nice place here." Her eyes followed his gaze and he winced a little. There was nothing special about this room, not aesthetically anyway. "I mean, it's good work that you and your family do. Have you lived in the *Neustadt* long?"

"Since I was thirteen," she answered. "So, eight years."

That made her twenty-one. He would've guessed that she was younger, maybe seventeen or eighteen. It was hard to believe she was only three years younger than he was.

"Nice." He waited for her to ask him a question. When it was obvious none was forthcoming, he asked another of his own. "Do you have another song?" He wanted to know if she was prolific. Did she take songwriting seriously, or was she just lucky with one good song?

"I'm working on a new one right now."

"Let me hear it."

"Oh. It's not really ready."

Well, at least that meant she wrote seriously. "Play me a finished one then."

She held his gaze. "I will if you will."

Wow, he hadn't expected that. Maybe the girl had some gumption after all. "You're on. But first, you know what? I'd really like to see your Duncan Africa. Is it possible for you to let me try it?"

Eva's green eyes flashed with a moment of anxiety, but then she nodded and handed Sebastian the guitar to put away. She reached for the cane hanging on the back of her chair—Sebastian hadn't noticed it before—and pushed herself upright. She limped ahead of him and he followed her through a door that led to a hallway and up a set of winding cement steps. He found himself jerking an arm outward, afraid that she might fall, but kept his hands to himself.

It was a slow climb, but they arrive at the next floor, and Eva opened the wooden door to their flat. It wasn't big. A living room faced the street and connected to a small kitchen that overlooked a quaint, overgrown courtyard. The flat was tidy, but lived in.

"No one's home?" he asked. It surprised him since the door was unlocked.

"Mama's in the kitchen downstairs cleaning up. Papa had a meeting. Gabriele, that's my sister, she's in university."

"You're not in university?"

Eva paused, then answered softly. "Not yet."

Sebastian wondered why, but he got the feeling it was personal and he didn't want her to feel like he was grilling her. She opened the door to a room that housed two narrow beds. It clearly belonged to a couple girls by the way it was decorated with floral fabric and lace. He spotted the guitar propped up on a stand in the corner and whistled.

"That's a beauty." He caught her eye. "Do you mind?"

"Go ahead."

He picked it up gently and examined the surface. "What kind of wood is it?"

"The back and sides are Indian Rosewood," she answered. "The top is solid cedar."

Sebastian whistled. "Nice."

Eva sat on one of the beds and Sebastian claimed the chair by the guitar.

"Is this where you write?" he asked.

"Usually. It's… easier if I stay here."

Right. Sebastian couldn't imagine Eva carrying the guitar down the stairs on her own. He ran his fingers along the strings, plucking out a familiar rift, closing his eyes as he absorbed the joy of it. The bright sounds rang from the wooden instrument like honey to his ears.

"I love that song," Eva said.

His eyes popped open, and he remembered where he was. "It's a crowd favorite."

"I'm a fan of your band," she added.

Sebastian grinned, and his eyes moved to the poster on the other side of the room. He remembered that photo shoot and that thousands of copies of that poster had moved in a week. Eva's eyes darted to where he'd been looking, and she covered her face with her hands.

"I'm so embarrassed."

"Why? I'm flattered."

"I just don't want you to think I'm like those groupie girls who follow you around."

Sebastian studied her. "Believe me. You're nothing like them. And I mean that in the best way." And that was the truth. Eva was like a breath of fresh air. She didn't want anything from him, didn't expect anything from him. He found himself relaxing for the first time in days.

He carried the guitar over to Eva. "Your turn."

She smiled brightly, and a strange quiver swirled in his chest. He lowered himself to the rug at her feet and waited. She pursed her lips together and looked up at the ceiling like she was deciding what she should play—a simple expression that on Eva was adorable. Sebastian shook his head. Where were these thoughts coming from?

Focus on the song.

He didn't have a chance to hear it because they were interrupted by a gust of wind and the shocked expression of a girl with short platinum blond hair who stood frozen in the doorway. She wore form-fitting jeans, a breezy blouse, and her arms were full of books. Her green eyes, the only thing that connected her to Eva, moved from the stunned face of the girl sitting on the edge of the bed, to Sebastian and back again.

She squinted at them. "Did I just enter an alternate universe?"

GABRIELE'S SHADOW

EVA ALMOST DROPPED HER GUITAR. She'd lost all track of time and wanted to kick herself for the lapse. She enjoyed having the sole attention of Sebastian Weiss. What girl wouldn't? It was a dream, a fairytale: she had to know it wouldn't last forever.

But she hadn't wanted it to end like this—with her beautiful, charismatic sister's charm luring him away. Eva and Sebastian had shared a moment. She hadn't imagined the admiration she saw in his gorgeous hazel eyes. Had she? She'd believed he was interested in her, at least as an artist. Maybe what they had wouldn't have lasted to the end of the day, but it had a chance before now.

Sebastian stood and offered his hand. "I'm Sebastian."

Gabriele set down her books on the dresser with the poise of the Queen of England. "I'm Gabriele, Eva's sister." She smirked and pointed to the poster of Sebastian on Eva's side of the room. "Of course I already knew who you were."

A red flare of mortification ignited in Eva's belly, and she wanted to crawl under her bed. Not that she wasn't already invisible. The scene had changed, and once Gabriele had stepped on stage, the spotlight had swung to her, leaving Eva blotted out by the shadows. If this scene were playing in a theater, Eva's character would be slinking out of sight on stage right.

Except there was no way for her to escape now. Gabriele blocked the doorway.

Gabriele propped a hand on her hip, and Eva swore she batted her eyelashes. "You can imagine my surprise," she continued, her eyes locked on Sebastian's face. "Finding you here… in my bedroom."

Sebastian jerked and looked at Eva, like he finally remembered she was there. "Eva was kind enough to show me her beautiful guitar."

"It is beautiful," Gabriele admitted. "Sadly, she won't let me play it."

"You have your own beautiful guitar," Eva said. "I didn't know you wanted to play mine."

Gabriele laughed. "Just teasing."

"Where's your *fiancé*?" Eva asked pointedly. Seriously. Gabriele was preparing to be married soon. Did she have to flaunt her expert flirtation skills?

Sebastian's gaze moved between the two sisters. "I should go."

"Probably a good idea," Gabriele said lightly. "Papa doesn't approve of boys in our room."

Eva rolled her eyes. *Oh my heart. Just kill me now.*

Sebastian surprised her by crouching in front of her so they were eye to eye. "Thanks for showing me your guitar and for playing your songs. You're a great songwriter, and I love your voice. Keep it up." He stood and grinned at Gabriele who hadn't moved from her spot by the door. "I can see myself out."

Eva may have taken Sebastian's admonishment to heart if she hadn't watched him brush past Gabriele in the doorway.

"Way to make room for him to get by," she said once

he was gone.

"Hey, it's not every day you find a hot celebrity in your bedroom." She snuggled close beside Eva. "Now spill. How did he end up here? Tell me everything. Don't leave anything out."

Eva sighed. No one was immune to Gabriele's charm, not even she. "He saw me play at the Blue Note."

"Wait," Gabriele pulled back. "The night you finally performed? And you never mentioned this?"

"It seemed so random. And I know I already come off as a lovesick fan. I didn't want to add to that." Eva shrugged a shoulder. "I really didn't think he'd follow through with his promise to look me up."

Gabriele gaped. "He promised you that?"

"Yeah. Kind of. He really liked my song. I just thought maybe he had too much to drink. Then he got recognized and raced away."

"Wow. Sebastian Weiss looked up my sister because he thinks she's talented." She squeezed Eva's shoulders and planted a kiss on her cheek. "Cool story. One for the Baumann family history books."

Eva felt her lips pull up. It was impossible to stay mad at her sister.

"Now that the surreal has passed," Gabriele said, pulling out her cell phone, "it's time to work on wedding plans." She gave Eva new instructions and Eva shuffled over to her desk where she could order some of the decorations online. She only peeked at Hollow Fellows website once or twice. Or three times. Oh, God. How was she supposed to concentrate on real life now? She closed her eyes and happily relived every moment that she shared with Sebastian Weiss that day.

"Eva!"

She jumped at her sister's voice. "I'm doing it, Gabi,

jeez." Eva had a sinking feeling that her life had peaked that afternoon, and it was all down hill from here.

Mama called for them to come for *Abendbrot*, a light meal of buns, meats and cheeses they shared in the evenings. The hot meal was eaten midday, and on soup kitchen days, the soup was considered their hot meal. Eva set the table with four plates and the necessary cutlery while Gabriele grabbed the glasses, the sparkling mineral water and the apple juice. Papa had already delivered the bread and quickly finished slicing a cucumber and tomato. This was a job Mama normally did, but Papa said she worked hard enough in the soup kitchen on soup days, and so he would oversee *Abendbrot* on those days.

Papa sat at his usual place at the head of the table with Mama at the spot to his right. Gabriele sat at the foot of the table and Eva beside her across from her mama. Papa cleared his throat, the sign that he was about to pray, and everyone closed their eyes and bowed their heads.

After the "Amen," Mama lifted the bun basket and passed it around. "How are the wedding plans going?" she asked Gabriele.

"Good." Gabriele sliced her bun and topped it with meat. "Papa, did you secure the Three Kings Church?"

He nodded. "I walked over this afternoon and settled things with the administration."

So that was where he had gone while Eva was with Sebastian. Her papa stared at her, like he was just remembering the occasion as well. She looked down and picked at the seeds on the top of her bun, but her papa wasn't thwarted.

"Who was that boy who came to see you today?"

"No one. Just a friend."

Gabriele scoffed. "Just a friend? That was Sebastian Weiss, Papa. He's gotten really big recently. On TV and the radio even. Eva's got a poster of him on the wall of our room."

"Gabi!" Eva hissed. What a traitor. She softened her expression and turned back to her parents. "He's not even a friend. Just a musician I met at the Blue Note."

Mama frowned and turned to her husband. "I knew it was a bad idea to let her go to a pub."

Eva muttered, "Oh, God."

Mama swung back to her. "Eva!"

"Sorry, Mama." Her mother felt that God's name should only be invoked if one were praying. "Oh my *heart*. But really, I'm not a child."

Mama clucked. "We know that, but, you still need to use wisdom. Is this boy even a Christian?"

Eva dropped her knife. "We're not *dating* for goodness sake. He just wanted to hear my song."

"And see your Duncan Africa," her sister added.

Eva seared her with a glare. Gabriele had the decency to flash her a look of remorse.

Papa raised a bushy eyebrow. "The boy was here? In our flat?"

Eva couldn't control the panic that was rising in her stomach. Her gaze cut back to Gabriele. *Help.*

"I was here, too, Papa," she jumped in. "They weren't alone or anything, and I brought the guitar to the living room. Who knows, maybe he'll buy one. Help support the Ugandans."

Gabriele's revised version of the truth was a successful deflection. Papa resumed eating in a relaxed fashion as if Eva's encounter with Sebastian as purely a promotion for a greater cause, which made more sense. Eva scowled. Of course Papa would find comfort in that thought. A guy like Sebastian Weiss couldn't possibly be interested in someone like his handicapped daughter.

SEBASTIAN RELUCTANTLY CHECKED his phone for messages. Five missed from Dirk. Nothing from Yvonne.

He felt strangely disconnected from that. Yesterday he hated her. Today he felt nothing. In fact, he couldn't seem to get Eva Baumann out of his head. What was it about her that intrigued him so much?

Sure she was talented, but there were a lot of talented young women in the world. Maybe it was the fact that she wasn't chasing a dream. Probably because of her leg. But if she wanted to and had the right public relations people behind her, she could use that in her favor. It made her different in a way that tattoos, piercings and dressing like a tart didn't.

She certainly was pretty enough—not like her sister who obviously spent more than a few minutes in front of a mirror to pull off that look. He actually couldn't believe those two girls were related. Not only were they drastically different in looks and style, but their personalities couldn't be more unlike.

Normally, he would've gone for the outgoing, made-up one, but now, well, he was done with superficial and anything that smelled of it. He liked authentic. Real.

He liked Eva Baumann.

But what about that leg? He chastised himself. Now who was being superficial?

Besides, it wasn't like he was a big catch. Once you pulled away the fame and the money—Eva Baumann could do better. Definitely. And she deserved better. Best to just toss all thoughts of her aside.

He called Dirk.

"Finally," he answered with a huff.

"Nice to hear from you again too." Sebastian smirked. He knew why Dirk was riled up. It had to do with his last text to him.

I quit.

"You can't quit. You know that right?"

"Why not?" Sebastian turned the corner and pushed the numbers to unlock the door to his building.

"Because you signed a contract. It's legally binding."

Sebastian swore softly. He figured as much, but he kept bluffing. "Find another lead singer. The deal was really with the band, right? Not me."

"It was with the band *and* with you. With each of you."

Sebastian went straight to his fridge, opened a beer and took a swig. "What happens if I just don't show? Karl is more than ready to take my place."

"Karl is an imbecile. What he did to you was unconscionable, no question. But he doesn't have what it takes to fill your shoes."

"Then fire him."

"I can't fire him for immoral behavior. He'd be the one suing next. I'm afraid you're just stuck with each other."

"Not going to work for me, Dirk. I quit."

"You're really going to face a lawsuit over this? Throw away your career?"

"I'll revive it."

Dirk went quiet, and Sebastian had to check to make sure he hadn't been cut off.

"Look," Dirk finally said. "I can probably postpone the next tour, give you guys some time to cool off and get your act together. It won't be pretty and you can expect fan and media backlash."

"I knew there was a reason we hired you."

"Yeah, well, the studio is still booked for October, so you're not on vacation. You better get writing. Ya hear me?"

"Yeah, yeah." Sebastian hung up without saying good-bye.

He flopped on the couch and put his hands behind his head. This was the best good news he'd heard in weeks. Six weeks off. Karl and Yvonne drama free. Sounded heavenly.

Sebastian heard Dirk, though. He had to write. He reached for the nearest guitar that was propped against the couch and ran his fingers up and down the strings, listening for something new to inspire him. Any random combination of things could ignite a new idea. He threw the strap over his shoulder and walked the guitar to the opened door to the deck. The view from his patio was familiar and comfortable, but he saw nothing that inspired an idea.

He went back inside and flicked on the TV. Normally, he avoided news channels. He hated bad news. It just reminded him of his own problems.

He flicked it off.

This was crazy. He wondered if he'd ever write a new song again. Dirk might get his court case by default at this rate.

Truth was, he wrote best in tandem with another writer. He didn't know why, but his best ideas came with collaboration. Like the song he wrote with Katja Stoltz or the dozen he and Karl had written over the years. The two of them were like John Lennon and Paul McCartney.

Sebastian groaned. He couldn't imagine spending five minutes in the same room with Karl again, much less writing another hit song with him.

Which made him think of Eva Baumann. She was a good writer. Maybe she could be his next muse? She certainly was on his mind a lot more than he'd expected. Even if she could just help him get started on a new song. He just needed a little help getting started.

Would it be weird if he showed up at her place again? Twice in one day? Her father would likely be there by now, and Sebastian was pretty sure he wouldn't be too pleased to see him again. He just missed running into him when he left their building that afternoon.

His stomach growled, and he went back to the kitchen to find something to eat. The three buns in a bag on the counter were hard, and the fridge produced a package of butter and a jar of mustard. Great. Now the question was should he go to the grocery store or eat out? He could order in, but suddenly he didn't want to stay home.

Italian food would hit the spot and he knew just the place. The open patio of the Italian restaurant that just happened to be right across the street from Eva's building. Yeah, a plate of pasta was what he needed.

He grabbed his sunglasses and his cap as a precaution, though the locals were getting used to him being around now and didn't pay him as much attention. There were still the tourists to avoid.

Luckily, there was an empty table tucked in behind a planter. The greenery shielded him from the foot traffic that walked by on the sidewalk, but he could see around it enough to keep his eye on the door of Eva's building.

A middle-aged waiter approached. "Hello, Herr Weiss."

Already recognized. "Good day."

"What can I get for you?"

Sebastian ordered fettuccine Alfredo with prawns and asparagus. His eyes kept darting to the second-story window—he could see the lace curtain billowing from the summer breeze. A dark head entered the frame, and he pulled back. He'd be mortified if she caught him gawking. He had to chuckle. Now he was the stalker? Usually he was dodging the crazy people and here he was, one of them.

He shook his head, disgusted at himself. He'd just eat his meal and head home. Leave the poor girl alone.

He no sooner thought this when he saw movement across the street out of the corner of his eye. The door eased open, and Eva stepped out. She'd changed into a knee length denim skirt that emphasized her narrow waist. Sebastian sat upright. Where was she going?

Eva carefully supported her weight with her cane and turned west toward the *Altstadt*. He waited, wondering if she was going to go into one of the shops. Maybe she was meeting someone? But she never turned in, just slowly made her way down the uneven sidewalk. Sebastian sprang from his chair.

"Hey?" The waiter called, just arriving with his meal.

"Pack it up for me," he said, pulling bills out of his pocket and dropping them on the table. "I'll come back for it."

Sebastian dashed down the street, dodging cyclists, skateboarders, women pushing strollers and couples walking linked arm in arm. He slowed up when he got within meters of her. What was he going to do now? Call out? Tap her on the shoulder?

Eva decided for him. For some reason she stopped and

looked over her shoulder. Her green eyes widened with confusion when she spotted him.

"Oh, I thought it was you," Sebastian said. He quickened his pace to catch up.

"The cane was a big giveaway?" she asked.

"No, well, yeah, maybe. Does it matter?"

"No, of course not."

"Can I join you?"

Her eyelashes fluttered. "Twice in one day. I'm honored."

"It's no big deal. Unless it is… for you. I can leave." A lack of confidence was not something Sebastian struggled with, but now in this moment, with this girl, he found he cared what she thought of him. It hadn't occurred to him before now that she might reject him. His empty stomach swirled.

Her face broke into a smile and relieved him of his fears. "You really must be bored."

She started walking and he moved slowly beside her. "Why would you say that?"

"I don't know. Don't you have *people*? Photo shoots? Studio sessions?"

"You could say I'm on vacation."

"And you're not on a plane to Italy because…"

"Okay, here's the truth. I want to quit the band."

Eva stopped and shot him a horrified look. He patted her shoulder. "Relax. The band's not dissolving. There are contracts. I have to stay. I just don't want to."

"Why? I thought making it big with your band was your dream?"

"It was. But that was before I found out my best friend was sleeping with my girlfriend."

Eva's mouth dropped open and her face turned a

shade of red. "Oh." She stared hard at her sandals and continued along the cobblestones.

"I'm sorry. Too much information." Sebastian gathered that she wasn't used to people being so forthright about personal things. He rushed on, hoping to smooth it over. "So yeah, I kind of hate Karl right now. We're on an imposed break for a month and a half." They reached the crosswalk at *Albertsplatz.* "Where are you going?"

She glanced up at him and then back at the street. "I don't know. My house can get kind of suffocating. Sometimes I just need to get out from under the microscope."

"Yeah, I know what it's like when everyone is in your business."

They managed to move through the crowd coming from the opposite side of the intersection and Sebastian worried they wouldn't make it to the other side before the light changed back to red. He pictured himself scooping her up to hurry things along, but they made it across just in time without his intervention. If he planned to hang out with this girl, he was going to have to work on his patience. Eva pointed to the statuesque fountain just past the rail stop. "I often sit here."

A couple vacated a bench so Sebastian jogged over to save it. He watched as Eva hobbled over. She eyed him tentatively and sat down. Her skirt inched up revealing a shapely thigh marred by a thick scar. She caught him staring and tugged at the fabric sharply.

"What happened?" Then he quickly added. "I hope it's okay I asked. If not just tell me to mind my own business."

Her fingers remained gripped on her skirt and he waited for her to tell him to take a hike. But instead she said, "It's fine."

"An accident?"

She nodded. "I was in a coma for three weeks."

"Crazy."

"Yeah." She gazed at the fountain. Large mermen intertwined with cherub and sea creatures wrapped around its thick base. "I don't remember anything," she added quietly.

Sebastian deciphered the code: Don't ask any more questions.

"So, anyway, it's kind of cool that I ran into you again," he said, like it was purely coincidental and that he hadn't been scoping her place. "I'm wondering if you'd like to try writing together sometime?"

Eva swung back to stare at him. "Are you serious?"

"Yeah, why not?"

"Because." She shook her head. "Because you're *Sebastian Weiss*."

"And you're Eva Baumann. A great songwriter. C'mon. Let's just try it." Sebastian hoped he didn't sound as desperate as he felt. He had to write a new song. He *had* to. Not just for Dirk or the band but for the sake of his own soul.

Eva's eyelashes fluttered. "I suppose I'd be crazy to turn you down."

"Yes," Sebastian encouraged. "You'd be crazy."

"My parents will freak though. I don't think you should come by again."

"Your papa get on your case?"

Eva sighed. "You could say that. And my dumb sister let it slip that you were in our flat."

"You could come to my place then." He half waved at her. "Obviously they let you out of their sight on occasion."

She grinned. "On occasion."

"Great. Give me your phone, and I'll put my number in it."

Eva wore a leather pouch with a long strap that ran from shoulder to hip. She pulled out a phone and dropped it into his open hand.

"Now you have my number." He pressed a button, and the phone in his pocket rang. "And I have yours. How does tomorrow at this time sound?"

She nodded, a stunned expression of disbelief crossing her cute face. Sebastian had to bite the inside of his lip to keep from smiling. "I texted you my address."

He saluted her as he left her sitting on the bench. He had a good feeling about this. Eva Baumann would help him break free from writer's block. He was going to write a hit song, he could just feel it.

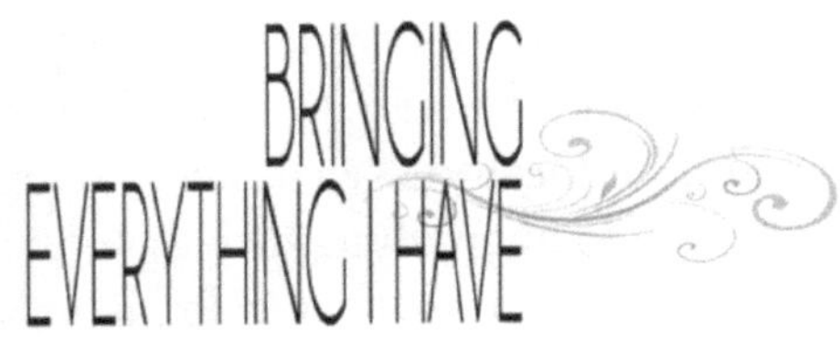

EVA'S MIND NEVER SLOWED, and she barely slept that night. From beginning to end the day had been outrageously incredible. She and Sebastian Weiss were practically friends. At the very least, they were writing partners. She pressed a hand over her heart. Be still.

She finally fell asleep just as dawn broke and the partiers outside quieted, but she woke abruptly to the beeping of the alarm on Gabriele's phone. Normally, the intrusive ping didn't bother her because she usually woke earlier than her sister. Today she groaned into her pillow.

"Are you sick?" Gabriele asked when she noticed Eva's form under the summer blanket.

"I'm fine," Eva croaked. She waited for Gabriele to finish in the WC before getting up. She willed the fog in her mind to clear, and then her eyelids snapped open. She remembered her encounter with Sebastian Weiss the day before and how she'd promised to go to his flat that evening.

What was she thinking?

She reached for her phone and pressed the contacts button. Sure enough Sebastian's name was there. She hadn't dreamed it.

And now she had the whole day to get through. It took her longer than "normal" girls to get ready for the day. She donned another summer skirt—she didn't like to wear shorts because it was hard to hide her scar and jeans were too hot—a blouse and leather sandals. She knew she wouldn't make the cut for the cover of a fashion magazine, but she had never cared about things like that. She brushed her hair, choosing to keep it down even though it would be cooler to pin it back or put it in a ponytail. She liked how she could hide behind it if necessary. It was an ostrich maneuver—hiding her cane and her limp was impossible —but it brought her a sense of ease in awkward moments.

Her parents didn't expect much from her when it came to cleaning the house, but she did insist that they let her do the dishes and make the short trek to the grocery store, at least when the weather was good. Pushing a cart wasn't that difficult, and she could get quite a lot in her backpack to bring the goods home.

She spent the afternoon working on the one university course she had recently decided to take online. Theoretically, she could get a degree this way, but it would take a decade or more. Gabriele and Annette were right. She should go to university this fall. Stop being a chicken and face the stares and questions. It wasn't just the people that frightened her: it was also the structure. How would she manage the crowded hallway and get to her classes on time? Everyone would stare if she arrived late. And there was a lot of ice in the winter. She could fall. She could miss the transit, stumble on slippery steps. What if one of the professors called her out in class?

Eva shook her head and sighed. Next year. She'd go next year for sure.

Eventually, the day passed. *Abendbrot* discussions mercifully moved from her to other topics like world events, neighborhood gossip, and of course, Gabriele and Lennon's wedding.

She excused herself afterward, announcing that she was going for a walk, and it hit her that she had no way of getting her guitar downstairs. How was she going to write songs without it? There was no way she could ask for assistance and even if she did get Gabriele's help, her parents would ask questions. She hoped Sebastian had an extra guitar.

She slipped her notebook into her large shoulder bag and threaded her arm through the strap. She was down the stairs and halfway to the address Sebastian had left her before she paused. Was she really going to do this? She didn't have to. She could just text him an excuse and maybe he'd leave her be. She furrowed her brow in thought. The guy seemed pretty intent on this writing experiment, and Sebastian Weiss didn't come across as someone who gave up easily.

Eva's heart raced as she pushed the button by his flat number on the door of the building. It buzzed and clicked open. Sebastian would have to live on the third floor.

He waited for her in the doorway of his flat and his face broke into a smile when he saw her. She wiped her brow of the moisture that had beaded there and smiled back. Sebastian wore knee-length shorts and a red muscle shirt. His feet were bare, and she wondered if she should take her sandals off when she entered.

He saw her reaching for the strap. "You can leave them on if you want." She did. "Can I get you a drink? I have water with and without bubbles. Or Fanta?"

"Water with bubbles, please."

Eva remained standing, leaning on her cane. Sebastian's flat looked lived in, with stuff everywhere, including a lot of instruments. She hadn't needed to worry about him having an extra guitar. There were several hanging from hooks on the wall and a number sitting on guitar stands on the floor.

Three hand drums of different sizes sat beside a sizable stereo system in the corner. A violin lay in an open velvet-lined case on the coffee table. A projector hung from the ceiling across the room from a pull-down screen for watching TV.

She wasn't sure what to do. She'd never been alone with a boy in his flat before. No, not a boy. A man. She'd never been alone with a *man* in his flat before.

Sebastian removed the lid from a bottle and poured the contents into a glass. "Have a seat," he said. She claimed the nearest armchair and he handed her the water.

She watched him over the rim of the glass. He grabbed one of his acoustic guitars and sat across from her on the couch. It looked like he hadn't shaved that day and Eva found herself wondering what it would feel like to rub her fingers over his jaw. He was better looking in real life than on TV, and he looked pretty good there.

"Eva?"

She snapped to attention. *Focus, Eva!* "Yeah?"

"I was wondering if you had any ideas?" He strummed a little riff. "Something to get us started?"

"Oh," Eva shifted, looking for a place to put her cane. She settled with laying it on the floor beside her chair. "I've never written a song with anyone before, so I'm not sure." She fished the notebook out of her bag. Her eyes fell on the lyrics she had scribbled there and she frowned. They felt good at the time, but now she wasn't sure.

"What is it?" Sebastian prodded.

"Just some notes, a few lines about an idea I had. More like a concept, really."

"Okay?"

"I was thinking about how humans are made up of more than just flesh and bone. That there must be something beyond…" She motioned to her bad leg. "…this."

Sebastian nodded and when he didn't say anything Eva hurried to fill in the silence. "I guess it's something I think about a lot, considering. We can scrap it if you don't like it."

"No, it's a good concept." He passed her the guitar. "Show me what you have so far?"

She accepted the instrument. "It's not much yet." She strummed a shuffle beat and hummed a melody idea, and then she sang softly.

I can't say what lies beyond my flesh and bone,
But for the pull here beneath
We reach to the sky

Here like shadows moving transience
Turning the fallow
Or building the gallows
To the certain uncertainty
Like an unremembered memory

She covered the strings with her palm. "That's all I have so far. It's not a rock song…"

He chuckled. "I can turn anything into a rock song. I like the groove. I was worried it would be mopey, but it comes across as an honest question."

She cocked her head. "Rather than preaching?"

His lip tugged up crookedly. "Well, the subject matter… along with your family's influence…"

"What do you mean by that?"

"Nothing, just that I'm not religious."

"Me neither."

He balked. "*You* don't believe in God?"

"I never said that. I said I wasn't religious… in the

sense that I'm not bound by the laws and beliefs of a particular denomination."

Sebastian's gaze narrowed, and his lips parted like he was going to respond, but then he stood and crossed the room. He picked up a second acoustic guitar. "I have some ideas."

He shared a few lines and Eva wrote them down. She added a couple. Sebastian played a harmony riff when they tested them out. Some lines, they agreed, needed to be crossed out and a couple they deliberated over.

When it occurred to Eva to check her phone for the time, she stammered, "Two hours! I have to go."

"Wow." Sebastian leaned back and said with a lazy grin, "You're on a tight leash. How old did you say you were?"

Eva swallowed a wad of embarrassment. He knew how old she was. "Don't judge me."

"Okay, sorry. It's just that I'm excited with the momentum we've got going."

"Yeah, well," she said coolly. She handed the guitar to Sebastian's outstretched hand and reached for her cane on the floor. She hated the way Sebastian watched her slow movements and how she felt his eyes on the back of her head as she limped to the door. He had no idea what it was like to be her. No idea.

"Eva?"

She turned slowly and caught his eye.

"I'm sorry. I don't mean to be a jerk."

THE CERTAIN UNCERTAINTY

He could be such a jerk. Here she'd come, acting against her family's approval, just to help him write a dumb song, and he had to go and make her feel stupid. He needed to make it up to her somehow. He didn't want her to feel like he was using her.

Was he?

No. They'd share songwriting credits. If it became a hit for Hollow Fellows, she'd make a lot of money. *He* was doing *her* the favor.

Still, she didn't seem to care about the money, and he could totally picture her quitting on him. She wasn't the one who needed a partner to write.

Eva Baumann was the best thing to happen to him in a long time. He enjoyed her company. She was smart and talented, and her innocence was refreshing. When the guitar was on her lap, covering her leg, it was easy to forget she was handicapped.

And she was cute. The way her eyes sparkled when they came up with just the right line, and the little lilt to her laugh. It was easy to be with her. No expectations. No drama.

Except for when he stupidly caused it.

Maybe he should take her out. Not on a date, just as friends. Somewhere nice. Somewhere she probably never goes. He drummed his fingertips on the tops of his thighs.

There was a tap on the door and he sprang to his feet to get it. Had Eva forgotten something?

He hurried to answer it but it wasn't the sweet face of Eva Baumann on the other side. It was the pinched face of Yvonne.

Sebastian huffed. "What are you doing here?"

Yvonne smiled like he'd just hit on her. She was dressed in short shorts and a revealing T-shirt. She tucked her short hair, tinted blue now, behind her studded ears and looked up at Sebastian from heavily made-up eyes. "I came to see you. We're still friends aren't we? She outlined the peacock tattoo with her fingernail.

He tugged his arm away. "You should go."

"Basti, let's be adults here." She strutted over to an armchair, slouched into it and draped a bare leg over the arm. "I know you're angry, and rightly so, but nothing actually happened between Karl and me."

"I saw you kissing him."

"Yeah, okay. We kissed. But we never went beyond that."

Sebastian leaned against the wall and crossed his arms. "Why should I believe you?"

"Because it's true. Besides, it didn't mean anything."

Maybe not to her, but it sure did to him. "It doesn't matter. You lied to me so you could be with him instead. That speaks volumes."

Yvonne pushed herself gracefully off the chair and walked toward him. "It was stupid, and I'm so, so sorry."

"I know. You told me that already."

"I just feel so bad. I heard the band broke up?"

"We're on hiatus."

She stepped closer. He could smell the hair products in her hair. "I feel responsible."

He kept his arms folded tight against his chest, a barrier. "You did have something to do with it."

Yvonne placed a manicured hand on his arm. "Basti." Her painted nails crawled up to the soft skin of his neck. She whispered, "Are you sure we can't start over? Just forget this ever happened?"

"Pretty sure."

She let her arm fall. "Don't tell me there's someone else already."

Eva's lips crossed Sebastian's mind, but he shook the thought away. "No. I'm just not interested in you anymore."

It was harsh, but it was true. Seeing her now and knowing she would follow him into the bedroom at the flick of a finger, it didn't stir anything in him. Her face blushed with embarrassment. She wasn't used to rejection. She stormed away and slammed the door, a move she'd made many times over the years when they'd fought. He'd always chased after her then, but this time he lowered himself onto the couch and let her go.

A soft chuckle escaped his lips. He was free of her.

IT'S NOT A DATE

ANNETTE SAT on the floor by Eva's feet while Eva tested out a messy, medieval-style braid Annette had found on Pinterest.

"You have gorgeous hair," Eva said. "I can totally picture you as an ancient queen."

Annette hummed. "I don't know if what you're doing looks good, but it sure feels nice. You have to let me try one on you."

"No thanks." Eva preferred to let her hair hang unhampered.

"Why not?"

"Have you forgotten about the disastrous bang affair?" Eva had succumbed to Annette's assurance that bangs on her would look cute. She hated them and it took five months for them to grow out.

"Eva, that was three years ago." Annette shook her head.

"Keep still," Eva admonished.

Annette froze everything but her lips. "Besides braiding doesn't involve a set of scissors."

"Done," Eva said, hoping that would end the discussion. Annette scurried to the dresser mirror.

"Where's the handheld one?"

"Near the corner of the dresser. Under one of Gabi's textbooks."

Annette lifted the book in question and retrieved the mirror. She turned so she could view the back of her head and examine Eva's handy work. "I like it."

Eva wasn't paying attention. She checked the messages on her phone, and stared at the name above the text.

"What is it?" Annette asked.

"A text." Eva looked up. "From Sebastian."

"Sebastian Weiss?"

"Yeah."

"Oh my goodness. Does he want to write with you again?"

Eva hadn't heard from him for three days. She was sure that he had found her to be childish and immature and probably boring, and that he had moved on to a more mature, sophisticated writing partner.

"Eva?"

"No. I don't know. That's not what he's asking."

"What's he asking?"

She handed Annette the phone.

Annette arched a brow. "He left three messages?"

Eva nodded, feeling stunned.

Sebastian Weiss

Can I take you out for lunch tomorrow?

Sebastian Weiss

I thought it might help if we got to know each other better. For writing.

Sebastian Weiss

Not a date or anything. Just friends. In case you're worried.

Annette squealed. "Sebastian Weiss wants to take you out!"

"It's not a date."

"So. You'd still be out. With him."

"I can't do it." Eva rubbed her forehead trying to erase the headache coming on. "My parents would never agree."

"Don't tell them."

"Annette!"

"Eva, you're an adult." Annette sat on the bed beside Eva, a serious expression crossing her freckled face. "If you want to go out with a guy, you should go. Hey, I'll cover for you. Tell your parents you're coming to visit me."

"I never visit you."

"I know. And it's time you changed that." She shrieked. "Oh gosh. He just messaged you again." She handed the phone back.

Sebastian Weiss

Eva?

"Not the patient sort, is he?" Annette giggled. "I guess when you're a rock star, you don't have to wait for what you want."

Eva fought a growing panic. She'd never been on a date before. Even if this wasn't a date. "What should I say?"

"Say yes, silly."

Showing up at Sebastian's place was nerve-racking enough, but at least she was free to leave when she wanted. They had two guitars between them and a song to discuss. Without the song and the guitars, what would they talk about? Her throat felt like it was closing up. "I can't," she muttered.

Annette snatched the phone from Eva's hand, and her thumbs raced across the keyboard.

"Annette!"

"There." Annette returned her phone. "You can't back out now."

Eva stared at the text her friend had written.

Eva Baumann
> *Okay.*

The phone buzzed again and she nearly jumped out of her skin.

Sebastian Weiss
> *Great. I'll pick you up tomorrow at noon.*

"Oh no," Eva stood and almost fell over. "He's coming here."

"Text him back. Tell him to meet you at Luther Square."

Eva's sweaty thumbs moved quickly across the keyboard. Moments later.

Sebastian Weiss
> *See you there.*

Eva collapsed back onto the bed and covered her face with her hands. She couldn't believe it. She was going on a non-date with Sebastian Weiss. She couldn't resist a tiny squeal.

Eva waited at Luther Square the next day at noon. She'd told her parents she was going to Annette's and they believed her because Annette actually came over that morning and walked her out. "Just in case you're tempted to ditch him," she'd said.

Annette helped her select a summer dress, yellow with lace trim around a boat-cut neckline and a narrow belt that tied into a loopy bow at the back. "It's feminine and not as frumpy as your other ones. The belt shows off your narrow waist."

Eva drew the line when it came to putting pins in her hair, but she had showered and shampooed. Annette spritzed her with some of Gabriele's perfume when she wasn't looking.

"Stop it," she said. "I don't want to look like I'm trying too hard."

"You don't want to look like you're not trying at all, either." Annette draped an arm over Eva's shoulders and kissed her on the cheek. "No worries. You look wonderful."

Just then a Hollow Fellows' song came on the satellite radio pumping through Eva's laptop and Sebastian's voice filled her bedroom.

Eva dropped her cane and sat on the chair by her guitar. "Oh my heart. What am I doing, Annette?"

Annette giggled. "You're going on a date with a rock star!"

"A non-date."

Her friend smirked. "It may be a non-date, but he's still a rock star."

Annette walked Eva to the square where Eva playfully shooed her away. "I don't want him to think I came with my babysitter."

So now here she was on a warm summer day, waiting for the one and only Sebastian Weiss. She looked around and wondered what he would be driving. She pressed her sunglasses against her face and leaned on her cane. She was about to head for the bench facing the rolling ball fountain when she heard a car horn beep.

Sebastian waved her over to an open taxi door.

"Hey," he said. Even though Sebastian wore sunglasses, Eva could tell he was checking her out, his eyes scanning her from head to toe. She was glad she'd taken the extra trouble with her appearance and promised herself she'd thank Annette later. Sebastian looked pretty good, too. He leaned against the open door, waiting for her, all suave and cool. He was every bit the celebrity. She saw a group of girls point and knew he'd been recognized.

He placed a hand on her elbow to guide her in, and his touch sent shivers throughout her body. Eva was Cinderella being helped into the pumpkin carriage by the handsome prince. Somehow her life had turned into a fairytale. She pulled in her legs and her cane and smiled, hoping she looked graceful and collected, and not like the unraveling wreck she actually felt she was.

Sebastian got in the other side. He slipped off his sunglasses and grinned. "You look nice."

"Thanks." She hoped he couldn't see her face flush. "Where are we going?"

"Königstein Fortress."

It was her turn to remove her sunglasses. "I thought we were going for lunch."

"We are."

"But that's at least a half an hour away." The taxi fare would be outrageous.

Sebastian shrugged a shoulder. "I don't have any other plans. Do you?"

She shook her head. "I'm surprised you didn't pick me up in a fancy car. I imagined you with a garage full."

"Nah. Some guys might do that, but I'm not really into cars."

"Guitars are more your thing."

"Yeah, that's right." He cocked his head and grinned. "You can't have too many guitars."

"So, why are we going to the fortress? There were plenty of places to eat close by."

"I wanted to take you somewhere different. Have you been there?"

"No." Eva's class once did a field trip to the fortress, but she had missed it because she was still in heavy physiotherapy. Her family stuck to home for the most part. They didn't even own a car. You didn't really need one once you mastered the transit system, and the railway lines across Germany were vast and efficient.

Sebastian rubbed his chin. "You're in for a treat then."

Music pumped in from the stereo in the dash, and Eva and Sebastian engaged in music talk: bands they liked, who's on top, who's on the bottom, their favorite songs and why they were great.

"Best song of all time?" Eva asked.

"'The Boxer', hands down."

"By Simon and Garfunkel?" She was surprised. She thought he'd pick a rock song. "Why?"

"First of all, the song is an example of a perfect match between music and lyric. The music arrangement captures the emotion of the stark pictures the lyric creates. It makes you feel like you are on the streets with the narrator, cold and alone."

Eva nodded in agreement.

"Secondly, the lyrics are very vivid and poetic. '*Seeking out the poorer quarters where the ragged people go, looking for the places only they would know.*' Words like ragged and quarters are not words normally used by street people, so it gives the feeling that the narrator is not from that world but he is consigned to it. It adds to the feeling of loneliness."

Eva loved how passionate Sebastian was when he spoke. His brows furrowed and he motioned with his hands for emphasis. She worked to keep from smiling inappropriately.

Sebastian continued, "The '*ly la ly*' tag makes it more of a folk song, which means it's a song for the common man. The last verse is unexpected because it breaks away from the narrator's voice. It's a vivid allegory of the narrator's predicament. It again paints a very clear picture and says things the narrator would not say himself but the listener hears it and gets a deeper picture. It's a perfectly written story song."

Sebastian eyed Eva with a smug expression like he knew he'd impressed her.

And he had.

"What about you?" he asked in return.

Eva had to think. She had a lot of favorites, but had never placed a single one on the top of the pile.

Sebastian patted her knee, startling her with his touch. He smirked at her reaction. "It doesn't have to be one of mine."

"I'm a Bob Dylan fan."

Sebastian's eyebrows jumped, but he waited for her to continue.

"I love how he paints pictures with words and doesn't

care if the message is clear on first listen. He writes songs you have to pay attention to."

"So, which one is your favorite?"

Eva hummed. "I'm going to say 'Chimes of Freedom.'"

Sebastian nodded like he approved. "Why that one?"

She stared at her hands. "It's about the underdog. I can relate."

"Everyone's the underdog at some point," Sebastian said.

"Which is why I love this song. Its themes are universal."

Eva barely noticed when they left the autobahn and drove down a road through thick forest. She was shocked when Sebastian announced they had arrived.

It looked like a giant hand had wielded a sword and sliced off the top of a mountain before placing the Fortress on top. Eva gaped at the massive stone structure high above them. It was far more intimidating in real life than in pictures.

"Impressive," Eva said. And it was a good thing there was a train to pull them to the top from the parking lot below. Though many people opted to hike, it would never be an option for her.

The train was actually a tractor that pulled several carts with forward-facing benches, much like Eva had seen on TV ads promoting theme parks. Sebastian paid the driver, an older man with a scowl and a big belly. He gladly took Sebastian's money.

The sheer height of the fortress wall could only be appreciated while standing at the base of it. Eva craned her neck up as she exited the train at the top.

"Those walls are made of sandstone," Sebastian said.

"They're as high as forty-two meters in some places, and yes," his hazel eyes glistened, " I did my homework."

Eva spotted the small outlines of people walking about high above. "How do you get to the top?"

Sebastian pointed to a lift. They walked toward it, Sebastian slowing his pace considerably to match hers.

"Oh," he said.

"What?"

He pointed to a sign. "Out of service. They're providing rides up on ATVs every hour for those who can't walk up." Sebastian checked the time. "Looks like we just missed the last one."

Eva swallowed her disappointment. Sebastian brought her to eat lunch and he must be starving. "I'm sorry."

"You might not be able to walk it, but I can."

She tilted her head in confusion. Was he seriously suggesting she wait for him?

He chuckled and bent low. "Get on."

"What?"

"Get on. I'll piggyback you up."

Eva's mind shut down. That would mean "touching" him. Like in a big way.

Sebastian glanced over his shoulder. "Are you going to make me wait all day? My knees are going to give out soon."

Eva gulped and stepped forward. She draped thin arms around Sebastian's warm neck, careful not to whack him with her cane, and wrapped her legs around his waist. Her head rushed as he stood. She was thankful that he couldn't see her face, and also that her dress had enough flare to spread out and keep her butt covered. She breathed in Sebastian's intoxicating scent and prayed she wouldn't pass out. Never in a million years would she have dreamed of this scenario, that she'd be pressing her body against Sebastian Weiss's back.

"Okay up there?"

She whimpered. "Yeah. Fine."

"Man, you weigh a ton. What are they feeding you?"

Eva smiled at Sebastian's teasing tone. She was slight and petite, weighing less than fifty kilos. Still, that got heavy in a hurry.

It was a long, steep climb through a dark cobblestone path. Eva couldn't imagine how horses pulling heavy carts managed the trip, much less the poor soul hefting her up. "Are you sure you want to do this?" she asked.

Sebastian huffed. "Remind me to renew my pass to the fitness center."

"We can go back."

"I'm fine. I see the light. We're almost there."

They passed the defunct wooden gate, now perpetually opened, that was once operated by an ancient pulley system, and finally reached the top.

He crouched and she peeled herself off. She glanced away, feeling shy, and smoothed out her dress. Sebastian pointed. Napoleon's Kitchen is this way.

"Napoleon's Kitchen?"

"It's a little outdoor restaurant by the wall."

They went straight to the kiosk when they got there and ordered the specialty: potato soup and a thick chunk of bread.

They slowed their pace after a few slurps of tasty soup. Eva couldn't stop watching her non-date who sat on the opposite side of the table. She was used to his public attire of a dark sunglasses and a brimmed hat pulled low. He wore a grey T-shirt and his peacock tattoo flexed as he lifted his spoon to his mouth.

"Is there a story behind that?" she asked.

He glanced down and then back at her. "Yup."

He didn't jump in to fill her in and she wondered if the meaning was too personal. She didn't know him well enough to pry, and so she filled her mouth with a piece of soup-soaked bread.

"You don't like it?" he finally asked.

She pursed her lips. "It's nice."

"Nice?"

"Yeah, what? It's nice."

He smirked and leaned in. "Most girls tell me it's sassy."

She almost choked on her soup. She pressed a paper napkin against her lips. "Fine. It's sassy."

He laughed. "You're just saying that now."

"No, I'm not used to saying things like that outright, but it's true." She paused, then forced the words out of her mouth. "It's sassy."

"Really? Eva Baumann thinks my tattoo is sassy?"

She rolled her eyes. "Now, don't get a big head about it."

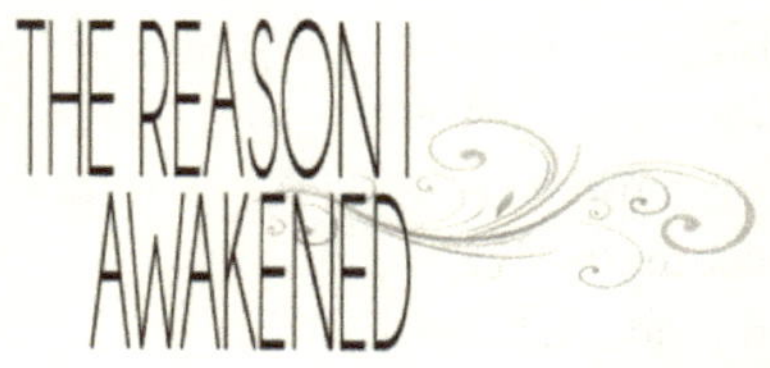

THE REASON I AWAKENED

EVA WAS FULL OF SURPRISES. A lot of girls flirted with Sebastian, told him he was hot and talented, and many were pretty forthright about wanting to do more than eat lunch, but none had ever pushed back like that.

He liked it.

The way the sun sifted through the trees onto her flawless skin, he found himself thinking she was beautiful. She wore a little makeup today, but not too much. She wasn't trying to hide behind a mask of foundation or eyes made unrecognizable by dark shadow and thick mascara.

With her legs hidden under the table he could forget that Eva was disabled. She wasn't pretentious. She didn't try to pretend she was something she wasn't. And she didn't want anything from him, wasn't using him as a step to gain hold of her own ambitions. He sensed she had a good heart and it occurred to him that he could trust her. He hadn't felt that way toward anyone in a long time.

"It's kind of a long story," he began, "but I'll give you the short version. My father's a doctor and my mother's a lawyer."

Eva failed to keep her expression blank.

"I know," Sebastian responded. "That info always surprises people. What happened to me, right?"

"I didn't think that," she said.

"Well, they sure did. They hounded me all through school to apply for medical or law. For a while I considered a career as a violinist in an orchestra. I was accepted for enrollment at the Conservatoire de Paris, and though that wasn't my parents' dream for me, they considered it an acceptable alternative.

"But in the end I decided I just wanted to play guitar in an alternative rock band. My parents thought I was being foolish and immature, but it was what I wanted to do. They didn't get me.

"When they finally realized I wasn't joking, that I wasn't going to pursue a path in academia, they kicked me out. Dad said I was a proud peacock, and not to come back until I got serious with my life."

Sebastian finished his beer and pushed the mug aside. "It's been my passion to prove him wrong ever since. I got this tattoo to remind myself not to give up."

"So what's it feel like?" Eva asked.

"What do you mean?"

"You've proved him wrong. How does it feel?"

Sebastian frowned. "Not as good as I thought it would."

He gathered their empty dishes and deposited them at the kiosk and then led her to the moss-covered stone wall that overlooked the valley below. The River Elbe snaked through green pastures and forested hillsides dotted with the red roofs of the village houses.

"It's stunning," Eva said.

"This fortress has been here for 400 years and has never been breached. It was used as a prison for much of that time until recently." Sebastian pointed and added, "Napoleon visited, which explains that."

A wooden panel painted like the portly Napoleon, complete with hand tucked in his vest, stood off to the side. There was a hole cut out where the face belonged that tourists took turns poking their faces through while their friends snapped pictures.

It stood empty now. "Take my picture," Sebastian said. He handed her his phone and jogged behind the fake Napoleon. He made a goofy face and she snapped.

"Your turn," he said when he returned to her.

Eva's smile tugged down. Sebastian could tell from where they were standing that she wouldn't reach the hole. "I'll lift you."

A woman and her teenage daughter hung by watching and Sebastian asked the mother if she'd take a picture. Sebastian scooped up Eva by the waist and hauled her to the back of the display. A fountain of laughter burst from her mouth. He laughed in return. He'd wanted to make her smile, and truth be told, he saw this as a good excuse to touch her again. Her waist was tiny but still soft in a womanly way. He hoisted her up so her head lined up with the hole and Eva's body pressed against his face.

He chuckled to himself. *Smooth move, Seb.*

Eva giggled. "You can let me down now."

Sebastian returned to the woman to retrieve his phone and walked back to Eva. The daughter had stood around looking bored, but now she stared hard at him. He knew that look. He'd been recognized. The daughter pointed and spoke excitedly to her mother.

"Hurry." Sebastian crouched low. "Get on."

The daughter had a camera of her own, a good one with a lens. "Keep your head down." He hoisted Eva on his back and galloped away. Eva burst out laughing as she bounced about hanging on for dear life, nearly choking him.

Sebastian didn't know why he cared if he was photographed with Eva on his back. Then he felt the warm breath of her laughter on his neck, and he realized that he didn't care. And now he wondered if he'd ever find another excuse to convince this girl to hold onto him again.

MYSTERY GIRL

EVA FELL into a happy daydream during *Abendbrot*. Her afternoon at the fortress with Sebastian was the highlight of her whole life. His body had felt so good pressed against hers. Even though it was in the friendliest of ways, it was the closest she'd ever been physically with the opposite sex. Every time he touched her was like an injection of energy and life. She couldn't remember the last time she'd laughed like that. She'd die with a smile because of this memory. Her non-date with Sebastian Weiss was definitely the best day of her life so far.

Snap, snap. "Eva?" Gabriele said, her fingers flicking in Eva's face. "Is everything all right?"

Eva's eyes fluttered as her mind returned to her present situation. Her parents stared at her with concern and Gabriele chuckled. "Where were you?"

"Oh, I was just thinking of something."

"Of what?"

"Just… Annette."

"Annette?"

"Yeah. It was good to be at her house again." Eva flushed with the lie. It wasn't something she liked doing.

"I'm glad you felt up to going," her mama said. "It's been a while."

The inference was there. Was she getting better? Her

body had recovered as much as it would from the accident, but she'd never quite recovered emotionally. Eva had withdrawn from society, creating a safe little world for herself.

A world she never imagined would expand—could expand—until Sebastian came into her life.

"I think I'm ready to go to university," Eva announced.

Her family worked to contain their shock. Her papa grinned. "That's great."

Eva surprised herself by her impulsive declaration. She had Sebastian to thank for that. He'd shown her she could be accepted the way she was. He made her feel smart and interesting. He looked at her like she was pretty or at least not loathsome.

If Sebastian Weiss wanted to be her friend, then other *regular* people surely would, too. She wondered why she'd been so afraid.

Gabriele clasped Eva's hand and squeezed. "I knew it was just a matter of time."

Eva had to bite her lips to keep the smile that wanted to take over her face at bay. It helped if she kept her mouth busy with food, and even though she was too excited to be hungry, it was better than inspiring another inquisition by her family.

After the meal she helped clean off the table. Her papa retired to the living room to watch the news, which was his habit. The news program had ended, and the introduction to an entertainment program began. Eva was passing by on her way to escape to her room where she could lie on her bed and let her thoughts roam freely.

"*...an amateur photographer sent us this. German rocker Sebastian Weiss spotted at Konigstein Festung with a mystery girl...*"

Eva stopped short, her heart halting. There she was riding on Sebastian's back. On TV! Her gaze cut to her papa. Thankfully, his eyes were closed and he appeared to have nodded off.

They'd zoomed in on her face! At least her hair covered her features, and her cane was in her opposite hand and blended in with the trees behind her.

"*…rumor has it this mystery girl is the reason the band broke up…*"

"*…apparently the band is still together, just on hiatus, but this mystery girl may know why the band suddenly postponed their latest tour…*"

"Is that *you?*"

Eva jumped at the sound of Gabriele's voice.

"Don't be crazy."

Gabriele pulled on Eva's dress. "Is this crazy? The *mystery girl* is wearing the same dress."

Mercifully, the show moved on to the next subject of gossip. Eva limped down the hall to her room. Gabriele followed and closed the door behind her.

"Spill, Eva. And don't even try to tell me you were with Annette."

Eva closed her eyes and sighed. She might as well tell her sister. Gabriele wouldn't let up until she did.

"It's not a big deal. Sebastian thinks I'm a good songwriter and he wanted to try writing a song together, so I went to his flat—"

"Wait. You went to his flat? Alone? Are you crazy?"

"Yes, and yes, and apparently. He's perfectly harmless."

Gabriele frowned, but waved a hand for her to keep going.

"We started on a song, but got stuck. Sebastian thought we couldn't finish it because we didn't know each other very well, so he asked me to go to lunch with him today."

"So you could get to know each other better?"

"Yes."

"And you went to Königstein Fortress… for lunch?"

"Yes."

Gabriele shook her head and smirked. "You've really surprised me, Eva. I didn't think you had it in you."

Eva smiled wryly in return. "Well, neither did I."

"But you're not going to see him again, are you? I mean, Mama and Papa would freak. He's not exactly the kind of guy they'd want you to date."

"We're not dating. We're writing songs. It's just business."

"Just business? Eva, you've been crushing on this guy for a year, and you want me to believe it's just business?"

"It is. He's not interested in me that way." She poked at her cane. "For obvious reasons. But this is a chance for me to do something. Think about it. I could have a song on the charts!"

Gabriele relaxed. "I suppose, if you look at it that way, it could be a good opportunity for you. Are you going to meet again to write?"

Eva nodded. "Tomorrow evening."

"But just as friends?"

"Yes, Gabriele. Just as friends."

ALL I WANT TO DO IS FIND LOVE

A week of the band's hiatus revealed one thing to Sebastian: he didn't have any friends. His life had revolved around his band for years, and particularly the last one. The band, Dirk, the road crew: they were his friends.

And not very good ones, it turned out. After his fall out with Karl, everyone had dispersed. Sebastian wasn't sorry about that. He needed a break from those guys. It was just that he discovered there wasn't anyone left outside of that circle. He wandered around his flat, moving from guitar to guitar, fighting back loneliness.

He should take off. Go to Italy or Greece, but the thought of traveling by himself depressed him even more. At least here he had Eva. Okay, he had one friend outside of the band, and she was coming over later that day. Maybe they'd finish that song. He'd love to shove that in Dirk and Karl's faces.

His phone buzzed in his pocket, and for a moment he worried Eva was canceling, but it was worse than that. It was his sister Leah. She was in town and heading over.

He scanned his flat. It was messy, and a pile of dishes filled the sink, but it wasn't so bad for a bachelor—especially one Leah considered irresponsible. He almost got up from his spot on the couch to start cleaning, but decided against it. It was just his sister. He'd clean up after she left. For Eva.

When the chime rang, he pressed the button to release the lock on the building door and then opened the door of his flat. He went back to the couch and plopped a guitar on his lap. He heard her steps echo in the stairwell. She paused in the door frame before coming in.

"Hi, Sebastian," she said. She wore Capris and a nice shirt and her brown hair was pulled off her face in a low ponytail.

"Looks like Spain's been treating you well," Sebastian said in greeting. "How are the fish?" Leah was a marine biologist and worked at an aquarium in Mallorca.

"Spain is great," she replied in Spanish. "So are the fish."

Sebastian knew a little Spanish, enough to make out what his sister said. He didn't bother trying to respond. He'd stick to German, thank you very much.

"What brings you here?"

"Just visiting. I have three weeks off, so I thought I'd drop in to see the family. You know how gleeful that is."

Sarcasm was a family trait they shared. "We're the happiest."

Leah made herself comfortable in one of the chairs and pointedly stared at the surrounding mess. "I've heard you're doing well."

"It's been a wild year."

"Yvonne must be ecstatic. Finally, all those years of putting up with your craziness is paying off."

"We broke up."

Leah snapped to attention. "Really? Now that you have a taste of fame, you dump her?"

Sebastian stiffened, and the phony smile he'd been flashing his sister's way disappeared. "You know, Leah, that's the thing about you and Mom and Dad. Always believing the best of me."

"What?" Leah's dark brows jumped. "She dumped you?"

"She cheated on me. With Karl. Then I dumped her."

"Oh, Sebastian. I'm sorry."

"Yeah, well."

"So anyone else on the horizon? A brunette perhaps?"

"Great. You follow the tabloids. All that feigned interest in Yvonne was just you digging?"

"Okay." Leah pulled her ponytail over her shoulder and played with the tip. "I admit I'm curious. Who's the new girl?"

None of this was any of his sister's business. Sebastian blew out in frustration and answered anyway. "She's just a friend. Someone I write songs with."

"She looked like more than a friend in the pictures. You were smiling, Sebi. I haven't seen you smile like that in years."

Sebastian blinked. Leah was right. Of course, he smiled when he was joking around, but mostly that was an attempt to hide the fact that he actually wasn't happy. Yesterday with Eva he felt genuine happiness.

"She's a great girl and I like her. But we only just met a little while ago."

"Yeah, how'd you meet?"

Sebastian chuckled. His sister was a diehard romantic. "I saw her play at the Blue Note. She's good. I asked her if she wanted to write with me. She said yes. The end."

Leah pouted. "That's all I'm going to get?"

"Yes, so stop probing. What about you? You still with that lug?"

Leah's expression fell. "No. I'm single. Otherwise, I'd be vacationing on the beach in Mallorca instead of coming back here to visit my brother who's still not talking to our parents."

"They're not talking to me."

"Someone has to make the first move."

"They kicked me out. Told me not to come back until I was ready to go back to school. I'm not going back to school, Leah, so I guess we're at a stalemate."

"He's not well, you know."

"Who?"

"Papa."

"I'm assuming his fingers and hands still work well enough to pick up a phone."

Leah sighed. "Fine. No one can say I didn't try." She stood and slung her purse strap over her shoulder. "I gotta run. Give me a hug, okay?"

Sebastian gave into her request begrudgingly, though if he were being honest, his sister's embrace felt good. Leah had sided with her parents when the ultimatum had been thrown down, but had since softened her stance. She hadn't exactly apologized, but she'd held out an olive branch on more than one occasion. Like she had by coming by today.

Now Sebastian cleaned up the flat in anticipation of Eva's arrival. He left briefly to pick up Indian takeaway and sat on his balcony to eat it. When he finished, he tossed the containers into the paper receptacle, and then went to brush his teeth. He put on a fresh T-shirt for good measure. Then he returned to his chair on the patio where he had a view of the street Eva would travel down to get to his place.

He sat up straighter when he spotted her turn the corner. She wore a red floral skirt and a white blouse. Her hair hung straight and shiny, like it usually did and a pair of sunglasses rested on her cute nose. She walked unevenly, gripping her black cane, but honestly, it was the last thing he noticed. It was like he'd stopped seeing the cane and the limp at all.

He stood and called out when she was close enough to hear. "Eva!"

The smile that crossed her face when she looked up and saw him made his legs feel shaky. He watched her slow ascent to the front door and then rushed inside to release the lock of the main door. Listening to her uneven, slow climb up the steps, it was the first time Sebastian wished his building had an elevator.

"Hey," he said when she reached the top.

"Hey," she answered.

He had water and sodas sitting out on the coffee table knowing she'd be thirsty from her trek.

They stood staring at each other for an awkward moment. Sebastian was surprised by the emotion he felt at seeing her again. Excitement. Anticipation. Joy?

"Here, have a seat," he said, waving at a chair. He had to look away for fear that his face would give away his feelings in an embarrassing fashion.

Eva gracefully sat in the chair Sebastian had indicated and helped herself to a glass of water. Sebastian had placed a guitar stand with Eva's choice of guitar in it within reach.

"I wanted to thank you again for yesterday," she said. "It was fun."

"Yeah," Sebastian said, staying cool. "Not a bad way to blow an afternoon."

"We made the news," she added. "But you must be used to that kind of thing."

Sebastian settled into the chair adjacent to Eva, about an arm's length away, and placed his guitar on his lap. "I don't think it's something you ever get used to. It's just there. Sorry, you had to go through that, though." He studied her. "You didn't get in trouble, did you?"

Eva shook her head. "My parents haven't put the pieces together. But my sister recognized my dress."

"And…"

"She's cool."

"Good. Well, let's see if our outing helped the muse."

They strummed and picked out the tune, reviewing the lyrics they'd come up with before.

"Do you have anything else?" Sebastian asked.

Eva pulled a folded piece of paper out of her small shoulder bag. "I wrote this down yesterday."

Sebastian read Eva's cursive scribble.

"It's to go along with our theme from before," Eva added quickly. "About the person looking for something outside of his or herself and thinking they might've found it. Except they're not sure. Her memory… or his… isn't very good."

"Sing it for me."

Eva brushed her fingers across the strings and closed her eyes.

> *You were the reason I had awakened*
> *I had placed you imperfectly*
> *Like an unremembered memory*
> *Oohhhh*

> *I can't say what lies beyond my flesh and bone,*
> *But for the pull here beneath*
> *I reach to the sky*

"And he… or she… finally realizes that being alone, hiding inside oneself isn't the answer."

Sebastian wondered if she was referring to herself, or

to him. Maybe both. He jazzed up the beat and had her sing it again. She came to the end, but Sebastian felt something was lacking. It needed more. He leaned forward to mention it, but stopped when he noticed the way Eva watched him, her eyes wide with curiosity and inspiration. She radiated pure joy and anticipation as they created together. His heart warmed and longed for her. He wanted more than flesh and bone. The space between them sizzled and his gaze moved to her lips once again.

He bravely sang out the only thing on his mind:

All I wanna do is find love
All I wanna do is find love
All I wanna do is find love
Forever now

Eva's lips parted slightly, and Sebastian imagined she was as surprised by his declaration as he was. He reached over and tucked the hair that stubbornly wanted to cover her pretty face behind her ear. She shivered at his touch, and heat exploded in his chest. His fingers moved to the back of her head, and he gently pulled her forward. She didn't resist. He closed his eyes as his lips found hers.

Eva was experiencing her first kiss, and her first kiss was with Sebastian Weiss! Was she doing it right? Sebastian was experienced. Oh, mercy! What if she was doing it wrong?

Another part of her brain told her to relax. Kissing was an instinct for humans. It wasn't something you had to study and learn. They were just lips.

She moved hers in rhythm with his. See? Kissing was easy. It was another type of music, their mouths another kind of instrument.

He pulled away gently, and she held her chest, trying hard not to pant like a thirsty dog. Now what? Was she supposed to say something?

He smiled and rested his chin on his guitar. "Sorry about that."

Eva's heart stopped. "You're sorry you kissed me?"

"No, Eva, I'm not sorry I kissed you. I'm sorry I surprised you. I should've asked you first."

"Oh."

"Next time I'll ask."

Her smile returned. So he planned on a next time. That sounded good to her.

"Let's finish this song," he said.

Eva stared at her feet. How was she supposed to

concentrate on the song now? She pinched her eyes closed and tried to concentrate on lyrics and melodies, but all she could think of was how her lips still tingled from the kiss.

"Are you all right?"

She snapped her eyes open, worried she was making a fool of herself so soon afterward.

"Yeah, fine. Really good actually."

He grinned. "I'm having a hard time concentrating now too."

"I probably should head home anyway," Eva said. If she got back too late, her parents would get concerned and start asking questions.

"I'll walk you."

Sebastian propped his guitar up against the sofa while Eva put hers in its stand. She retrieved her cane and glanced toward the door. For her to get to it, Sebastian would have to move so she could scoot by. His eyes glistened as he stared down at her, like he knew he had her trapped.

"I like you, Eva," he said, not breaking his gaze.

Eva's heart fluttered. These were the kind of words she'd dreamed of hearing from Sebastian, but she never dared to believe it could happen. She wasn't the kind of girl a guy like him usually went for.

"I didn't think I…"

"Was my type? Me, neither. I'll be honest. But I *like* you. You're sweet and cute and talented. You get music and songwriting. You understand what it's like to dream, but you're still grounded somehow.

"Also, it's nice to be with a girl who's not throwing herself at me. Not that I wouldn't like you to throw yourself at me—I actually would like that—but I like that we have something more than that, something deeper."

Eva's legs trembled, and she almost lost her balance.

Sebastian stepped closer, placing a hand on her back, preventing a humiliating tumble.

"I got you."

"Uh, thanks." She felt silly and wondered if Sebastian ever planned on moving out of the way. Apparently not.

He leaned in and whispered hotly into her ear. "I said I would ask you next time so this is it. Can I kiss you?"

Eva nodded mutely. She didn't think she'd ever be able to say no to that question. Ever.

He swept her hair behind her ear and for the second time he undid her with the tenderness of his kiss.. Her nerves shot off and she grabbed his shoulder, certain she would collapse otherwise.

Sebastian's lips moved to her ear and he whispered, "Okay, I have to stop now or… I might not let you go home." He took her free hand and led her out of the flat and carefully down the stairs to the street below without letting go of her hand once.

He kissed her quickly before pushing the door open. "One for the road."

And then he released her hand and tucked his fists in his pockets.

Right. He was a celebrity. She remembered how she'd been photographed with Sebastian the day before and all the speculation it had caused in the entertainment world. She understood how he'd have to watch himself when he was with her in public, but somehow it pinched a little.

Sebastian chatted, keeping the conversation light, and Eva nodded in all the right places. Her mind was going a million kilometers an hour: what were they now? Friends? Better than friends? Boyfriend and girlfriend?

It didn't matter to her. She felt insanely happy. If she weren't holding on to her cane, she'd float away through the trees.

Sebastian *liked* her. He *kissed* her. Three times! She breathed in deeply as she remembered how his lips felt on hers.

"Eva?"

She blinked at the sound of his voice. Had she really been daydreaming about Sebastian in his presence? If she wanted to continue to impress him, she had to be more mature about things and not act like a silly schoolgirl with a crush.

They turned left at the corner and Sebastian nodded with his chin. She looked for what he was motioning to. Then she saw it. Or rather, she saw *him*.

"Oh, no."

Sebastian spoke under his breath. "He doesn't look happy."

It was her papa heading toward them. She didn't know if he was just out for an evening stroll or if he'd been looking for her. Either way, Sebastian was right. He didn't look happy.

"Hi, Papa," she said when he reached them.

"Eva." Papa stood in front of them, and his bushy brows furrowed as his dark eyes flickered between Eva and Sebastian. His thick shoulders straightened as he puffed out his barrel chest. "What are you doing?"

"I was just out for a walk and ran into Sebastian. You remember, he came to the soup kitchen once."

"He didn't eat any soup."

"Yeah, he came to talk about my song."

Papa narrowed his eyes and pierced Sebastian with his gaze. "I trust you got the information you needed?"

"Yes, Herr Baumann. Eva's been very helpful."

Eva would've burst out laughing if the situation wasn't so awful.

"I was just walking her home," Sebastian added.

"How gentlemanly of you. I can walk her from here. Thank you."

Eva blushed with humiliation. "Papa!"

"What? Shall he accompany the two of us? The sidewalks aren't that wide." He pressed against her elbow prompting her to start walking.

"Auf Wiedersehen," Papa said tersely to Sebastian as he turned his back to him.

Eva threw an apologetic glance over her shoulder. Sebastian raised his thumb and little finger to his ear, signaling he would call her later.

 BUILDING THE GALLOWS

HERR BAUMANN WAS A BIG MAN. He had a broad back with a thick waist and stump-like legs that shuffled to match his daughter's slower gait. He rested a thick hand on Eva's shoulder protectively.

Sebastian stroked the shadow on his chin as he watched them walk away until they disappeared in the crowd. He'd never had to deal with a girl's father before. Yvonne's parents just pretended he didn't exist. They let their daughter date whomever she wanted as long as she was home by midnight, and they never bothered her with questions about what she did when she was out.

His own father hadn't been part of his life for the last three years.

This was unfamiliar territory and Sebastian was unsure of how to manage it. What he did know was he wasn't going to let Eva's father push him around. Even if he was a pastor.

"Sebastian!" He turned toward the female voice calling him. A pretty girl with long blond hair and an enhanced chest waved wildly. He didn't know her. Two other women saddled up beside her. The leader and her friends. He'd seen this group of three many times on his tours.

They ran across the street and he considered dashing away, but decided that would be unnecessarily rude.

"Sebastian Weiss! It's really you!" she gushed.

Sebastian nodded politely. "Hello." Normally when fans approached him on the street they asked him to autograph something. He was afraid to offer in this case. There was a good chance the exposed skin would be the choice spot. It had happened before, and it was an awkward situation he'd rather avoid, especially in the middle of the street.

Instead the buxom blond waved toward the Mexican restaurant halfway down the block. "We're just going to lunch," she said. "Come with us!"

He was going to say no, but it wouldn't hurt for him to do a little PR, especially after the bad press his band had been getting.

He plastered on his rock star smile. "Sure, ladies. Lead the way."

The large, street-side windows were open in the summer, giving the illusion that there was no outside wall at all. Sebastian took the seat nearest to the door so he could make an easy getaway if necessary. The blond brushed her bosom along his back as she maneuvered for the chair beside him. He groaned inwardly. This was a bad idea. He should've known better.

The three women started asking questions all at once.

"I read you broke up with your girlfriend."

"I hope that mystery girl is a hoax? Is it?"

"Did Hollow Fellows really break up?"

He faked interest and answered their questions as vaguely as he could. He was thankful to be interrupted by the waiter when he came. The blond was less than subtle with her body language, twisting completely in her seat to face him, twirling yellow strands of hair around her finger, batting eyelashes. Sebastian knew she would go home with him if he asked.

He wondered why he wasn't interested. He was a red-blooded, heterosexual guy. Even so, one-night stands had never appealed to him. He'd always been faithful to Yvonne, though now he wondered why he'd bothered.

No, he knew why. His burden of guilt was already so big. Adding cheating to that would be more than he could take.

Besides Eva deserved better. She was everything these girls were not. She was worth waiting for and worth dealing with her overbearing parents for.

He reached for his phone and stared at the screen, careful to make sure the blond couldn't see it was blank. "Ah, man. I forgot I have an interview to do in twenty minutes." He stood and waved the waiter over. "So sorry, ladies. I gotta run. Lunch is on me."

IS IT A GOOD TIME TO CALL?

EVA'S FATHER gently squeezed her shoulder. He glanced down at her with soft eyes, his lips pulled inward in a slight smile—his pastor face.

"*Schatz,*" he began. "You must stop seeing that boy."

Eva's heart lurched. "We're just friends," she lied. Her heart squeezed a little more. She never used to lie to her parents. To anyone at all for that matter. That habit began recently. With Sebastian.

"He's not the right kind of boy for you. You must see that, right? He is one kind of person, and you are another. Remember how the Bible tells us not to be unevenly yoked. You know what that means, don't you?"

She did. She heard all the sermons, but she knew he would tell her anyway.

"The farmers of old depended on oxen to plow their fields. They had to make sure that the oxen they yoked together were equal in size and strength, or the team would not be able to succeed. One would pull the other, and they wouldn't be able to walk in a straight line. It's the same with two people who marry. If they don't approach life in the same way, share the same values and beliefs, one will pull the other one along in a direction she doesn't want to go."

"Papa, he was just walking me home. We're hardly talking marriage."

"Yes, but I know how young men think."

Eva wrinkled her nose. *Please, not the talk.*

"First it's holding hands, then kissing, then—"

"Papa!"

Her father sighed. "Don't forget what the Bible teaches you."

How could she forget? The lessons had been hammered home since she was a child. Honor your mother and father. Forgive your enemies.

Forgiving her enemies was something else. She'd never forgive the person responsible for her handicap, the one who was responsible for the physical and emotional pain she dealt with daily. The person who had stolen her confidence and made her afraid. She didn't think God could fault her for that.

Honoring her mother and father had been easy until now. Her father wanted her to give up Sebastian, the very person who was giving her back some of the things she'd lost. Confidence. Courage.

Passion.

How could her papa make her choose?

Her father pressed the code to their building when they reached it.

"Be careful with your heart," he said as he held open the door for her. "That's all I'm saying."

The problem was Eva was tired of being careful. She'd been nothing but careful for the last five years.

Gabriele was hunched over her laptop when Eva made it back to her room. Eva flopped on her bed, suddenly exhausted.

Gabriele didn't look up.

"Homework?" Eva asked.

"Exams."

"You're almost all done, Gabi. I'm proud of you."

Gabriele looked up then, and a smile drew across her face. "I know. I'm getting married in three weeks, Eva. Three weeks!"

Eva laughed with her sister. "I'm happy for you." And she was. Her heart felt larger and warmer toward her sister. Eva really wanted her to be happy.

Eva's phone buzzed. She pulled it out of her purse, and her insides tingled. Sebastian had texted already.

Sebastian Weiss

Is it a good time to call?

"Who is it?" Gabriele asked.

Eva ignored her and texted back.

Eva Baumann

No. Sister here.

Sebastian Weiss

Fine. We can text. I just want you to know I'm thinking about you. Your lips mainly. But you. Yes, definitely you.

"Eva? You should see your face. You're blushing!"

Eva huffed. "Don't you have exams to study for?"

"Is that Sebastian Weiss? Is he *texting* you?"

"Can you just chill?" Eva said through tight lips. "Everyone is treating me like I'm twelve."

Gabriele clammed up after that, but her eyes kept darting to Eva.

Eva tucked her phone out of sight and texted Sebastian back.

Eva Baumann

You're creating quite a stir around here.

Sebastian Weiss

That seems to be the effect I have on people. Are you okay with it???

Eva Baumann

I'm totally okay.

Sebastian Weiss

Whew. I really want to see you again.

Eva Baumann

I really want to see you again, too. Might need to wait a day or so. Let things cool down.

Sebastian didn't text back right away and Eva wondered if she'd just killed their relationship before it had a chance to get started.

Then finally he responded.

Sebastian Weiss

I hate waiting. But you're worth waiting for. Good night, Eva

Eva bit her lip to suppress the squeal that bubbled up. Gabriele flashed her another worried look, but Eva just turned and faced the other way allowing her lips to stretch out into a big, sappy smile.

BETTER THAN GREAT

IT WAS like Eva's kisses had unlocked the song vault in Sebastian's heart. He spent most of the afternoon scribbling down lyric ideas and plucking out new melodies. He hated that he had to wait to see her again, but if he could keep this up, the time would fly by.

Dirk would be happy. Sebastian hadn't thought about Dirk or the band in days. He'd promised Dirk he'd spend the band's hiatus writing. At the time, he thought he was just blowing off his manager, but here he was with several great ideas and a few strong songs started.

Sebastian reached for his phone and pressed Dirk's number.

"Hey, man," he said when Dirk answered.

"Sebastian, how's it going?" Dirk sounded reserved, like he was afraid Sebastian would lay on more drama.

"Actually, it's going great. Better than great."

"Really?" A relieved breath. "What's up?"

"I'm writing, man. And I think I've got some good songs to work on. You should set up a rehearsal."

"You realize that Karl is still in the band, right? Aren't you still pissed at him? You know, the reason we're on this sabbatical in the first place."

"Yeah, but whatever. The past is past."

"The past is past? You weren't talking like that two weeks ago. What happened? Did you meet a new girl?"

Sebastian chuckled. "Yeah. I did. Yvonne is so yesterday."

Dirk laughed. "Okay, great. I'll set up a rehearsal. You can't imagine how relieved I am to hear you got your head back on straight."

No one was more amazed than Sebastian at how quickly he'd turned around. He wondered if he'd ever really loved Yvonne. He thought he had at the time, but she never stirred him like Eva did. She never made him want to dig deeper creatively or grow as a person. She was kind of just there, which was what he needed at the time— someone to lean on when his family abandoned him. She was like a wall or a fence. She kept him from falling over, and he felt immensely grateful. But were those feelings love? They'd gotten physical quickly after getting together. Yvonne never held back, never said no. He was able to release a lot of his emotional pain with her body. But he realized now his feelings for her weren't love. They were loyalty.

She stood by him. He would stand by her. Until she didn't.

It was amazingly easy to get over her, and maybe this was why.

Not that he was in love with Eva. Though he could imagine falling in love with her one day. Maybe.

His phone buzzed and he assumed it was Dirk getting back with rehearsal times. Or maybe it would be Eva saying she could see him sooner after all.

The name that flashed shocked him. Then angered him. Stefan Weiss, his father.

What did he want? He hadn't tried to contact Sebastian in years. Not a birthday greeting. Not a congratulations when his songs hit the charts.

Sebastian pressed ignore. As far as he was concerned, he didn't have a father anymore.

REACH TO THE SKY

EVA SERIOUSLY THOUGHT she had died and gone to heaven. The last two weeks—wow, her life had changed so radically! Before she was an invisible cripple with nothing more pressing in her life than making sure to take her pain medication and watch Gabriele have the life she thought she'd never have. Today Eva felt alive and… hopeful.

Last month each wedding-related task assigned to her was like a needle in the heart, poking and taunting her with envy and pity. But now she made ribbons for the table decorations with enthusiasm. One day she would have her own wedding.

Even if it wasn't to Sebastian (*Oh my heart, please let it be him!*), he'd shown her that she was worthy of adoration and affection. Of love and devotion.

Not that he'd declared his love to her. But he obviously really, really liked her. Every time she'd gone over to his flat (sneaking away while her parents were busy with the church, and Gabriele with Lennon) with the guise of writing a song, Sebastian struggled to keep his hands off her. She'd had a lot of practice at kissing lately (!), and more than once she had to gently move his hand when it crept too high or too low.

"Eva?"

"Huh, what?" She'd become the queen of

daydreaming lately. Gabriele stared at her across the kitchen table with consternation. "You've made one bow in the last five minutes. We'll be here all day at that rate."

Gabriele's friend Julia and Eva's mother were seated around the table, helping as well. Her mother just *tsked* and kept her eyes on her own handiwork. Julia had short dark hair, and a severe side part. She raised a brow and nodded subtly, like she was signaling that she found the bow-making task boring too.

"I've done three in the time that you've done one," Gabriele continued.

"Okay, I'm working," Eva said.

"Give the girl a break," Julia said. "I'd find it hard to concentrate too, if I had the attentions of Sebastian Weiss." She grinned wickedly at Eva. "You must be going crazy!"

A hush descended on the table. Her mother's head shot up. "She's not seeing that boy anymore, Julia," she said.

Her family didn't know she was still seeing Sebastian, but that didn't mean they hadn't been spotted together. The *Neustadt* was relatively small.

Julia narrowed her eyes at Eva, and Eva could tell that she knew. She'd seen them. "Oh, I'm sorry," she said tactfully. "My mistake."

The door chime rang, and Eva was thankful for the distraction. Gabriele sprang from her chair to let Lennon in. She stepped into the hallway and the women left behind at the table could hear Lennon's footsteps stop in the stairwell and the subsequent passionate greeting.

Eva rolled her eyes. Her mother and Julia studied the ribbons in their hands like they couldn't hear the smacking of lips coming through the open door.

Gabriele led Lennon in by the hand and waved at the mountain of bows on the table. "The big ones are to decorate the end chairs in the rows in the church," she explained. "The little ones are to decorate the chairs at the party."

Lennon's eyes crinkled closed as he smiled. He dressed casually in jeans and a button-down shirt. His style was different from Sebastian's: more clean-cut and preppy, but a perfectly attractive counterpart to fashionable Gabriele.

"Nice work, ladies," he said in German.

Eva smiled at his British accent. Lennon was a man of few words and didn't try to talk to anyone. Maybe because his German wasn't very strong. It was a good thing that Gabriele's English was excellent. Eva wished she could say the same for her own English. She understood most things and liked English better for songwriting—it was just more lyrical and more commercial—but in practical, everyday conversation, she wasn't very good.

She added another bow to the pile before checking her phone for messages. Her heart jumped at the sight of a new text from Sebastian.

Sebastian Weiss

English movie playing at the Arthouse Theatre this afternoon. Can you go?

Perfect timing. Just when she was thinking she needed to work on her English.

Eva Baumann

We must speak English only.

Sebastian Weiss

The whole time?

Eva Baumann

The whole time.

Sebastian Weiss

Good idea. Meet me there in one hour?

Eva Baumann

Yes

Eva was becoming a master at hiding the fountain of joy that continued to bubble inside. She kept her hands busy, making bow after bow. They were almost done. Mama had work to do downstairs, and Julia left with Gabriele and Lennon. Such a relief to be left alone and out of scrutiny.

Eva put on a fresh sundress, combed her hair and applied a little makeup. She grabbed her cane, locked the door behind her and shuffled down the circular stairwell. Once outside, she headed in the direction of the Arthouse Theatre. Her sunglasses hid her eyes, but she could no longer hide her smile.

 English Lessons

Sebastian had Eva Baumann on the mind: the way her hair smelled and the fresh scent of her skin, and the way her soft, body felt under his fingertips and how she gently kept them from roaming too far. She was intoxicating. Her conservative nature was part of her appeal. She kept her blouse buttoned up one notch more than any other girl he knew, and she blushed at the slightest amount of flirting.

He had assumed she was still a virgin, though now that he knew what it felt like to want her he didn't know why he assumed that. But when she confessed that he was actually her first kiss, he was stunned. Surely some suave Christian boy would've broken that seal before now.

When the shock wore off he felt honored and pleased. It made him ridiculously happy that no other guy had touched his girl before.

Yeah, *his girl.*

He wished he could offer Eva the same gift, but that ship had long since sailed.

It also made him want to be extra careful. She was precious and pure of heart, not jaded by bad love affairs. He didn't want to be the one to screw that up. That meant he had to slow himself down. Way down. Which meant he needed to stop bringing Eva to his flat and to take her out instead, to public places where he'd be forced to behave himself.

He just happened to walk by the Arthouse Theatre and spotted the posters for showing English language films showing this week. He acted on impulse, knowing that Eva might not be able to drop everything and meet him, and he felt ridiculously giddy when she said yes. He waited now, outside the door of the theatre, cap pulled low, aviators on. He felt his lips tug up when he saw her at the intersection waiting for the light to turn. He walked to meet her as she crossed over to his side.

"Hi," he said, taking her in. He'd never known a girl who wore so many skirts and dresses, but Eva hinted that she liked to keep her scar hidden, and shorts wouldn't do it. He liked the look. Very sweet and feminine, and kind of retro.

She smiled back. "Hi."

He bent down to kiss her and it felt like the whole street blurred away, as if they were the only two people left on the planet. The only people that mattered anyway.

He took her left hand. He always walked on her left because of the cane.

"Just to warn you," he said. "It's a romance. I know how you hate that sort of thing."

She smiled. "I love romance. But I imagine this is a big sacrifice for you."

"I'll do anything in the name of education. Hey, we're supposed to be speaking English."

"Right," she said in English. "How are you?"

"I am fine. How are you?"

They laughed at the use of their first English conversation learned long ago in school.

The Arthouse Theatre was an old hole in the wall, a small film house that had seen better days. The old décor was dingy and the vintage wallpaper sagged with age. It smelled musky, but despite the aging appearance it had a rustic appeal.

A couple about their ages stood in front of them to buy tickets. They spoke fluent English to each other and it was obvious by their loose-fitting clothes and the backpacks that hung on their shoulders that they were tourists.

He whispered into Eva's ear. "Here is our chance to practice English."

"Hello," he said when the couple turned with tickets in hand. "We overheard you speaking in English. I hope you don't mind if I ask where you are from?"

"Not at all. We're happy to speak English with anyone who's willin'," the guy said. "We're from Idaho." He said it like Sebastian and Eva should know where that was. "I'm Ben and this is my wife Emma."

She giggled when he said that. "We're on our honeymoon," she said. "It's still weird to hear him introduce me like that."

"Congratulations," Sebastian said. "I am Sebastian, and this is my girlfriend, Eva."

It was the first time he'd called her that, and he watched her expression carefully. Her lips twitched slightly, forming a little smile, and her eyes twinkled. He guessed she liked it.

"Do you live around here?" Emma asked.

Sebastian nodded. He was relieved that Ben and Emma hadn't recognized him, especially after he gave his name. It didn't surprise him though. He was well-known in Germany, but Hollow Fellows hadn't made it across the Atlantic. Yet. A certain, unnamed pressure lifted off him. He could breathe and be himself without feeling like he was being idolized.

"How long have you been in Germany?" he asked.

"One week," Ben answered. "We started off in

Barcelona, worked our way through France and now here."

"We were so excited when we walked by this theatre and saw they were playing movies in English," Emma said. "After three weeks of foreign languages, I'm just so homesick to hear my own again."

"I have never been to America," Eva said. "I cannot imagine how it feels."

"Your English is very good," Ben said appreciatively.

"Thank you," Eva said. "I wish it were better."

"We're just so happy to meet people who even try," Ben said. "The only other language I speak is redneck."

Sebastian and Eva stared at him blankly.

Emma slapped Ben's arm. "They don't know what that is, babe."

"Just joshin' ya. Anyway, we should go in before it starts. Nice meetin' ya."

"Nice to meet you too," Sebastian said, and Eva nodded in agreement.

Sebastian bought their tickets and led Eva into the darkened room. It was long and narrow with only a scattering of attendees. Sebastian chose seats near the back, several rows behind their American friends, letting Eva have the aisle.

"Did you want something to eat?" Sebastian asked, sticking with their commitment to speak English. "They sell candy here."

"No, I'm fine. I ate at home."

"Okay." Sebastian wrapped an arm over her shoulders. "You're sweet enough."

She giggled, a sound that was sweet music to his ears. "Am I really your girlfriend?" she asked.

"I hope so."

"Then that would make you my boyfriend."

"That would. Are you okay with that?"

She snuggled more deeply under his arm. "I'm very okay with that."

The lights dimmed, and the movie started. It was a light romance that barely kept Sebastian's interest, and if it weren't for the fact that he was using it to improve his English, he might have fallen asleep. Eva seemed thoroughly enthralled. She nudged him during a scene where the couple was riding bikes through a park.

"I miss that."

"What? Bike riding?"

"Yeah."

There wasn't much Eva couldn't do, but the accident she was in had wrecked her leg to the point where she'd never run a race, or apparently ride a bike. She'd told him that her femur had broken through the skin and that her hip had also been fractured, but he picked up that she didn't like to talk about it, so he didn't bring it up. He just hoped he never met the guy driving the other car. He'd punch him in the face.

Halfway through the flick, Ben and Emma started making out.

Eva giggled. "Well, they *are* on their honeymoon."

"I think they have the right idea." He twisted toward her and drew her chin up with his fingers. The bluish light flashing from the film reflected off her face, her eyes full of admiration for him. He couldn't resist kissing her lips. If he were a kid again, this would be the part where he'd make a move, but he remained a grown-up and a gentleman and kept his hands to himself.

The movie finally ended, and they had to put on their sunglasses quickly as they adjusted to the bright summer afternoon light. They were walking happily hand in hand toward the park, not quite ready to say good-bye to each other yet, when Eva came to a sudden stop.

"Uh-oh."

Sebastian saw a girl with short dark hair approaching them. He didn't recognize her, but Eva obviously had.

THIS IS MY BOYFRIEND

EVA WAS TEMPTED to untangle her fingers from Sebastian's but stayed resolute. She was tired of hiding. And something more. A burning rope tangled in her gut, and she clenched her jaw. Sebastian was the best thing that ever happened to her, and she was going to fight for him. Starting now.

She forced a smile. "Hi, Julia."

Julia's dark brows arched, and her lips turned up in a wry smile. "Hi, Eva." Her eyes moved to Sebastian's questioning face, and then down to the couples entwined hands, prompting Eva to make formal introductions.

"Julia, this is my *boyfriend* Sebastian. Sebastian, this is Gabriele's friend, Julia."

Sebastian released Eva's hand to shake Julia's causing a blush to flush across her pale face.

"I'm a fan," she gushed. She seemed to have forgotten she'd just caught her friend's younger sister with her forbidden beau. "I watch your music videos all the time."

Sebastian nodded and took Eva's hand again. Eva noticed his smile looked tight and forced, a marked difference from when they conversed with the Americans who didn't know who he was. She was starting to understand how being famous shaped you into something you weren't meant to be.

"Eva and I spent the morning helping her sister

prepare for the wedding," Julia continued. "Are you coming?"

Eva almost gasped. Whose side was she on? Surely Julia understood that Gabriele wasn't in favor of this relationship. And her mother had made her opinion clear during the bow-tying project.

"I think I'm out of town that weekend," Sebastian said, covering.

Eva tugged on his hand. "We have to get going. It was nice to see you again, Julia."

Julia giggled and waved. "Nice to formally have met you, Sebastian."

Eva frowned. She was certain Julia would pull out her phone the minute she was out of sight and call Gabriele.

"Busted," Sebastian said.

Eva stopped and stared questioningly at him. "Will you come to my sister's wedding with me?"

His eyebrows jumped above his sunglasses. "Seriously?"

"Yes. I'm done pretending to my family. You are an important part of my life now and I can't hide it. I don't want to hide it."

He pulled her close and set his forehead lightly on hers. "I'd go anywhere with you."

Eva trembled at his touch, and his words fastened themselves to her soul. She believed him. And it was true for her as well. She was prepared to follow Sebastian Weiss anywhere if he asked.

He kissed her tenderly and she responded in kind ignoring the passersby who gawked or brushed against them. He pulled back and grinned. "I guess I have to buy a suit."

Her parents were going to kill her.

But she wanted him by her side at Gabriele's wedding.

She wanted to show him off. *Sebastian Weiss* was her boyfriend.

As luck would have it, Eva's mother exited the church at the same moment Eva and Sebastian reached the front door of their building. Mama's eyes widened, and her lips formed a hard, thin line when she saw Eva's hand in Sebastian's. Sebastian started to tug his away, but Eva clung tighter.

She smiled at her mother, then turned to Sebastian. "I'll see you later?"

"Of course," he said. His eyes rested briefly on her lips, but he left without kissing her. She was glad. Seeing them hold hands was already more than her mother was ready for.

"Eva," her mother said, "You're looking for a world of trouble."

Eva braced herself for the confrontation to come. Her mother headed upstairs ahead of her and Eva could picture the emotional conversation soon to take place between her mama and papa. What had become of their sweet, compliant daughter?

"Eva!" Papa summoned her to the living room before she'd stepped all the way inside their flat. She limped over to where he was sitting and collapsed into an empty chair. Papa closed the book he was reading and set it aside.

"Mama says you were holding hands with that boy."

"That boy has a name."

"Don't talk back to me, Eva."

She folded her arms and sat upright. She'd started this battle and she better be prepared to see it to the end. "I'm not talking back. I'm pointing out a fact."

"This Sebastian boy. He's wild and worldly. He's *experienced.*"

Eva kept her expression blank. These were the exact

attributes she liked about Sebastian. He brought her out of her shell. Couldn't her papa see that?

"He's not like that with me," she said, hoping to calm him.

He softened his eyes. "What about our talk? Didn't you hear a word I said?"

"I did hear you. And I appreciate your concern. But it's my life and my choice who I spend it with."

"*Schatz*, he will break your heart."

"It's my heart, Papa. It's a risk I'm willing to take."

Papa breathed in long and hard. His jaw clenched but he said no more, just waved her off with his fingers. She'd won this battle, but she wasn't a fool. The war was still brewing and she hoped there wouldn't be any casualties when all was said and done.

FALLING FOR HER

Sebastian felt like he'd abandoned Eva to the firing squad, but Eva knew her parents best and knew how to handle them. The way she stared her mama down and refused to let go of his hand made him proud.

He had to get going anyway. Dirk had scheduled a rehearsal, and Markus was picking him up in an hour. It would be the first time he'd faced Karl since Sebastian forced the band on hiatus. His stomach clenched at the thought of seeing his ugly mug again. If he could avoid another personal encounter with him, or with Yvonne for that matter, he would. As it was Karl was an occupational hazard. At least Sebastian had some new tunes to bring to the floor.

His phone rang as he reached the steps to his building and he almost answered it without looking, thinking it would be Eva reporting back. Good thing he checked. It was his father again. Twice in one week? It made him think there was something wrong. It stopped on the third ring. Couldn't be that urgent.

Sebastian went straight to his fridge and grabbed a drink. The fizzle sound it made as he removed the cap ignited his thirst and he gulped back a couple swallows before settling on the sofa and putting his feet up.

He turned on the sports channel to watch a soccer match to pass the time, but kept checking his phone every ten seconds hoping to hear from Eva. Finally, he texted her himself.

Sebastian Weiss

You still alive over there?

Eva Baumann

Yeah. It's tense but it'll be okay.

Sebastian Weiss

Sorry you have to go through this.

Eva Baumann

Me too.

Sebastian Weiss

Heading out to rehearsal soon. First time since…

Eva Baumann

Nervous?

Sebastian Weiss

Nah. Well, a little. I just need to focus on my guitar.

Eva Baumann

:)

Sebastian Weiss

See you tomorrow?

Eva Baumann

Yes

She seemed all right. Definitely not very chatty, but…

Not for the first time Sebastian questioned himself. Eva's family was more important than he was. She needed them more than she needed him. He hated that they'd put her in a position where she felt like she had to choose. The thought of breaking up, even after this short time cut him. It just didn't feel right. It didn't feel fair. Besides, his heart was lassoed. He couldn't walk away unless she asked him to leave.

He really hoped she wouldn't do that.

The door chimed, and Sebastian startled. He ran a hand through his hair and told himself to get it together. His electric guitar was in its case, and he grabbed it and headed downstairs. Markus had returned to his car, which was idling at the curb.

"Hey, man," he said.

"Hey." Sebastian threw his guitar in the back seat and hopped in.

Markus tapped his fingers on the steering wheel. "You've been keeping busy."

Sebastian cocked a brow. "What do you mean?"

"You're in the news. First with a brunette on your back and then eating out with a busty blond."

Sebastian shook his head. "What busty blond?" Then he remembered being accosted by fans at the Mexican restaurant. Someone had taken a picture? He let out a frustrated breath. "That was nothing. Just an annoying fan."

"And the brunette? Also an annoying fan?"

Sebastian smirked. "No. That one I like."

Markus chuckled. "You don't know how happy I am to hear that. Really, man. Glad you've moved on."

"Yeah, me too."

Karl's fancy new car was parked in front of the warehouse. Sebastian inhaled and steadied himself. He had nothing to be nervous about. Karl was the jerk in this situation. At least he had the decency to have the sound system set up and turned on by the time Sebastian and Markus arrived. Karl's expression was guarded as he watched Sebastian cross the room to where his mic was set up and ready. Sebastian didn't utter a greeting, just went directly to his amp and plugged in.

"I got some new tunes to try," he said.

They made it through the whole rehearsal without bickering or throwing a punch. Sebastian didn't know if Karl was still with Yvonne. He never offered the information and Sebastian never asked.

Sebastian left Karl to clean up and at least for this time, he didn't protest. His uncharacteristic amiability was a lame sort of apology. Sebastian wasn't sure if he was ready to accept it.

He and Markus picked up fast food on the way home, which Sebastian wolfed down before Markus dropped him off at his place.

Sebastian gripped his trash in one hand and collected his guitar with the other. "Thanks for the ride."

He'd just finished brushing his teeth when the door chimed. He wasn't expecting anyone. Especially not the person who identified himself.

"It's Herr Baumann. Can I come in?"

Sebastian groaned. Eva's father was paying him a visit. This couldn't be good. He pressed the buzzer and braced himself for the worst. A quick scan of his flat confirmed that it was too messy to tidy up in the minute it would take the middle-aged man to climb the stairs. He was glad his roommates had taken down their posters of half-naked girls and that he'd removed his inappropriate wall hangings the first day he'd invited Eva over to write songs.

Herr Baumann didn't burst into his flat like the raging

bull he'd imagined. Instead he looked tired and defeated. His thick shoulders hung forward as he clasped his hands in front of him.

"Hello, Herr Baumann. Would you like to sit?"

"Thank you, but I don't plan on staying long."

Sebastian was glad to hear it. He slid back onto the sofa. "I hope you don't mind if I sit."

"I'll get right to the point," the man said. "I want you to break things off with my daughter."

Sebastian snorted. Were all fathers the same? Egotistical and manipulative? "I expected as much."

"Will you?"

"No."

Herr Baumann raised his palms. "Why would you want to hurt an innocent girl like Eva?"

"I don't think I'm the one hurting her."

"Surely you are aware how all the young women of Europe are in love with you. The celebrity you. Every one of them dreams that she could gain your attention and your affections. Eva is no different."

Sebastian frowned. He remembered the poster of him and Hollow Fellows on Eva's wall. But that was then. She doesn't see him like that anymore. She sees the real him. And she still wants to be with him.

"Eva is special," Herr Baumann continued. "She's been through a lot. I couldn't bear to see her hurt again. Please, would you consider it?"

"You don't want to see her get hurt again but you're asking me to do just that."

"Yes, I know. But the pain now will be far less than the pain later."

Sebastian bristled at his words. The man was so sure that he would leave his daughter hanging.

"I've already told her I'd accompany her to Gabriele's

wedding. Do you want me to rip her heart in two right before that joyous event?"

Herr Baumann stared at him and pinched his lips together. "No, that's not the memory I want her to associate with her sister's happy moment. You can come to the wedding, but then the next day it's time to say good-bye."

"What if I don't want to say good-bye to her? Ever?" Sebastian stood and stared at Herr Baumann, man to man. "I think I'm falling in love with her."

Herr Baumann's eyes widened under his thick eyebrows. He rubbed his forehead as if he could scrub the shock off. "If you love her you'll let her go."

Sebastian returned his challenge. "If you love her, you'll let her go."

Herr Baumann sighed. "Perhaps we should both let her go. Just think about it, that's all I ask. Will you? Do what you know is best for her."

YOU SCARED ME

Sebastian Weiss

I have a surprise for you.

Eva Baumann

I love surprises.

Sebastian Weiss

Meet me outside.

Eva Baumann

Now?

Sebastian Weiss

Now.

EVA QUICKLY CHECKED her image in the mirror, ran fingers through her hair and smoothed her skirt. Her stomach bubbled with anticipation. What kind of surprise did Sebastian have? And how brave of him to come to her door. Her parents were working in the flat but they could go out at any time.

Papa looked up from the computer at his desk in the corner of the dining room and pushed his reading glasses up on his nose. "Where are you going?"

Eva hesitated. She could spin a lie, tell him she was going to visit Annette, but she didn't want to lie anymore, especially to her parents. She lifted her chin. "I'm meeting Sebastian."

Papa's face flickered with disapproval, but he only grunted, then went back to whatever he was working on. Interesting. She would've stood up to him long ago if she'd thought it would be this easy.

She was greeted with warm August air that smelled spicy from the mixed aromas of the open restaurants on her block. Her eyes widened with, yes, surprise, when she saw Sebastian standing there. With a two-seater bike.

He disarmed her with his smile, the way he always did. "What do you think?"

"It's... nice."

"It's more than nice. It's perfect. See, I had the bike techs disengage the back pedals."

"So, you do all the work?" Eva asked.

"It's not much work. It's not like you weigh much, and the bike trail along the river is flat."

A smile took over her face. Sebastian had listened to her when she told him she missed riding her bike. He found a way to give her back her dream. Her heart swelled with gratitude. She limped over to him and pushed up on her toes to meet his lips.

"This is so sweet of you. I love it." *And I love you.*

Sebastian straddled the front seat and braced the bike between his legs. "So, get on."

Eva hoisted herself onto the back seat, setting her cane across the handlebars and placed her feet on the pedals, allowing her bad leg to straighten as it rested on the lower one. "Okay. I'm ready."

Sebastian pushed off, and Eva squealed with delight, hanging on tight. They headed toward the river, dodging pedestrians and hitting the cross lights just as they turned green. Her ribs rattled as they skimmed over the cobblestones until they reached the smoother section along the pedestrian street of *Neustädter Markt*.

They walked the bike toward the bridge and down to the bike path that ran along the River Elbe, before taking off again. Eva breathed in deeply and released a happy sigh. The sun on her face and the wind in her hair, coasting along as if on air. This was what she missed. She only wished she could participate in the pedaling, feel the burn in her thighs and the stretching of her lungs as she exerted her body.

But this was a worthy second-place prize with the added bonus of being able to stare at Sebastian's strong shoulder muscles rippling under his shirt.

After a while Sebastian stopped by an empty bench. "Do you want to rest here a bit?"

Eva wasn't the one who'd been working, so she wasn't in need of a rest, but she got off for Sebastian's sake. The bike had a water bottle attached, and Sebastian removed it and took a swig before handing it to Eva. "Want some?"

She reached for the bottle and drank. "Thanks," she said as she handed it back.

Sebastian sat beside her and draped an arm over the back of the bench behind Eva's shoulders. He shifted his sunglasses to the top of his head, closed his eyes and stretched out, basking in the sun.

"I love summer," he said.

"Me, too."

He opened the eye closest to her and stared. "How'd it go last night? With your parents?"

"It was tough. But I think they respect me enough to let me do what I want."

"Which is what?" he asked playfully.

She nudged his leg. "Be with you."

"Ah." He sat up straighter and turned to her. "That was it? I thought you'd get the third degree or an ultimatum or something."

"I think if Papa thought he could get away with that, he would."

"Your Papa…" Sebastian's eyes flickered with… something. Indecision?

"My papa what?"

Sebastian pushed his sunglasses back onto his nose. "Nothing. Just… I'm sure he's worried about you."

His voice tightened when he said that and it scared her. "Is something wrong?"

"Eva, are you sure this is worth it?"

"Am I sure *you're* worth it? Yes. Without hesitation."

Oh, no. Was he breaking up with her? Her blood went cold then hot at the thought. Tears immediately welled up behind her eyes.

Then he smiled. "And you are absolutely worth it."

She let out the breath she was holding. "Oh my heart. You scared me."

"Scared you. How?"

"I thought you were leading up to a break-up speech."

Sebastian took both of her hands in his and stared hard in her eyes. Eva's eyes fluttered with nervous apprehension. What was he going to say?

"I don't want to break up," Sebastian said firmly. Then he smiled. "In fact, I think I'm falling in love with you.

 HEART TO HEART

THAT DIDN'T GO AS PLANNED.

Sebastian had meant to give Eva one last good memory of them together so she wouldn't hate his guts completely the day after Gabriele's wedding when he'd planned to make good on Herr Baumann's request and say good-bye. He'd spent a sleepless night thinking about Eva, her goodness, and how he fell so short. He wasn't worthy of her.

He would be leaving to go on tour for two weeks shortly after so it was perfect timing. She could hate him for breaking up with her, and he could hate himself for the same reason. A perfect hate fest.

But instead he declared his love.

And it was true. He did love her.

"I love you, too," she said through her kisses. Her arms tightened around his neck. "I've loved you for a really long time."

His hands grabbed her waist, stroking the soft skin along the waistband of her skirt. "Thanks for waiting for me."

They were creating a scene in a public place. That meant a photographer with a long-range lens could be lurking. He had to be more careful. He didn't want Eva to be a tabloid target. He pulled back and twisted his cap lower over his eyes. He lifted Eva's hand to his mouth and kissed her knuckles.

"You know things will get tough if you stick with me."

"Tough in what way?"

"Paparazzi. Rumors."

"Like the blond with major cleavage you had lunch with?"

So she saw that and didn't say anything. "Yes, just like that. I was having lunch, and they were very annoying."

"They?"

"Yeah. The pictures only showed the one girl to make it look intimate, like we were on a date, but she had two friends sitting across the table."

"Interesting."

"And once the media gets wind that I have a serious new girlfriend, they'll hound you. Not like Kate Middleton or anything. But the paparazzi are out there like vultures looking for their next meal."

She smiled in a flirty way that made his heart melt. "I'm kind of stuck on the words 'serious new girlfriend.'"

He leaned in and worked his lips along her neck. "I'm kind of stuck on that, too."

She kissed his forehead. "I'm up for it."

"You're sure?"

She pulled back and stared at him sternly. "Stop asking me that. Yes, I'm sure. One hundred percent."

He laughed. "Okay then."

TRUTH FOR TRUTH

HER HEART SOARED. Sebastian loved her! She loved Sebastian! They were *in love*! She held on to the back seat handlebars as Sebastian pedaled. She tilted her face appreciatively toward the sun. They approached a riverside café decorated in a Hawaiian theme and Sebastian pointed, speaking loudly over his shoulder, "Wanna stop?" She nodded yes.

The patio was shaded with a grass-thatched roof and ukulele music played through a stereo system. They found an empty table, and when the waitress approached, a cute little Asian girl with a flower tucked in her hair, Sebastian ordered a Panini with ham and pineapple and Gouda cheese. "Are you hungry?"

Eva shook her head. Her stomach was in a knot with excitement. "I'm thirsty though." The waitress suggested a pineapple and banana smoothie, and Eva ordered one.

Sebastian reached for her hand as they waited. "If you could go any place in the world," he said. "Where would you go?"

Eva was stumped by the question. She couldn't imagine leaving Germany. Or Dresden for that matter. The thought of traveling frightened her. What about robbers? Bad water? Terrorist attacks?

She didn't want to go anywhere new. Just crossing a busy city street in a neighborhood she knew well was hazardous enough for her. Her heart palpitated.

"Don't worry," Sebastian said with a furrowed brow. "I'm not going to go buy tickets. I'm just making conversation."

Eva blushed at her stupidity. Of course. It was a hypothetical question. "I'm not great with crowds. Or hills."

"Okay, so somewhere flat and unpopulated. A desert?"

Her eyes darted to her cane. "Sand can be difficult."

"So, no sand. Not even a beach?"

"Beaches are fine, as long as I'm lying on them and not jogging across them." She smiled, trying to make her comment light.

"Swimming's okay, though, right? Water makes you buoyant."

She nodded. "Swimming's okay." She'd spent a lot of time in pools during her rehabilitation.

The waitress arrived with their order, placing the hot sandwich in front of Sebastian and in front of Eva, a frosted glass that had a little umbrella stabbed through a cherry resting on top.

"So a flat beach town with few people?" Sebastian asked after swallowing his first bite.

"Yeah," she said. "I want to go there. You know of a place?"

"Not off the top of my head. But you can bet I'll be looking." He reached over and squeezed her hand. "Not that I want to see you in a bikini or anything." He grinned suggestively.

Oh my heart! What was she thinking? She couldn't wear a bikini in public. Her leg! Her *scar*.

"Eva? What's going on?"

She blinked and forced a smile. "I'm fine. I just have to go to visit the toilets."

She smoothed her skirt as she stood and gripped her cane, her eyes searching for the restroom sign. She could feel Sebastian's eyes on her as she walked away. Her shoulders weighed heavy with a new realization. This relationship with Sebastian *would* be a challenge to her and not for the reasons he worried about. She could care less about the paparazzi. They were by far her lesser enemy. Her imposing nemesis was fear. And if she didn't conquer it she'd lose Sebastian for sure.

And now she'd just added a gigantic new fear to her already massive pile.

Eva used the facilities and washed her hands. She examined her reflection in the mirror. Two people lived inside the face that looked back. The one who was buoyed by love and wanted to scale mountains (metaphorically speaking, of course). That Eva was like Joan of Arc in full armor, ready to conquer anyone who was a threat to herself and those she held dear.

And the other Eva was like a turtle who was terrified of getting thrown onto her back. She shied away from anything that could expose her tender underbelly to harm. Even if it was the one person she wanted to love and trust with all her heart.

This constant inner battle exhausted her. She splashed water on her face and pinched her cheeks. She had to shake off this mood. It didn't help that her leg was throbbing. Even though she didn't have to pedal, the vibrations wracked her tender nerves and her leg grew stiff from the unnatural way she had to balance it on the pedal.

She dug a pain reliever out of her shoulder bag and downed it with water before returning to her table.

Sebastian looked at her with concern in his eyes. "Is it your leg?"

"It's fine. The painkiller will kick in soon."

He reached over and squeezed her shoulder. "Do you struggle a lot? With pain, I mean?"

She grimaced. She didn't want this to become a pity party for her. "Sometimes. It's manageable with enough rest and a good prescription." She forced a laugh.

A table nearby grew excited, and a quick glance showed Eva that a group of girls had recognized Sebastian. They had their cameras out. "Looks like it's time to go."

Sebastian noticed and waved the waitress over. He paid the bill and then helped Eva back to the path where he unlocked the bike. Eva was determined to enjoy the rest of the day and pushed back her earlier dark thoughts. Their romance had just started. It was stupid of her to throw cold water on it before it barely had a chance to flame.

She was quiet on the ride home. She almost wished that Sebastian had picked her up in a scooter. At least that way she could lean against his back and wrap her arms around his waist. But scooters were dangerous, too. The temptation to swerve in and out of traffic. You could easily get hit.

Eva never said anything to Sebastian about her worries. It was bad enough that she was physically weak. She didn't want to be emotionally weak, too. She put on a smile when they returned to her building and hoped she looked stronger than she felt.

She wrapped her arms around Sebastian's neck and whispered, "Thanks so much for the bike ride. It was so sweet and thoughtful of you. She kissed her way from his earlobe to his mouth and her joy reignited as she felt him quiver against her. He gripped her waist and pulled her close and then rested his chin on her head.

"What's the plan for tomorrow?" he asked. "Do I pick you up or meet you at the church?"

Gabriele's wedding day had arrived so quickly.

"I'll be very busy all day until the ceremony. I wish we could go together, but I have to stay with my sister."

Sebastian looked relieved. "I'll arrive a little late and slip in the back."

She frowned but understood. Someone there could recognize him and it would be less distracting if they didn't see him arrive.

"Okay. I'll see you tomorrow," she said.

He kissed her softly. "Don't forget that I love you."

The happy bubbles sprung up again. He loved her! Why was she so worried? "I love you, too."

She hummed a tune on her way up the stairs, even though her leg was still killing her. Soon she'd be lying on her bed resting it and there she'd be free to relive the entire day.

The warm air of her flat couldn't thaw the frosty wall she encountered the moment she entered. Her parents stood with grim expressions and folded arms.

Dread percolated up her spine. They were upset and she had a feeling it had something to do with her. "What's up?"

Papa pointed to his computer screen.

Already?

Her face heated up as she took in the pictures: Sebastian and her on the bench by the river. His mouth was on her neck, and her eyes were closed and lips parted with the passion she couldn't hide. Sebastian's hand rested on the bare skin of her waist, his fingers reaching under her shirt.

Oh my heart!

"The whole world can see this, Eva," her mama began. "Already, we're getting emails from members of the church letting us know."

Eva felt her mother's embarrassment roll off in waves. Eva had always been the quiet child. The obedient child. The child everyone pitied.

"Is this the life you want?" Papa asked, his skin red

with the anger he fought to control. "You look like a floozy."

Slap.

So this was what real mortification felt like. Blood rushed to her head. Her heart stopped. Sweat broke out under her arms and on the top of her lip. Tears pooled behind her eyes.

New fear alert! She *was* afraid of paparazzi. Very afraid.

She couldn't look her parents in the eye. She muttered, "I'm sorry," and lumbered to her room. She closed the door tightly, crawled onto her bed and cried into her pillow.

 THE FIRST TEST

SEBASTIAN WAS BARELY HOME ten minutes when he received a text from Dirk alerting him to the photos. "Congratulations! Hollow Fellows is back on the public radar thanks to you. Good work!"

Dirk believed that all publicity was good publicity. That may be the case for the band, but it was a disaster for this fledgling relationship. Worse yet was the journalists' speculations, that Sebastian had set up the shot to boost publicity.

Hollow Fellows were now trending on twitter all over Europe.

He immediately called Eva. "Hey, just a heads up…"

"I've seen it."

"I'm so sorry. I didn't know. Honestly."

She didn't respond right away and Sebastian's stomach clenched. She said she didn't care about the paparazzi. Here was her first test.

"It's okay."

He let out a long breath. "I should know better. I'm really sorry. No more public displays of affection from now on, I promise."

"I hate that. But, you're right."

He could hear the pain in her voice. Already he had cut her. He'd dreaded leaving her when he went on tour, but maybe it was for the best. Give the hounds a chance to find something new to talk about. Give them time to forget about Sebastian Weiss's "mystery girl."

"Has anyone else seen it?" Sebastian was thinking about Eva's father and wouldn't be surprised if he had another visit from the man tonight—this time with serious threats.

"Yes. My parents. Probably my sister. The whole country, I think."

Sebastian paced the floor and gripped his hair. "These things have a short shelf life. Someone else will do something way more scandalous by the morning, and we'll be old news." He hoped to comfort her, but she was the one living in the same house as Herr Baumann. It couldn't be pleasant.

"Yeah, I'm sure you're right. Anyway, my sister is turning into Bridezilla. I have to go help her."

"Okay. Good. Get your mind off this. Like I said, it'll blow over before you know it."

They hung up, and Sebastian collapsed into a chair and rubbed his face with his hands. He was certain Eva would be getting an earful along the lines of "our house, our rules." Her parents would insist that she end things.

The thought was a knife to his heart.

But he knew they were right. This was just the tip of the iceberg. Hollow Fellows was positioned to get bigger, even worldwide. Especially with the new CD and their new songs.

Eva's songs.

Staying with him would mean greater heartache for her.

He picked up an empty beer bottle on the coffee table and threw it across the room with a roar.

The bottle crashed and splintered, sending green

shards across the tile floor. He stared at the mess, groaned and then went to the closet to search for the broom.

RUMORS

Eva expected a verbal storm, but it didn't come. She guessed Gabriele's wedding was providing a temporary shield and that the onslaught would arrive the next day.

Gabriele had shaken her head at her when she got home the night before. "I never in a million years thought you'd manage to upstage my wedding day."

"Gabi."

"Save it, Eva. You managed to not only embarrass yourself, but our whole family. Not to mention the church."

Eva crumbled. "It's not that bad."

"If you say so. I'm just glad this is the last night I have to sleep in this house. Have fun dealing with Mama and Papa without me here to buffer you."

Annette was the only one who thought she'd done something cool. She'd texted: *oohlala. E and S for the win!*

That was right. Eva and Sebastian for the win. They would survive this. It would blow over in a few days. Maybe less time than that. Everyone would be talking about Gabriele and Lennon soon enough.

She'd texted Annette back: *Thanks. You don't know how much I needed that.*

Now she sat on the chair by her guitar with a sage green satin dress that ended just below her knees. It had two thin straps that ran over her shoulders and crossed along her bare back. She had to compensate for weak legs with her upper body, and as a result she had shapely arms and back muscles she rarely got to show off. Her hair had been done, a messy up-do with curls that escaped around her face. Her hair was by nature, stubbornly straight, so it was an unfamiliar look. The curls were hard fought for by the hairdresser, and Eva worried the girl was going to burn Eva's hair off with the curling iron. She swore they went through a half bottle of hairspray to keep the curls in place.

Julia had given Eva an exaggerated wink when she arrived earlier to help Gabriele get ready but didn't say anything. None of Gabriele's friends said anything, and Eva had the feeling Gabriele had issued a gag order.

Eva's nerves were taut with anticipation. She couldn't wait to see Sebastian again and especially looked forward to seeing him in a suit. The thought brought a smile to her face. She grabbed her guitar and began picking. The tune brought a calm to the room, and more than one girl glanced at her appreciatively.

Gabriele was last to get her hair done. She shot a look at Eva. "You're wrinkling your dress with your guitar."

Eva stopped plucking and gently put the guitar away. She sighed. It was going to be a long day.

From the pedestrian lane of *Neustäder Platz*, the Three Kings Church was just a flat stone front with a large wooden door. On the other side, the structure loomed tall with a blackened clock tower that shot up to the sky. Tall, narrow doors opened to a vast cobblestoned space dotted with trees and benches focusing on a tall stone fountain in the middle. Eva watched from an upper-floor window as the guests arrived. Her eyes searched for Sebastian's familiar form though she knew she wouldn't see him. He'd said he'd arrive late.

At 14:00 precisely, the girls escorted Gabriele down to the back of the sanctuary where Lennon was waiting. The room was smaller than one would expect from looking at the outside, and not nearly as ornate as the *Frauenkirche*, but another story was about to be added to its ancient white-washed walls. The chairs were decorated with the ribbons Eva had helped to make, and candelabras burned brightly adding an ethereal touch. White cherub statues hanging from the upper balconies looked down on the ceremony as if to bless it.

Lennon's handsome face was awash with emotion: excitement, pride, anxiety—

Weddings were nerve-racking (!)—and love. His eyes glistened with deep adoration as he gazed at his bride.

Gabriele was simply stunning. Her blond hair was styled and decorated with diamond-like Zirconia pins that reflected the candlelight. Her chiffon gown draped beautifully over her curvy body and landed in a delicate pool on the stone floor.

They walked down the aisle toward Papa who waited for them at the front and then sat in the two chairs facing him.

Papa officiated the ceremony. He led Gabriele and his soon-to-be son-in-law through the vows of marriage before man and God. "… until death do us part."

Papa smiled at the couple with fatherly affection and pride. Here was a daughter who was doing it right, Eva thought. *This* daughter married a good Christian boy. Papa could boast to his friends about *this* daughter.

The crowd exploded in applause when her Papa

pronounced them as husband and wife. Eva had never seen Gabriele happier, and the crowd roared as Lennon kissed her passionately. Gabriele broke away with an enormous smile and a rosy blush on her face. She beamed as she walked hand in hand with her perfect new husband down the aisle and into the spacious foyer. The guests emptied the chairs, family first, which comprised of Gabriele's side only, as Lennon sadly had no family.

Eva had been given a white cane decorated with a white, silky ribbon and a matching carnation to use for the occasion. Her eyes scanned the back row for Sebastian and she broke into a huge smile when she spotted him. She nodded subtly to the foyer, indicating that she wanted him to meet her there.

She was trapped behind a crowd as guests came to congratulate the couple. A commotion grew on the other side of the foyer and caused Eva concern. A group of girls, and some older women too, had created a circle around Sebastian and were making a scene. Their giggles and requests for autographs echoed in the cavernous space. Soon the attention of the people had turned from her sister to her boyfriend.

Eva willed him to look at her, and when she finally caught his eye, she waved him over. There was no way she could navigate this crowd and steal him away, which was exactly what she wished she could do.

Sebastian managed to escape—he had a lot of practice dodging fans—and made it to her side. Gabriele glared at both of them.

He leaned over and muttered, "I think I should go."

A pit grew in her stomach. She didn't want him to leave. Didn't want him to leave her. "Sebastian."

He smiled gently. "This is your sister's special day. I'm stealing her thunder."

"But…"

"It's okay." He gave her a quick kiss on the cheek and whispered in her ear. "I'll meet up with you later. Oh, and by the way, you look gorgeous. Save that dress, okay? I want to see you in it again. When we're alone."

Eva blushed and held a hand over her mouth to conceal her sly smile. Sebastian looked amazing himself, and she'd like another private occasion to see him in that suit again, too. She waved weakly as she watched him sneak out the side entrance. Once all the handshaking and kissing ended, the bridal couple headed out to the park in front where more pictures would be taken before everyone headed to the wedding party celebration.

Eva was already exhausted from this day and still had several hours ahead of her to endure. She hung back from her family so she could sneak into the public WC to freshen up. She was drooping like the flower on her cane, and she let out a long sigh. She locked herself into a stall just as a couple of girls came in giggling loudly.

"I would die if Sebastian Weiss showed up at my wedding," one of them said.

"I'd probably leave my groom at the altar and run away with him." More giggling ensued and Eva's heart lightened. Even though she and Sebastian had been official for only a short time, she had loved him for much longer. If he asked her to marry him tomorrow, she'd say yes.

"Did you see the girl he was with? The one with the cane? I saw him kiss her cheek."

"That's Gabriele's younger sister."

"Really? They don't look anything alike."

"Yeah, so sad about that accident. She's going to need that cane for the rest of her life."

"What does Sebastian Weiss see in her? She doesn't

have Gabriele's looks or her charisma. If Lennon weren't so hot, I'd say Sebastian hooked up with the wrong sister."

"I know what you mean. Maybe it's a publicity stunt. You know. Famous rock star dates cripple girl."

"I saw that on Facebook. I didn't know the mystery girl was Gabriele Baumann's sister. That's so random."

The girls left and Eva turned to the toilet and dry heaved. Her eyes blurred and she gasped for breath, bending over like someone had punched her in the gut.

People believed what they read in the news and it stung. And it was partially true. Sebastian could do better. He could be with someone who could ride her own bike. Could hike up hills and ski down mountains. What would happen when Sebastian decided he wanted to do those things? She knew he skied the Alps in the winter. She'd faithfully followed his adventures on his blog last year.

And worse yet, what if the story were true? She didn't really know Sebastian all that well. What if he was using her to boost his publicity?

She bent over and dry heaved again.

 COME WITH ME

Eva hadn't been the same since the wedding, and Sebastian was concerned. He kept asking her if anything was wrong and she kept shaking her head and saying no. But Sebastian could see it in her eyes. The sparkle was missing when she looked at him. Was she pulling back already?

He hadn't gotten another visit from Herr Baumann, but that didn't mean he'd given up on seeing his daughter break free of him. He asked Eva about it, if she was being pressured by her parents to end things, but she insisted that she wasn't.

Something was scaring her and if it wasn't her family, then he needed to find out what it was.

Maybe it was the tour coming up? He'd be gone for two weeks. Was she worried about that? He knew what they said about him in the tabloids. That he was a womanizer, that maybe that was what had driven Yvonne to cheat.

Did Eva believe he'd cheat as well?

It must be so hard for her, being bombarded with mixed messages and untruths from every side. He didn't blame her for feeling confused. What could he do to assuage her fears?

He'd love to take her along on tour but never asked because he knew what kind of fallout that would have with her family, and he didn't want to put her in that position again.

But maybe she wanted to be put in that position.

Maybe she needed to know he wanted her with him, even if she had to say no.

The pressure in his chest eased a little. That had to be it. He just needed to give her the option to say no. Then she'd know she could trust him. Two weeks wasn't that long.

He grabbed his phone and texted her: *Come with me on my tour.*

SUFFOCATION

MAMA AND PAPA were killing her. Now with Gabriele married and in Greece on her honeymoon, Eva was the sole point of attention. It seemed they were everywhere, watching, probing, frowning. Even the needs of the house church didn't seem to distract them from her life. Or rather, her love life.

Eva had spent most of her twenty years envying her sister and there was never a time when she envied her more than now. What she'd give to run away with Sebastian. She was willing to go anywhere just about now.

But she hadn't forgotten what the girls in the WC at Gabriele's wedding had said about her. Maybe her parents were right about her and her "obsession with the rock-star boy." Maybe she was just making a big fool of herself, and her father's premonition would come true, that this relationship was bound to end in heartbreak and disgrace. Her heart felt like it was on the verge of exploding right now. What would she do if Sebastian ended it? He might. He was leaving soon. Maybe she had just been a distraction for him while he licked his wounds over Yvonne's betrayal. She couldn't get the thought out of her head. Maybe she *was* a PR stunt.

Her stomach rolled so much these days she could barely eat, but she had to fuel herself sometime. She pulled herself off her bed and headed to the kitchen for breakfast.

She heard her parents talking in low tones and stopped when she heard her name.

"We'll only make things worse if we try to force her to leave him," her mother said. "We just need to let it run its course and pray it doesn't go on for too long."

"He told me he'd end it," Papa said.

"What do you mean?"

"I went to see him shortly after he started coming around to see her. I asked him to be reasonable. To imagine the future and how it could only end badly for our Eva."

"And he promised to end it?"

"Well, not in so many words."

Eva felt sick. Her father had asked Sebastian to end things? Anger stirred hot in her gut. She couldn't believe he would stoop so low. She could barely breathe. She inched back to her room quietly and folded into her chair. She was trapped. If only she hadn't dropped out of university, she could be well on her way to acquiring a career and a way to providing for herself. As it was, she depended on her parents for the roof over her head and food in her belly.

Her phone buzzed. She hobbled to her night table wanting to see one name. Part of her was scared to death that he was texting to end it, that her father had gotten to him somehow. But instead she read his invitation and her heart leaped with relief. She didn't give herself a chance to think it through, to talk herself out of it. She typed one word.

JUST ONE WORD

HE SENT THE TEXT, and she responded two seconds later. His heart stuttered to a stop. No argument. No questions. Just one word.

Okay.

Things must be really bad over there. The tour started tomorrow. The guys were busy today packing up gear and the personal stuff they'd need for the duration. He had booked off a couple hours in the evening to say good-bye to Eva. Looked like he didn't have to do that now.

Sebastian Weiss

We leave at eight tomorrow morning.

Eva Baumann

Can you pick me up? I need help with my bag.

Sebastian Weiss

Yes. For sure. See you then.

He stared out the window feeling stunned. Everything had changed again. So fast. Eva was coming on tour with him. It could mean sharing a hotel room. Heat burst through his body at the thought of that. They hadn't even slept together yet. He worried that things were moving too fast for her, even if she didn't realize it herself. He'd let her set the pace. If she wanted her own room, he'd spring for that, his own personal expense.

He rubbed his face hard. His door chime rang, and he buzzed to let in Markus.

"Hey," Markus said, heading straight for the gear Sebastian had packed up. Sebastian grabbed two guitars and followed Markus out. Most of the gear was stored at their rehearsal space, and that was where the tour bus was parked.

"I need a favor tomorrow morning," Sebastian said.

Markus gave him a bored look. "Let me guess. You need a ride to the bus."

"Well, yeah, but then we need to pick up Eva. She's coming along."

Markus shot him a hard look.

"I don't care about the 'no girlfriend' rule. If you remember, I never voted for it."

"Yeah, sure, but… man, why do I have to be the one to break the news."

"Break what news?"

"Karl is bringing Yvonne."

Sebastian felt sucker punched. "What?" He didn't even know the two of them were still seeing each other.

"Yeah, it's true. Sorry, man."

Sebastian let his head fall back and groaned. Just what he needed. More drama. Now the question was should he tell Eva before or after he picked her up.

He better call her right away. The sooner she knew the better. She might change her mind about coming and he didn't want to deal with that scene in the morning. He pressed her number, but she didn't pick up. He texted her instead: *Bad news. Karl is bringing Yvonne. In case that changes anything.*

Markus eyed him again. "You look like crap."

"Thanks. I feel like it, too." He kept his phone in his palm, hoping Eva would respond soon.

They arrived at the warehouse and Sebastian could see Dirk and Karl loading gear onto the bus.

"Don't say anything to them about Eva coming along, okay?" he said to Markus. "She might change her mind now."

He snorted. "No problem. I wasn't planning to step on that landmine anyway."

Sebastian kept silent as he joined in with loading the gear. If he said anything to Karl he might end up punching his face in. Instead, he kept his ill feelings to himself. The bus had several rows of forward-facing seats behind the driver, a small kitchen area behind that with a little fridge, microwave and food storage space. A closet-sized bathroom was tucked in behind that and then a section of cots, two deep on each side. That was where they packed the gear. None of their trips necessitated sleeping overnight on the bus, which was a good thing since there were more people than cots.

He jumped out of the bus just as he felt buzzing in his pocket. His breath hitched as he pulled it out. The moment of truth. Was she coming or not?

Eva Baumann
I'm coming for sure now.

Sebastian grinned. He loved it when she got territorial with him.

Sebastian Weiss
That's my girl.

Eva Baumann

:)

Sebastian pushed the phone back into his pocket and let out a breath. Somehow it was all going to be okay.

At ten to eight the next morning, Eva exited her room with her cane in her right hand and dragging a rolling suitcase in the other. She was dressed in a fresh blouse and skirt, her hair was washed and brushed, and she wore a little makeup.

Her parents sat at the table eating breakfast and looked at her with quiet, stunned faces. Her papa held a piece of buttered toast in mid air. He asked the obvious question. "Are you going somewhere?"

Eva swallowed hard and nodded. "I'm going on tour with Sebastian."

Papa slowly lowered his toast. "If you go, don't…"

Mama quickly grabbed his arm and shook her head sharply. "Eva, you haven't thought this through."

"I have Mama, and I'm going. Nothing you say will talk me out of it."

Papa stood sharply. She could see the hurt in his eyes, and she felt a moment of regret. But she held her resolve. He shook his head and disappeared down the hall.

Mama's torment was no less. Her eyes grew glossy and she held a hand to her chest. "Where are you going?"

"Salzburg. Then Munich." After that she wasn't exactly sure. "I'll be back in two weeks."

Her mother's eyes fell to her suitcase, and Eva knew what she was wondering. How was she going to carry that out? "Sebastian is coming up to get it."

Mama walked over to Eva, her face twitching as she held back her sadness. "I'll carry it for you."

"Mama."

"It's okay."

Eva followed her mother down the steps and not for the first time, she admired her. She didn't always agree with her mama, but she had to admit she was a strong woman. She waited with Eva until Markus and Sebastian arrived in Markus's car. She didn't spare a glance or a "hello," to the boy who was taking her daughter away. She held Eva tight. "I love you no matter what. And so does Papa."

She turned, and Eva's heart ached at the pain she knew she was causing her. It couldn't be helped. She was almost twenty-one and needed to cut the strings as hard as it might be.

"Bye, Mama," she whispered as the woman disappeared into the building.

Sebastian placed her suitcase into the trunk and helped her into the backseat before crawling in beside her.

"I'm a chauffeur now?" Markus quipped.

Eva pushed back at the swirl of emotion that was overwhelming her. Sebastian draped an arm around her shoulders and kissed her tenderly on the lips.

"Are you okay?"

"I will be."

"So Markus," Sebastian called, "I haven't officially introduced you to my girlfriend. This is Eva."

Markus eyed her from the rearview mirror. "Hi, Eva."

"Hi, Markus," she said softly. "Nice to meet you." She knew his face, of course, from the website and from seeing him on TV, but now that she knew Sebastian the way she did, she wasn't fazed by his celebrity status.

A short time later, they drove into a neighborhood of

brick warehouses, most of them abandoned with small yards overrun by weeds, and pulled up beside the tour bus.

Eva saw Dirk and Karl waiting for them. Like Markus, Eva hadn't met them personally, but she knew who they were. Karl had his arm around a short girl with spiky blue hair. Eva remembered Yvonne from the previous year when it was Sebastian's arm that had been draped around her. Only then, the girl's hair had been pink.

She reached for Sebastian's hand and held on tightly.

Yvonne scowled when her gaze landed on Eva, moving from her face to her cane. She rolled her eyes like the sight of Eva disgusted her. Eva's feelings toward Yvonne were less than amiable, too, and she couldn't imagine a more awkward tour situation. Sebastian had been with Yvonne for a long time, *years*, and Eva knew they'd had a physical relationship. Sebastian had told her outright that he'd asked Yvonne to move in with him, but for some reason she'd refused.

Eva could thank her for something.

Dirk waved to Eva, and Karl nodded an acknowledgment. Sebastian's eyes darted between Eva and Yvonne, his expression one of discomfort and displeasure. He smiled faintly at Eva as if he hoped to encourage her before pitching in with the other guys to load up the final pieces of equipment.

Eva found herself standing alone with Yvonne and she felt mild dizziness, like she was trapped in a twisted, surreal alternate reality.

Again, Yvonne scanned Eva from head to toe and narrowed her eyes in contempt. "You must have a really nice personality."

The first jab in record timing.

"Charm is deceitful, and beauty is fleeting," Eva quipped. Yvonne's eyes fluttered, like she didn't understand, and then she left her suddenly to help the guys. Eva regretted her sharp tongue. Yvonne had lost Sebastian. Eva pitied her.

Yvonne carried a guitar in each hand and stepped onto the bus. Eva's heart sunk. At least Yvonne could be helpful. Eva was just dead weight.

Sebastian returned and pulled Eva's suitcase out of Markus's trunk. He eyed her softly. "How are you doing?"

She shrugged. Her stomach had twisted into a hundred knots. She was dishonoring her parents by running off with a boy she loved but hadn't known for that long, and his former longtime girlfriend, who still obviously had a thing for him, was coming along.

"I'm fine."

He kissed her head. "I'm really glad you're here."

Sebastian introduced her to the bus driver, a middle-aged guy called Florian, and then she followed him onto the bus.

"Where should I sit?"

"Anywhere you like."

She took a seat in the second row by the window and waited anxiously for Sebastian to join her. She needed the comfort of his presence. The warmth of his arm alongside hers. His fingers weaving through hers and squeezing. She closed her eyes and metered her breathing, slowly in and out. Her heart raced, and she worried she was going to have a panic attack. That was too humiliating to consider, which made her pulse jump even more erratically.

She let out a long breath when Sebastian settled in beside her. "Here." He handed her a bottle of orange juice and a small plate with a croissant. She accepted them gratefully. She'd skipped breakfast, which wasn't helping with her drop in blood sugar levels.

Florian drove them out of town and merged southward

onto the autobahn. The mood on the bus was somber. Karl and Yvonne sat together on the opposite side of Eva and Sebastian, one row ahead. Eva noted how both Karl and Yvonne often glanced back at them. Eva couldn't feel more out of place and unwanted as she did now in their presence. Dirk and Markus were friendlier. They'd offered her an understanding smile before each had claimed his own row, Markus behind Eva and Sebastian, and Dirk across from him. They reclined on their backs, feet hanging into the aisle, and fell asleep.

Eva's phone buzzed. A text from Gabriele: *Mama told me what you did. Are you crazy?*

She shoved the phone back in her purse. Gabriele was on her honeymoon. Surely she had more to do than interfere in Eva's life.

Eva watched the scenery pass by: pastures and rolling hills, villages with their red-tiled-roof homes clustered together. She'd rarely been out of Dresden, and the world beyond both excited and frightened her. Her goal for the year was to face her fears, one by one, and speeding out of town was one of the easier ones.

After a while, they stopped at a rest stop to refuel and use the restrooms. Eva noticed that Sebastian only talked with Dirk and Markus, even about band stuff, adeptly ignoring Karl, and Karl did the same thing. The tension on the bus wasn't Eva's doing, she realized. It would've been thick even without her presence. She waited for Yvonne to exit the WC before taking her turn. They would never be friends, and avoiding close quarters and the pressure to engage in small talk was pertinent.

They took the opportunity to eat lunch at the restaurant there, again in three groups, with Florian sitting at a table with Dirk and Markus, Karl and Yvonne, and Sebastian and Eva on the other side of the room. Sebastian paid for the two of them, even though Eva offered to pay for hers.

He grinned and shook his head. "You're my guest."

Did that mean he was going to pay for everything for her? It wasn't like she had a lot of money of her own. She didn't get paid to work at the kitchen, and she never had a job. All she had was limited access to an insurance claim from her accident, and it wasn't really a lot of money when she considered she had to finance the whole rest of her life somehow.

For the first time since her impulsive move to join Sebastian on this tour did she think about what her life was going to be like *after tour*. It was a big, blank page and the emptiness of it scared her to death.

She shook her head and refocused on her meal. There would be time to think about that later.

"Sorry about this somber bunch," Sebastian said between bites. "Normally, we're a lot more lively."

"It's fine."

"The energy levels will rise as we get closer to Salzburg. Have you ever been there?"

Eva shook her head. "I've heard it's beautiful. I had an American nurse when I was in rehab. When she heard I was a musician and music lover she gave me a DVD of a movie called *The Sound of Music,* which was filmed there. So you could say I've been to Salzburg vicariously."

"I've never heard of that movie."

"I hadn't either, but apparently it's very famous in America."

"What's it about?"

"An esteemed general from World War I hires a nun to care for his seven children. The nun trains them to sing— they all happen to be great singers, and the music in the movie is fabulous—and the unruly children along with the general fall in love with her." Eva paused and grinned. "She decides she doesn't want to be a nun anymore and marries the general."

Sebastian arched a brow. "Sounds like a chick movie."

"Except the Nazi party is taking root and expects the general to play nice. He doesn't want to so he plans a daring escape with his family of nine across the Alps into Switzerland—a plan that almost fails because of a secret and forbidden romance between the eldest daughter and a young Nazi soldier."

"Ah, that sounds better."

"Don't forget it's based on a true story."

Sebastian reached across the table for her hand and winked. "True stories are the best kind."

Eva agreed. She smiled warmly at Sebastian. They were in the middle of writing their very own.

SALZBURG

"We're in Austria now," Sebastian announced. He grinned at Eva's eager expression as she pressed her face against the bus window.

The white-stone fortress spread across the top of the hill in the middle of the old city, glowing like a magical light in the summer sun. The perpetually snow-covered Alps lay majestically like broken teeth in the distance. Eva's eyes never moved from the scene outside as the bus drove into the city center. Colorful row houses lined the banks of the River Salzach that sparkled like a jeweled bangle in the sunshine.

Eva sighed happily. "It's so beautiful."

Sebastian squeezed her shoulder. "I can't believe you've never been to Austria before."

"I haven't been anywhere."

"I'm definitely going to work on changing that. Tomorrow, before we head to Munich, we'll take a tour of the fortress. There's a gondola that goes right to the top, and the view is spectacular."

Eva turned to him and smiled widely, and Sebastian couldn't stop himself from kissing her forehead.

Florian parked the bus at their destination and everyone jumped out. They were greeted by the concert organizer, a young guy with spiky hair and an eyebrow ring, and they followed him inside the old building.

Sebastian loved the musky scent of ancient music halls.

The worn wooden steps that led to an elevated stage, nicks in the walls from people hauling sound equipment and not quite navigating the turns, the peeling paint in the nooks and crannies—all echoing the performances of hundreds of artists who had played there before Hollow Fellows. Artists that dated back to Bach, and Mozart who had been born in Salzburg.

He set up his guitar stand onstage and unsnapped the case. Tech guys buzzed around him, setting up sound equipment and lights. He stood to gauge the empty space in front of him. The crew set up a few rows of chairs near the front, leaving the rest clear for the fans to stand and watch.

Eva sat in a chair stage left, waiting. Sebastian nodded and saluted. His excitement to play tonight grew as the hour to begin drew nearer and Eva's presence just highlighted it all. This tour would've sucked without her.

His eyes darted to the other familiar figure on the opposite end of the row. Yvonne. Her eyes weren't on Karl like they should be. They were on Sebastian. Her gaze followed him as he walked across the stage. It irked him to no end that she agreed to go on tour with Karl when she consistently refused his request for her to join him in the past.

The way she stared at him confirmed what he suspected. She wanted him back. "That's not going to happen," he muttered under his breath and turned away from her. Sebastian worked efficiently, making an extra effort to avoid Karl.

It was impossible to ignore him completely, and at one point Karl backed into him.

"Hey," he said.

Sebastian grunted.

Karl grabbed his arm. "Are we cool?"

"You stole my girlfriend."

"But you got a new one you seem to like a lot. It's fate, Seb. Let's just chill."

"Fine. But we're not friends. We just play in the same band."

Once the stage was set up, another hour was spent on sound checking vocal mics, guitars, the drum kit, the monitor system. Over and over again. This was the grunt work. Sebastian felt bad for Eva. She'd pulled an e-reader out of her bag and was reading.

He jumped off the stage when the sound check ended.

"How are you?" he asked. "I know it's a long wait."

Eva slipped her reader back into her bag. "I'm fine. Nice to catch up on my reading."

"The greenroom is ready. You must be hungry."

"I am. Lead the way."

The greenroom wasn't actually green. It was just the standard name used by all musicians for the room where they waited before a gig. It usually had food and beverages, and this one was no different. A broad selection of buns, meat, cheese and salads, along with water, fizzy drinks and beer filled a table along the back wall. Everyone loaded up plates and sat at a second table to eat.

Sebastian excused himself to use the facilities, and when he returned he walked up behind Eva who was conversing with Yvonne. It freaked him out. His old girlfriend and new, talking. The expression on Eva's face told him she wasn't enjoying it very much.

"He's just with you to get back at me," Yvonne said.

"If he wanted to be with you, he'd be with you."

"You don't know him like I do. Sebastian isn't all that you think…"

"Yvonne!"

The girls spun, and Yvonne forced a smile. "Sebastian, Eva and I were just getting to know each other a little."

Sebastian threaded his arm through Eva's. "I heard you, Yvonne. You're not my spokesperson."

He led Eva away before Yvonne could respond. "Don't listen to a word she says."

Eva answered, "Don't worry. I'm not."

Tension filled the greenroom as the clock ticked. The band had changed into stage clothes, basically just cleaner versions of what they all wore earlier, and waited while the local opening band finished their set.

Finally, there was a knock on the door. "You guys are up."

Sebastian stopped to kiss Eva just before he went backstage. "Are you going to be all right?" he asked. He'd made sure a seat in the front row had been reserved for her, but he hated leaving her alone with a thousand strangers.

"I'll be fine," she said. "Have fun."

Sebastian climbed onto the stage and the crowd started yelling. He breathed in deeply, loving the moment. Nothing like a full house of half-crazed fans calling your name. The house lights were blinding, so it was tough seeing anything past the first couple rows. He searched for Eva and felt relief when he spotted her claiming her chair, hanging her cane on the back before sitting down. She flashed him a thumbs up, and he laughed.

He screamed out, "Hello, Salzburg!" and the cheers grew deafening.

"You may have heard this one before, but I promise you, our version is different!" Sebastian strummed the first chord of their rock remake of Katja's folksong, "Sun & Moon."

God, won't you calm my mind

> *I feel like it will implode*
> *The difference between them and I*
> *Is like the sun and the moon*

Sebastian's voice blasted the room, full and growly, increasing in intensity as he neared the bridge.

> *I'll take the long way around*
> *sling shot around what I thought was the darkest side of the moon*
> *Coming round took so long*
> *Sun light nearly stole my eyes*

Sebastian screamed out the high note on "stole my eyes," and the fans went wild. Sweat broke his brow, and he jumped energetically across the stage, making love to his guitar. He never felt more alive than he did on stage playing before a full house of enthusiastic fans.

They played all their hits and some of their new ones, too. As usual, the crowd demanded an encore, and Hollow Fellows were prepared to give it to them.

When the show ended, the fans stormed the stage, pushing empty chairs out of the way, calling their names.

"Sebastian! Sebastian!"

The smile fell off his face when he saw them push around Eva. She was walking toward the stage and was overcome by bodies. She lost her balance and fell to the floor.

"Eva!" Sebastian jumped off the stage, pushing back at his fans. "Back off, everyone!" He heard the girls gasp, but he didn't care. "Eva!"

He reached her and helped her back to her feet. "Are you okay?"

"Yeah, I'm fine. I just couldn't move fast enough to get out of their way."

"Sebastian, Sebastian! Can I get your autograph?"

Sebastian helped Eva to the front of the stage. "I can make it from here," she said, looking sheepish.

"Are you sure?" He felt terrible that she'd fell. She could've been trampled.

She smiled at him, and his heart melted. "I'm sure. Go make your fans happy."

THE ROOM

THE HOTEL WASN'T FANCY, just a boxy, four-story building off the autobahn on the Austrian/German border. Eva shivered in the cool early morning darkness and stifled a yawn. A meal had been set up in the greenroom for the band where polite conversation was made with the concert promoters. The act Sebastian and Karl had performed on stage—best friends rocking together—ended when the fans disappeared. Fatigue wrestled with the clamoring voice in Eva's head that recited she was dead weight, a waste of space, and deserving of Yvonne's constant sneering. Eva had offered to help with the CD table, a position Yvonne had claimed and ran with obvious experience and expertise. Yvonne had waved her away with a demeaning flip of the hand.

Eva stifled another yawn. Not only was she physically spent, but her ego still stung from her embarrassing fall. She wasn't glamorous or Goth. She wasn't graceful or hip. She was plain and backward, completely out of her element.

Eva felt small and invisible and when Sebastian asked her if she was ready to go, she nodded sharply.

The hotel lobby was empty at that time of night, and Sebastian walked directly to the night clerk at the counter. His arm rested on her shoulders and he drew her close.

"I have a room booked for me," he said softly in her

ear. "You are *more* than welcome to stay with me, but I can book you your own room if you prefer."

Eva's stomach flipped and flipped again. She had considered that leaving on tour with Sebastian would mean sharing a hotel room. Could she really expect him to pay for an extra room for her every night? Besides, she wanted this, right? She wanted to be with Sebastian. She whispered back, "I'll stay with you."

The corner of Sebastian's lips pulled up in a way that made Eva's knees melt. Sebastian accepted the keycard from the clerk and pulled both of their suitcases to the elevator. The bell rang as the doors opened to an empty space, and Sebastian waited for Eva as she entered first. They stood side by side facing the door, arms brushing. Eva could smell his heat and concert sweat. She swallowed hard as she watched the numbers climb to the fourth floor. She was really doing this.

Sebastian unlocked the door and held it open for her. She limped inside and exhaled. The room was nice. Burgundy carpets, dark wood furniture including a desk, a table with two chairs, a flat screen TV on the wall… and a lone, king-size bed. Her legs trembled as she sat in one of the chairs.

Sebastian dragged in the two suitcases. He put hers on the suitcase bench and opened his on the floor. He glanced at Eva as he plucked out clean clothes. "I'm going to have a shower." His eyebrows jumped as he waved to the room and he grinned crookedly as he teased, "Make yourself at home."

Eva smiled back, feeling her lips stretch unnaturally as she fought her nerves. She caught a glimpse of herself in the floor-length wall mirror. She was sitting straight-backed and stiff with her hands clasped on her lap like she was an old nanny applying for a job. No wonder Sebastian disappeared into the bathroom as fast as he could. She wasn't exactly emitting the message, *come get me.*

Eva checked her phone and found the expected message from her sister. She'd changed her name and it took a moment for Eva to make the connection.

Gabriele Smith

Can you at least let me know that you're okay?

Eva Baumann

I'm okay. Safe and sound in Salzburg.

Gabriele Smith

Are you sleeping with Sebastian?

She ignored that last text. It wasn't any of her business. Eva never asked Gabriele personal questions like that about Lennon, though she was pretty sure her sister was a virgin on her wedding night. They were both raised to believe that sex was a sacred act reserved for the marriage bed. It was a value Eva had always espoused. It just made sense to her. If you love someone, make it official and plan to be together for a lifetime. Her parents were a good example of that. They were sure to let their daughters know that they had waited (the memory of "the talk" still made her squirm) and were glad that neither had a history with anyone else but each other. And they've been happily married for twenty-four years.

But wasn't that an old fashioned belief? People just didn't wait anymore and… it was already too late for Sebastian. Yvonne would always be a part of Sebastian's memories. A shadow. There were two women on their bus and Sebastian had seen one of them naked many times. The wrong one.

Eva sighed. The past couldn't be changed. She could only make her own memories with Sebastian now. The question was what would that look like? Eva decided it was time to throw caution to the wind. She needed to live her own life. She respected her parents' values, but that didn't mean she had to share them. She'd spent too many years being afraid. Tonight she needed to be strong. Fight back at fear.

The bathroom door opened and Eva's breath hitched. Sebastian stood there in his pajama pants, no shirt, just his beautiful bare chest slightly damp. His hair was darker and shiny, clean but still messy. Eva didn't think he owned a brush, and she was glad. She loved his unkempt look.

Sebastian tilted his head and smiled slyly. "I take it by the way you're staring that you like what you see?"

Eva snapped her slack jaw closed. "I need to brush my teeth."

Sebastian laughed and claimed the side of the bed opposite the window. He reached for the remote and turned on the TV. Eva collected her toothbrush and paste from her suitcase and made use of them in the bathroom. She wasn't ready to change into her pajamas yet. Her nerves were jumping, and she didn't want to look pretentious or overly eager. Another deep breath before exiting the bathroom.

Sebastian eyed her blouse and skirt. "Are you going to sleep in your clothes?"

"No, I'll change. I'm just… not tired yet." She climbed onto the bed beside Sebastian and let her cane fall to the floor.

Sebastian lowered the volume on the TV then flipped onto his side. He propped his head onto his hands and grinned at Eva. "You're really cute when you're nervous."

Eva wiped her hands on her skirt. "I'm not nervous."

Sebastian snorted. "Yes, you are. I've never seen you more nervous."

"Shut up."

He laughed and poked her in the ribs. "It's true."

"Well, maybe it is. We both know I'm venturing into new territory."

Sebastian ran a finger along her arm sending shivers up her spine. "And I'm impressed, Eva. You have a way of surprising me anew every day. I admire your bravery."

He admired her *bravery*? Eva almost laughed out loud.

She turned on her side to face him. The room was dark except for the bluish light flashing from the TV and a faint glow of white from the outside street lamp that lit up Sebastian's face. She drew a finger over his brow and along his cheekbone. "You were fantastic tonight."

"We haven't done anything yet," he joked.

She smacked him playfully.

"Oh, you meant the concert," he said. "Thanks."

Eva's skirt had inched up when she'd twisted over to her side, and the tip of her scar peeked out. Sebastian touched it with his finger, and she froze.

He held onto her gaze. "Can I see it?"

She winced. "It's ugly."

"There's nothing ugly about you, Eva. Not even this." He slowly traced the line of her scar, and she stopped breathing. The tip of Sebastian's finger was like a hot iron, scorching her skin, burning her, but in the best kind of way. He gently pushed up her skirt, higher and higher, and internal fireworks exploded in her body. Her heart thudded in her chest as she watched his hand. *Stop, go, stop.*

Go.

Sebastian paused for a moment and smiled at her, his eyes locking on to hers with intensity and desire. Eva's heart was about to burst. Heat birthed in her belly and flared up her neck. She felt the burn of flush on her face.

Was she really going to do this?

Sebastian leaned in, his breath hot on her cheek. "You're so beautiful. Every part of you." His lips traced a moist course down the curve of her neck. His hand remained on the bare skin of her hip and she shuddered. His lips found hers and she responded eagerly, taking him in, loving his scent and the taste of his mouth.

He flipped himself on top of her, his body tense and hard along the length of hers, bracing his weight on his forearms to keep from squishing her. Eva's breaths came in short bursts. She could feel Sebastian's pulse rapidly beating against her skin, his breath, hot and fast under his kisses.

Her heart beat so rapidly she felt dizzy, and sweat broke out on her forehead. The frightened little bird that lived inside her screamed, flapped its wings and pecked away at her ribcage.

"I'm not ready," she whispered.

Sebastian stilled, and his kisses stopped. He eased off her and flipped onto his back. Eva heard him struggle for composure.

"I'm sorry, Sebastian." Tears of frustration and humiliation burned her eyes. "It's like I'm delayed," she explained. "The accident put everything on hold and even my own ability to function normally in a relationship is handicapped."

"*Shh.*" Sebastian turned onto his side and stroked her face. "It's okay. You got me a little excited, I admit, but I've always said that you control the pace. We can go as slow or as fast as you want."

"I love you," Eva said. "I'll catch up. I promise."

"I love you, too. And it's not a competition. We have

our whole lives ahead of us."

Eva couldn't love him more than she did right now. His gentleness and understanding were everything she needed. She couldn't believe she'd found someone so perfect.

She tugged on her skirt, once again covering her scar.

"Why don't you tell me about it?"

"About what?"

"About the accident. I know you don't like to talk about it, but maybe it will help."

Eva twisted her finger around the hem of her skirt. "What do you want to know?"

"Who was driving the car?"

"I don't know."

"Was it your mama or papa? A friend?"

"No, it wasn't anyone I knew."

Sebastian's brow furrowed. "You were with someone you didn't know?"

"I wasn't *in* the car, Sebastian. I was *hit* by a car."

Sebastian's voice hitched. "I thought you were in a car accident."

"I was in an accident involving a car, but I never said it was a car accident. I was hit while riding my bike. It's common knowledge in my circles. I just assumed you knew."

The light from the street lamp shed a ghostly glow on Sebastian's constricted face. He looked like he was choking.

His expression frightened her. "Are you all right?"

"When, exactly, did this happen?"

"Five years ago, on the ninth of May."

"Were you wearing a red coat?"

Eva blinked. "Yes. Why?" *And how did he know?*

Sebastian leapt off the bed and raced to the bathroom. Eva grabbed at her heart and shivered with foreboding. Something was wrong. Something was terribly wrong.

WHAT REALLY HAPPENED

Please God, no.

It was *her!*

Five years ago. The timing. How had he not put two and two together before? O

Sebastian flipped the toilet lid up and vomited. He twisted the sink tap on to try to cover the sound of his heaving. He slunk to the floor and wiped his mouth with toilet paper and flushed the toilet.

He ran both of his hands through his hair and leaned his forehead on his knees. This was bad.

His mind flashed back to the day after that rainstorm. A strip of red fabric in the grill of his car. He remembered plucking the piece of fabric, torn from something, and wondering what it was and how it had gotten attached there.

He had to tell her. She'd hate him, but he had to tell the truth. And he'd probably go to jail. So much for Hollow Fellows. The guys would really hate him now.

A light tapping on the door was followed by Eva's voice. "Are you okay?"

"Yeah," he called. "I'll be right out."

He brushed his teeth and washed his face. He could just pretend it was food poisoning. Not tell her at all. What she didn't know wouldn't hurt her, and all that.

But she was bound to find out one day. Some sleaze bag journalist would eventually decide to look for dirt on

Sebastian and find the skeletons in his closet. It was just a matter of time. If she found out he knew and didn't tell her, she'd never forgive him. Ever.

He opened the door with a shaky hand. Eva stood in the middle of the room—she had turned on one of the lamps—and leaned on her cane. Sebastian forced back a sob. He'd done that to her. He'd given her that scar, put her through the pain of rehab. He was the one who had stolen simple joys like hiking and bike riding.

"I'm sorry, Eva."

"What's wrong, Sebastian?" Eva's eyes were wide and glassy. "You're scaring me."

Tears ran down Sebastian's face, and he pushed at them with the back of his hand. "I thought it was a dog. I thought I hit a dog."

Eva's free hand went to her chest. Her face contorted like she knew what he meant but didn't want to believe it. She took a small step back. "What are you talking about?"

"It was me. I was the driver who hit you and ran."

UNREMEMBERED MEMORY

N*o, no, no.* This couldn't be happening. Black spots swirled around her peripheral vision and her legs gave out. She landed on the carpeted floor with a thud.

"Eva!" Sebastian raced to help her.

She held up a palm in warning. "Don't touch me!"

He jumped back like he'd touched an electric fence.

"Eva."

"Don't you dare touch me."

She wrestled to get herself off the floor and into the closest chair, wincing at the pain that seared up her leg, an echo of the shattering of her glass heart. With three hard breaths and eyes pinched closed, she relived the night she was hit. Dusk had fallen and she'd forgotten her bike lamp. She was riding home from a friend's house, having left later than she intended. It was before her family had moved to the *Neustadt* and taken the flat above the soup kitchen. Back then they'd lived in the outskirts of the city. It grew dark and started to rain, pointy drops that poked her face as the wind picked up. The road wasn't well lit and she'd kept as far right as she could to allow the occasional vehicle to pass. Water splashed up from their tires, soaking her left leg. She remembered being cold and wet, and pedaling hard, just wanting to get home.

She'd told everyone that she never felt a thing—that one moment she was riding her bike along the road and the next she was lying in a bed in the hospital.

But that wasn't true.

The truth was she clearly remembered the moment of impact, and the fear that whipped her like a cat of nine tails when her back wheel skidded out from beneath her. Her breath stopped and her pulse pounded loud and heavy in her ears for those long, surreal seconds as she hurled through the air, and her mind registered, *I've been hit.* She cried out in agony as she landed on a jagged rock, her leg twisting beneath her. Her hand reached for the source of her pain and sprang to her chest when she realized she'd touched her own broken femur *bone*, jutting through her skin. She heard the unbearably loud thudding of her heartbeat in her temples as she passed in and out of consciousness. The certainty that she was dying. Would die. The twisting, stabbing, choking *fear of death*.

Then blackness.

She woke up three weeks later in the hospital and remembered every terrifying detail, but they were too horrific to share. Her parents' faces and Gabriele's, they looked so fragile when they peered down at her. Eva couldn't add to their pain. She wouldn't soil the obvious relief and joy they were experiencing at her awakening.

"I thought it was a dog, I swear."

Eva cut Sebastian with a glare. "And you left a family pet to die?"

"No, I wasn't sure. It could've been a raccoon, or a rock. It was raining hard and it was dark. I couldn't see."

"But you didn't think to check to make sure? If it weren't for a farmer caught in the rain while walking his dog, I would've *bled out*."

Sebastian collapsed onto the bed. "I'm so sorry. I've regretted not going back more than you can know."

"When did you know it wasn't a dog you'd hit, but a person?"

"The next day. I found a piece of red fabric stuck in my grill."

"From my coat."

"I checked the news and read about a hit and run. But they said the injuries were… survivable. I couldn't see the point of turning myself in. I couldn't change what happened. And I didn't want to go to jail."

"That is the most cowardly thing I've ever heard."

Eva's heart hardened to stone. A switch snapped from on to off, from hot to cold. Whatever love Eva thought she'd had for Sebastian Weiss seeped out with his confession. She no longer loved him. She hated him. *Hated him.* He'd left her to die in the dark and in the cold rain. She could forgive anything but that.

"I want to go home."

"Eva…"

"Now!" Eva handled her cane with a shaky hand, eyes focused on anything but the stricken look on Sebastian's face. Good. He hurt. It was nothing compared to the pain she'd endured these last five years. She pushed by him to the bathroom to collect her toothbrush. Thankfully, she hadn't unpacked anything else. She stuffed it in her suitcase and zipped it shut.

Sebastian let out a long hard sigh. "There aren't any flights until morning."

"I'll take the train." Eva didn't fly. The autobahn was scary enough. The thought of traveling through the air in a steel tube made her blood freeze.

"There won't be any trains leaving until early morning either."

Eva speared him with an icy glare. "Then I'll wait at the train station." There was no way she was spending the night here. With him.

Another heavy sigh came from Sebastian as he grabbed

her suitcase. He held the door of their room open, and she limped by him. The ride down the elevator was unbearable. Standing side by side, she could feel the heat of his body next to her, a hot invisible wall of separation. The elevator beeped, announcing their arrival to the lobby. Sebastian walked ahead and Eva heard him order a taxi.

Eva continued to the waiting area outside where a taxi pulled up. Sebastian put her suitcase in the trunk as she crawled into the backseat. She couldn't contain her surprise when he got in next to her.

"I don't need a chaperone," she snapped.

"I'm not leaving you alone overnight at the train station."

She spoke through tight lips. "I'll be fine."

"I'm sure you will. I'm still coming."

Eva huffed and stared out the window. The oncoming traffic blurred by in white and red ribbons of light. Her chest squeezed with the heaviness of a steel drum locked tight. Her face pulled down like hard leather. The back of her eyes burned as she held back angry, resentful tears. She wouldn't let Sebastian see how deeply she was wounded, how lethal his injury was to her. She carefully stitched up the festering sore in her soul, ignoring the poisonous pus.

Eva insisted on pulling her suitcase when they arrived at the station, but she didn't fight him when Sebastian refused to let her buy her own ticket home. He owed her that much anyway.

"I'm checking your suitcase through," Sebastian said, "but you have to change trains in Munich and Nuremburg."

Eva swallowed. What if she got lost? What if she couldn't find the right platform in time and missed the connection?

Sebastian seemed to read her mind. "Just follow the

directions on the ticket," he added gently. "The platform numbers are listed there."

Eva snatched the tickets and slipped them into her shoulder bag and followed the signs overhead to the appropriate platform number. See, this was easy. Whatever trial lay ahead of her as she made her way home alone would be a million times easier to face than staying on tour.

Eva had hoped for a crowded waiting area with only a single empty seat that would force Sebastian away from her, but the platform was nearly empty. Not many people opted to spend their nights on uncomfortable plastic chairs waiting for the 5:00 am train.

Exhaustion ripped through her being and she slumped into an empty seat and closed her eyes. She heard the sound of another body easing into a chair opposite her and she knew it was Sebastian. She could feel his eyes on her, staring. Remorseful.

A lump formed in her throat, soft and gooey. The burning in her eyes felt wet and a tear escaped. She jumped to her feet, turning her back to Sebastian. She didn't want him to see her cry. She left for the restroom she'd spotted on the other side of the platform. Her leg felt like a dead weight, a ball and chain she dragged with her everywhere she went. A middle-aged man with greasy hair and dirty jeans watched her until she disappeared behind the restroom door.

She double-checked to ensure she was alone before allowing the tears to flow. She pressed a paper towel to her mouth to suppress the sobs that escaped from a deep place, like lava bubbling stubbornly to the surface. She thrashed at her chest. Her heart hurt so much!

The one person she dared to love was the only person she'd vowed to hate. And she hated him even more for putting her in this impossible situation.

SIX MONTHS LATER

SEBASTIAN FINISHED the tour before turning himself into the Dresden Police. He owed the band that much and had waited until the bus ride home from their final date in Stuttgart on the last day of August to break the news.

He'd never forget the stunned looks on their faces, especially Karl's and Yvonne's. Everyone had expected drama, but not *that*. Immorality, diva-like demands, a lame explanation (finally) as to why Eva left so abruptly a day into the tour, but not a confession to a crime.

They tried to talk him out of it.

"You'll go to jail," Karl said, "throw our band off the rails."

Sebastian shook his head. "The band? That's what you're concerned about?"

Karl shrugged. "Well, sure. I mean, that was then, this is now. Let it go."

"He's got a point," Dirk added. "What's to gain by turning yourself in? Your career is on an upsweep. A confession like this would kill momentum. And for what?"

"It's the right thing to do."

"Did Eva ask you to do it?" Markus asked. "I mean, I can see why she'd be mad, but can't you just pay her off?"

"Yeah," Karl said. "It's not like you can fix her leg by doing time."

They didn't understand and quite honestly, Sebastian would've been surprised if they had.

"She didn't ask me," he said. "I need to do this for myself. Look, I laid down my voice and guitar tracks for the new songs at my home studio. Use those to record while I'm… otherwise engaged."

"You could be otherwise *engaged* for two or three years," Karl stated.

"Maybe, but I'm hoping they'll take my youth and inexperience at the time into consideration, and the fact that I'm freely surrendering myself."

"That's a big assumption."

"I know."

Eva had been "imprisoned" by her injuries for five years already with no chance of parole. He'd man up and do a few years if he had to.

That was fifty-eight days ago. The judge gave him twenty-two months in a minimum security prison, a three-thousand-euro fine, and ordered him to pay "damages to the victim for pain caused." He was more than happy to comply with the latter, and he was glad that his recent success gave him the financial ability to do so.

His celebrity status meant nothing to the men he bunked with now. He worked during the day and read at night. They were allowed to watch TV in the dining hall, and he spent the first two weeks glued to the reports of his arrest—not because he cared about what the media said about him, but about how they hounded Eva. He curled his fists and scowled at the images of photographers camping outside the Baumann's building, intruding on the soup kitchen, nearly tripping Eva as she pushed passed them down the sidewalk. The camera zoomed in and froze on Eva's face, always twisted with anxiety.

"That your girlfriend?" one inmate asked.

"It's the girl he hit, moron," another offered.

"She's cute."

Sebastian pushed away from the table and waited by the door for a guard to take him to his room.

The days were long and boring and ran like molasses into each other. The only highlight was visiting day. Despite his crime, his popularity hadn't slipped, and it was brought to his attention that he had fans creating a scene at the entrance of the prison.

Sebastian smirked a little at that. The only visitors he got were the ones he okayed. To date the list consisted of Dirk and Markus, and his sister who'd dragged their mother along once. He wished Eva would come, but he knew hell would likely freeze over before that happened. He was surprised by the visitor listed on the roster today. His father. Sebastian's first inclination was to deny him, but then he wondered why. In light of everything that had been going on, he now saw how silly and childish it would be to continue their feud.

He was sitting in the chair behind an empty table when Sebastian arrived with the guard. His father sat straight and tall, his usual stance, but Sebastian noticed his shoulders were thinner and his face, though expressionless, had looser skin around his mouth and chin. His father had aged. Time didn't stop for anyone, but despite the change in appearance, Sebastian immediately felt like he was fifteen years old again under the man's scrutiny.

"Hi, Papa," he said.

"Sebastian."

The silence that descended between them was fat and awkward.

"I tried calling," Herr Weiss began. "Before."

"Yeah. I should've returned your calls."

Herr Weiss shifted uneasily. "I wish you would've told me. About this. When it happened. I would've helped you.

I'm a lawyer. I know lawyers. It was an accident. You would've got off without jail time."

Sebastian nodded. He could see the wisdom in it now, but back then, at eighteen, he not only hated his father he feared him.

"Thanks for coming," Sebastian muttered. It felt lame to say it, but he didn't know what else to say. And his coming was a nice gesture, just a little too late. Sebastian was ready for them to say their good-byes already.

Herr Weiss stared at him with brown, watery eyes. "I'm sick."

A patch of cold spread through Sebastian's chest. "What kind of sick?"

"A bad kind."

"How bad?"

"Cancer bad. Pancreas."

Sebastian didn't like his dad, but he didn't want him dead, either. He forced a dry swallow. "How long?"

"Weeks, months. They aren't promising anything. I just thought you should know." He stood to leave and nodded good-bye.

"Papa?"

The man stopped and twisted to look back.

Sebastian licked dry lips. "I'm sorry."

His father lifted his chin. "I'm sorry, too."

ON CAMPUS

Eva had returned from her short stint on tour a drastically changed person. The first thing she did when she got home besides ignore the probing questions from her parents and the intrusive text messages from her honeymooning sister was rip the poster of Sebastian Weiss off her wall. This was followed by removal of any trace of his presence on her laptop. Swift and efficient swipes and clicks on her mouse deleted all Hollow Fellows albums, cleared their website from her bookmarks and unsubscribed her from their newsletter and all their social media updates.

She'd lain on her bed and rubbed the throbbing in her leg. A glance at her empty chair and her guitar next to it brought Sebastian to her mind's eye, sitting there that first day when she let him in to play her Duncan Africa. She rubbed her temples. She had to forget him. That was her priority. She needed to be distracted. It was then that she signed in online and registered for university. She needed a new environment, new friends, a new focus. *New, new, new.*

She chuckled humorlessly. She didn't know why she

had been afraid to go back to school before. Not going was the thing that suddenly frightened her.

Sebastian had given her something—popularity. She hadn't known he was going to turn himself in. She didn't asked him to, so it was a shock to wake up one morning to find a pack of media people outside their building looking for her.

At first she was furious at Sebastian. Everything he did ruined her life. She was his girlfriend for a minute, and now it was all the nation wanted to gossip about. She'd become a subject of intrigue. The story about Sebastian Weiss was scandalous and sensational. The rock idol had tried to soothe his guilt by seducing his victim. *Can you believe it?* Front page tabloid material.

Her family was mortified and so was she. Eva even agreed to an interview, hoping to clear up the falsehoods, but it'd just made things more twisted. She remained the Victim of the Celebrity.

She was practically famous when she arrived for her first day of school. Her papa had to drive her because public transit was no longer safe. She acknowledged that it was a nice change of pace from invisible, though she questioned the sincerity of her new friendships. But she didn't care. In a way, they were using each other. At least she had one real friend in Annette.

Unfortunately, even six months later, Sebastian's popularity hadn't fallen with Eva's climb. Hollow Fellows songs continued to dominate the charts, and Eva almost had a heart attack when "Flesh & Bone" was released recently as a single. She hadn't realized Sebastian had recorded it. Turned out he could rock up any kind of song. Eva barely recognized her version, but it soared to number one in just a few days.

When word got out that Eva was listed as a co-writer

of the popular hit, it was almost impossible for her to walk the halls. Her cane saved her from several falls.

Annette worked as her bodyguard. "Back, people! Let the girl through. Do you really want to be responsible for causing *Eva Baumann* to fall?"

Eva smirked. Her friend said her name like it meant something. Like she was *someone*.

They made it to study hall without incident. Other students would pause and stare when they spotted her. Others would shyly wave and say, "Hi, Eva."

Annette scowled and muttered about how she was being ignored and threw her mane of red hair over one shoulder. "What am I? Chopped liver?"

They pulled out chairs at an empty table and sat. "It is a reversal of roles, isn't it?" Eva commented. She patted her friend's shoulder. "Don't worry. It'll pass. I'll become a has-been and you'll continue to be the beautiful one."

Annette puffed. "You *are* the beautiful one, Eva." She opened a book, but her eyes remained fixed on something across the room.

Eva looked for what had caught Annette's attention. A table full of boys. "Which one?" she asked.

Annette's eyelashes fluttered. "What?"

"Which one do you like?"

A flush of red crept up Annette's neck. "Was I staring?"

Eva removed a textbook from her bag. "Uh, yeah."

"Xavier."

"Which one is that?" Eva asked, searching.

"Black hair, beautiful dark eyes."

The guy in question happened to look over at them in that moment. Annette ducked her head. "Oh mercy. Did he see me staring?"

Eva smiled at the handsome, olive-skinned boy, and

they locked eyes. "I don't think so," she said without turning away. He cocked a brow, and she raised her chin.

He looked away when Annette glanced up. "He's so cute," Annette whispered, "and I think he likes me."

Eva tried not to sound surprised. "You do?"

"We share a class together. He's borrowed my books. I think he did it just to have an excuse to talk to me. We're going to go for coffee sometime."

"Like a date?" Eva asked.

"I hope so." Annette giggled. "I really like him."

Sebastian didn't know Dirk had released the song until after it had hit the charts.

Dirk visited him with unconstrained excitement. "It was a risk, I know," he explained. "But when your arrest didn't snuff out the band's fan base like I thought it might, I figured we had nothing to lose. I mean, you're not going to be in here forever, right?"

Sebastian forced a smile. "No one's more surprised by the song's success than I am," he admitted. A small part of him actually hoped he'd see the end of fame, or in his case, infamy, but Dirk's enthusiasm was contagious. Besides, "Flesh & Bone's" climb up the charts benefited Eva. Their short-lived, emotionally tearing relationship would at least have a financial payoff for her. If the song gained long-range traction, she wouldn't have to depend on her parents to support her forever.

Dirk rubbed his balding head and leaned forward. "Is there any chance you'd get out early? You know, for good behavior and all that?"

Sebastian chuckled. "You watch too much TV." He'd served six months of a twenty-two-month sentence. He saw a lot of forest brush clearing in his future, not guitar playing. Guitar strings were considered a health risk. If a guy got it into his head that he'd had enough of this life, they could be used to self-inflict injury. Sebastian hated how the tips of his fingers had become soft. At least there was an old piano in the dining room and the guys didn't seem to mind when he played it, even though it was slightly out of tune.

An hour after Dirk left, Sebastian was surprised by another visitor. Herr Winkle was a tall, thin man who introduced himself as one of Sebastian's father's lawyers. He wore a sweater-vest over a white shirt and tie, and a designer winter jacket. He removed his satin scarf as he sat in the seat across from Sebastian.

Herr Winkle pushed glasses with dark, pricey frames up on his nose and got right to the point. "Your father has friends in high places, Herr Weiss. The judge has agreed that you've shown sufficient remorse and aren't any danger to society. He has reduced the remainder of your sentence to six months and is permitting you to serve it under house arrest."

Sebastian shook his head, flustered at the news. That was a ten month reduction.

"Why would Papa do that?"

Herr Winkle studied him. "I'm not privy to your personal relationship with your father, but I'm a father myself and I know I'd do anything to help my son, no matter the problem."

The lawyer obviously didn't know his papa, at least not the side Sebastian usually saw. This move was uncharacteristic and could only mean one thing. His father didn't have much time left and he didn't want to die with his son in jail.

"What's next?" Sebastian asked.

"Your release will happen in three days. You will not be permitted to leave a six-block radius around your place of residence. You're required to work thirty hours a week for three months doing community service without pay. A parole officer will be in touch daily and make random drop-in visits to ensure you comply."

"Where?"

"The judge has left it up for you to choose. Do you have something in mind you'd like to do or should the courts appoint you with a task?"

Sebastian leaned back in his chair and grinned. "I know exactly what I want to do." Herr Winkle stood. "Great. The next half year won't be that exciting for you, but it'll be better than what you'd experience if you stayed here."

 IMAGINARY LINT

"PASS THE BUTTER, PLEASE, EVA," Papa said. Eva pinned her smile on and handed the dish to her father. Her eyes grazed over Gabriele and Lennon who'd joined them for the occasion. Lennon was a handsome attraction to the family. And a nice guy, Eva thought. Gabriele was the luckiest girl on earth. She didn't have to worry about Lennon lying and keeping huge secrets from her.

"How's work?" Papa asked him while passing the basket of buns.

Lennon worked at a small IT company. He was pretty tight-lipped about it, saying no more than it was boring computer work, so no one was exactly sure what it was he did there.

"Good," Lennon said. He selected a bun covered with poppy seeds. After a short lull in the conversation he offered, "I'm grateful for steady work in this economy."

"Don't you miss England, though?" Eva asked. "Do you think you and Gabriele will move there one day?"

Lennon shook his head. "There's nothing left for me there." He patted Gabriele on the knee. "Everything important to me now is here in Germany."

"Are you still enjoying your studies?" Lennon asked Eva, changing the subject.

Eva nodded, smile firmly in place. "Oh, yes."

A flash of concern swept over Gabriele's face before

she returned Eva's smile. "We're so glad things have worked out for you. And that song—"

Eva flicked her hand, her eyes widening slightly as she rushed to stop her sister from going there. "It's nothing. My life is so full of other things. Terrific other things."

She heard her mother clear her throat. The new Eva was an improved Eva. Mama made sure no one rocked the boat. "How's your job search going, Gabi?" Mama asked.

Gabriele's English and International Studies degree had yet to land her a job. "I have an interview on Tuesday." Eva smiled and showed concern in all the right places.

"Eva," Papa said, "Can you play for the soup kitchen service on Sunday?"

Papa always asked and Eva always agreed. "Of course."

Eva helped with cleaning up and made pleasant conversation when it was necessary. She was determined to be the perfect daughter, the perfect sister.

Also, the perfect student. "I have a lot of studying to do," she said lightly. "Good night, everyone."

She disappeared down the hall and into the room she no longer had to share. She eased onto her bed, propping the pillows up behind her back and let out a thick breath. Keeping up her cheerful, carefree façade was exhausting. A knock on the door forced her to snap back to the happy child. Gabriele stuck her head in.

"Hey."

Eva cocked her head. "Hey?"

"Is everything all right? You just seem…"

Eva kept her expression soft. "Seem?"

"Different."

"I thought that was what you wanted." Eva didn't bother reminding Gabriele of all the times she lectured her to face her fears and get on with her life. That was what she was doing.

Gabriele's shoulders sagged. "I want you to be happy, Eva. That's all."

"I am happy, Gabi."

"You'd tell me if anything was wrong."

Eva pushed back her discomfort. Gabriele was too discerning and Eva had to be more careful around her. Eva smiled brighter. "Of course." She brushed imaginary lint off her arm while adding, "And I'm fine. Don't worry about me."

 HOUSE ARREST

SEBASTIAN HAD BEEN ESCORTED to his flat at 23:00 in order to avoid public attention. He managed to stay under the media radar for three days before a small contingent began camping outside his door. The warehouse was outside of his permitted six-block radius so the band had to meet at his flat. Tonight would be the first time they would be gathered together in one spot since his arrest.

Sebastian tidied the place up. Washed dishes. Swept the floor. It was odd to be home. After six months of never being alone, he appreciated the quiet. But he also felt lonely. He glanced out the window again and watched the small group of fans. It was cold outside, which limited the size. Not many had the stamina to wait more than an hour at a time and Sebastian was glad for that.

"Just go away," he muttered. Fortunately, there was a back way out of his building, through the courtyard, and if Sebastian waited until after dark he could make it to the corner store or pizza place to get food when he was hungry. He wore a pair of reading glasses and a wool cap along with a thick winter coat to further his disguise. So far it had worked. He hadn't been recognized.

He spent most of his time alone playing his guitar. He hadn't played since the summer and he was rusty. The tips of his fingers were soft and pink like a baby's. He pushed through the discomfort. He had to get back in shape.

The buzzer sounded, and he let the boys in. There was

an awkward reunion of handshaking and back-patting. Karl cautiously extended his hand and Sebastian gave it a quick, professional shake.

"It's good to see you in a friendlier environment," Dirk said.

"It's good to be home," Sebastian admitted.

He offered beer and put out a bowl of chips. "So," he began. "What'd I miss?"

"We've been doing small venues without you," Karl said. He kept his expression flat, but Sebastian suspected that he had enjoyed not having to share the spotlight.

"Great," Sebastian offered.

"We know you can't leave the *Neustadt*, but hey," Dirk said with a grin, "the *Neustadt* is the best place to play anyway. I can book a concert in a different venue every other week. I guarantee it will sell out each time because it's the only place your fans can come to see you. Plus, everyone is dying of curiosity."

Sebastian shrugged. "I suppose. The fans have been great. Who am I to deprive them of what they want? The only thing is I'm outta practice. And we can't rehearse here. My neighbors would complain. Loudly."

"Dirk's already looked after that," Markus said. "The Blue Note."

"Maurice will let us rehearse there?" Sebastian asked. "Isn't he busy running a business?"

Dirk answered with a grin. "The Blue Note is closed in the mornings. You can meet from eight to ten."

Nothing like jumping back into the raging river feet first. "Fine. But I have community service from eleven to five, five days a week. Starting tomorrow.

Dirk reached over and slapped him on the back. "You'll be a busy boy."

Sebastian nodded. "That I will." He was glad of it. It

would make his sentence go by faster and give him less time to think and stew.

Now that the business end of things was worked out, an uncomfortable break in conversation settled in the room. Markus answered a call on his phone. Dirk messed around with his tablet, supposedly updating their calendar and responding to emails.

Karl tapped his knees with his fingers. "I should probably tell you that Yvonne and I broke up."

"Oh." Good. Now he didn't have to worry about dealing with her. She'd tried to visit him when he was in prison, but he'd declined her request.

"And I want to say sorry," Karl continued. "I was a jerk."

"Yeah, you were," Sebastian said. Then he smiled. No sense hanging on to grudges. Karl had actually done him a favor, even if he was a selfish idiot. "Hey, it's the past. Let's move on."

The next day's rehearsal just proved that they needed to keep rehearsing, but it felt really good to be back at music and to play hard and loud. Sebastian hadn't lost himself in anything like that in ages, and he almost lost track of time.

"Man!" Sebastian unstrapped his guitar. "I have to get going."

"Go," Karl said. "We'll clean up."

Sebastian threw on his heavy black jacket and matching wool cap. He wrapped his grey, knit scarf around his neck, covering half his face. It made for a good disguise along with its practical usefulness to block the bitter wind. He broke into a jog, dodging other pedestrians in a hurry to get to their destinations and out of the wintery weather. The crisp air froze his lungs and focused his mind, not on where he was going, but on the fact that he needed to get there on time.

With only a minute to spare he turned the corner onto *Alaunstrasse*, almost slipping on a patch of ice, and arrived, just as the graffiti-covered metal outer blinds were rising. Herr Baumann stared at him with a solemn expression from the other side of the glass.

Sebastian figured the guy regretted agreeing to this assignment, but it was too late now for either of them to change their minds. Sebastian would be working at the soup kitchen for the next three months.

Herr Baumann opened the door and growled, "Come in before you freeze to death."

Sebastian entered, clicking the door shut and the cold with it. He pulled off his gloves and cap and waited. Herr Baumann pointed to a closet at the end of the hall. "You can hang your things here."

Sebastian did as instructed and followed the quiet man to the kitchen. So there'd be no small talk. No welcome speech. Not that Sebastian expected any of that. Frau Baumann was there when they entered, with her hands in a deep, stainless steel sink. She glanced at Sebastian and frowned, then turned her attention back to the sink, like the dirty pots soaking in it held immense fascination.

"Thanks for agreeing to have me," Sebastian offered.

Herr Baumann grunted. "Don't give us a reason to regret it." He pointed to his wife. "You can start by relieving Frau Baumann of dish duty. Everything but the larger pots can be run through the dishwasher. I'll instruct you on how to do that later. You do know how to wash pots?"

Sebastian nodded. He'd done his fair share of kitchen work at the prison.

Frau Baumann dried her reddened hands on a tea towel and made room for Sebastian. He rolled up his sleeves and thrust his hands into the hot, sudsy water.

Sebastian heard Frau Baumann say in a low voice behind him. "This is a mistake."

"Perhaps, perhaps not," Herr Baumann mumbled back. "Time will tell."

Sebastian wondered why they had agreed to this situation if they were both so obviously uncertain about his working there. Maybe Eva had convinced them to take him on? The thought that she'd rallied in his favor gave him hope, and he returned to his task with vigor.

Another woman joined them as they prepared the soup. Frau Vogel was a stout, red-faced woman in her fifties. She glared at Sebastian when she spotted him and rolled her eyes. Sebastian certainly didn't have any fans here. He could only hope to win their good graces by working hard. He scrubbed potatoes and carrots, peeled and cubed them and added them to the pot of broth. He chopped onions until his eyes burned and tears dribbled down his face. He wiped down the tables and chairs and welcomed the hungry indoors from the cold with a friendly hello.

He noticed Herr Baumann watching him and thought he caught a hint of approval in his eyes. Progress.

Sebastian wondered if Eva would arrive in time to play guitar, but he was disappointed when a middle-aged man Herr Baumann called Jörg took a spot on the small stage and picked up the instrument. The room was now full of what Sebastian imagined were homeless or at least unemployed—men, women and a couple of children. They waited respectfully as the man played, and not that well, Sebastian couldn't help but notice. Most of them joined in, familiar with the words of the songs that were meant for heaven. They didn't seem to care that the guy's playing and singing were below par.

No one there seemed to put it together that it was alternative-rock sensation Sebastian Weiss of Hollow Fellows who worked quietly around them. This would be the last place people would expect a guy like him to be. He kept his gaze averted most of the time, just in case.

Afterward, when everyone had cleared out, Sebastian cleared tables and ran dirty dishes through the washer according to Herr Baumann's clipped instructions. The words spoken in the kitchen between Sebastian and the others were few, but at least by the end of the shift, the animosity toward him had tempered.

The last task of the day was to sweep the floors. His back was turned to the door when he felt a whoosh of cold air come with the person who entered.

He turned and the girl froze, her mouth falling open.

Eva.

Sebastian had longed to see her for over half a year and now here she was only meters away. Her hair was longer, hanging loosely under a winter hat. She wore tights under a knee-length dress and high tie-up boots Her cheeks and nose were rosy from the cold. Sebastian's heart flipped. She was adorable and vulnerable and it took everything in him not to drop the broom, throw himself at her and kiss her face.

"Hello," he said softly.

Eva's eyelashes flickered. "What are you doing here?"

"I'm working off my community service."

"H-here?" she stammered.

"You didn't know?"

Her mouth flattened into a straight line and she leaned on her cane as she walked purposefully to the kitchen at the back. "Papa!" she called.

Sebastian rubbed the back of his neck. Eva was obviously surprised by his presence. And unhappy about it.

# STUPID BAD LUCK

Eva stood in front of the mirror in one of the many campus washrooms. She washed her hands while watching Annette apply peach-colored lipstick.

"Are you going to wash your hands right off?" Annette asked Eva's reflection.

Eva paused and turned off the tap. She found it difficult to concentrate on the simplest tasks. "I just can't *believe* he's working in the soup kitchen." She shook her head sharply. "My father knew he was coming and didn't say anything to me."

"You've mentioned."

"He could do his community service anywhere. Why did the judge appoint him to us? Stupid bad luck? Did he think it a form of poetic justice?"

"My bet is on Sebastian."

"Shh!" Eva didn't permit Annette to speak his name.

"Eva, really. I'm sorry it upsets you, but maybe it's time you cut the guy some slack."

Eva's mouth dropped open, and she considered her friend with disbelief. "Look at me." Eva waved her cane in the air with one hand and swept the other along her body. "*He* did this to me."

"Eva, it was an accident. And he panicked. It could've happened to anyone."

"Well, it didn't happen to anyone," she said sharply. "It happened to me."

Eva squeezed her eyes closed, wishing she could just make this whole thing go away. She wished she'd never met Sebastian Weiss. Despite the act she put on, she wasn't over him and she hadn't spent one second truly free of him. He dominated her dreams at night and lingered on the edge of her consciousness during the day. He was always there when she tried to write music. The very act of playing guitar with a pen in reach thrust her back to their writing sessions together. To her first kiss.

It wasn't fair.

"You don't know what it's like," she whispered, barely concealing the anger that constantly simmered under the surface. "You don't know what it's like to have something taken from you. To cope with chronic pain. You don't know what it's like to be truly afraid."

"Maybe I don't, Eva. But my life isn't perfect, either. And there are a lot of people in the world who have it harder than you. I just think it's time you stopped playing the victim."

Annette's accusations were a slap in the face. And for the first time since Eva's return to the university, Annette left her alone to fend for herself. Eva gripped the edge of the counter and breathed in deeply, pushing back the jagged pain of betrayal she felt. The chatter from a group of girls entering the room interrupted her, and she carefully attached her smile before turning to them.

"Hi, Eva," they said, looking stunned to catch the object of so much gossip alone.

Eva nodded hello and gripped her cane as she reached for the door. One of the girls held it open for her.

"Thanks," Eva said. She headed down the busy hallway to her next class, working hard at minimizing her limp, pushing down at the pain.

She almost made it without bumping into anyone. Her

shoulder pressed into a toned chest. "I'm sorry," she said, looking up.

Xavier grinned down at her with straight white teeth. His eyes sparkled as he took her in. "No, it was me. I wasn't paying attention."

Eva couldn't help but return a smile. Annette was right. Xavier was very attractive. "Not a problem." She heard the flirtatious lilt in her voice as she cocked her head and stared back brazenly. "At all."

COMMUNITY SERVICE

EACH DAY at the soup kitchen for Sebastian was pretty much a copy of his first day, with the exception of Eva's appearance. Sebastian hadn't caught a glimpse of her once since she'd been surprised by his assignment. She obviously despised him. Her rejection settled in his chest like a soggy sandbag. But, even if Eva wouldn't forgive him, he would still try to make amends with her parents. He'd put them through hell as well, and though he couldn't change what he'd done, he could make sure they knew he was sorry for it.

At the moment, he focused on cleaning and chopping up the five-kilo bag of carrots in front of him. Frau Baumann and Frau Vogel chatted in a friendly manner on the opposite side of the kitchen. They'd either gotten used to him being around or had decided to just act like he wasn't there. Either way, Sebastian was fine with it. At least they weren't stabbing him with sharp glares anymore.

Herr Baumann arrived and greeted the women. Then he surprised Sebastian by saying, "Take a ten minute break and have a coffee with me." Sebastian washed and dried his hands and followed the older man into the front sitting area.

Herr Baumann surprised him further by insisting that Sebastian take a seat and by pouring his coffee for him. He returned to the coffee station to prepare his, then sat in the chair opposite. He stared pensively at his mug, stirring the cream in with smooth, circular strokes. He took a sip and then looked at Sebastian.

"Since we're going to be working together for the next few months, I thought we should get to know each other a little. Besides... the reason you are here... I know very little about you."

"What do you want to know?" Sebastian asked. What exactly was Eva's father after?

"Tell me about your family. Did you grow up in the *Neustadt?*"

"Yes. I have one sister—Leah. She's a marine biologist and she lives in Spain. My father is a lawyer and my mother is a doctor."

Herr Baumann raised a bushy eyebrow. "And you're a musician?"

Sebastian smirked. "I think I'm adopted. Or at least that's what I tell myself to try to explain things, except I look a lot like my mother."

"You managed to become successful in your chosen field," Herr Baumann acknowledged. "They must be proud of your accomplishments."

The smile slid off Sebastian's face. "Quite honestly my life choices have been a point of contention. My parents kicked me out of the house when I refused to go to university. They think I'm careless and irresponsible." Sebastian inhaled. "I suppose they're not wrong about that."

"Any career choice can be honorable if pursued with integrity. My parents didn't want me to become a pastor, so I know what it's like to go against one's parents when it comes to the big choices." He grinned. "But they liked my choice in a wife, so that helped to ease their minds. This many years into it, it's no longer an issue."

"My father came to visit me when I was in prison. It was the first time I'd seen him in six years."

Herr Baumann's face softened. "Did it go well?"

Sebastian shrugged. "I suppose. He's not the same as he used to be, not as stubborn. I think that's because he's dying."

"I'm sorry to hear that. Can I ask what ails him?"

Sebastian sipped his coffee and pushed back at the emotion that snuck up on him. "Cancer."

"Such a horrible disease."

"Can I ask you something?" Sebastian leaned forward slightly. "Why did you agree to let me fulfill my community service here? I mean, I know why I wanted to come, but why did you agree?"

Herr Baumann lowered his mug. "Tell me why you wanted to come, and then I'll answer you."

"I'm in love with your daughter." Sebastian tried to read Herr Baumann's face as he made his confession, but the man was an expert at keeping his expression blank. "I wanted to see her again. I'd hoped she felt the same way, but it appears that she doesn't."

"I said yes to your request because I love my daughter as well. She's hardened her heart, and I fear she's headed for a life of unhappiness if she doesn't reconcile what happened to her with God. And with you."

"So, we both want the same thing, sort of. How do we get what we want if she refuses to come to the soup kitchen as long as I am here?"

Herr Baumann tented thick fingers and rested them on the slight round of his belly. "We can only pray and do our part by being here for her when she's ready."

JUDAS'S KISS

ANNETTE HADN'T STOPPED WALKING with Eva, but her demeanor had grown cooler, as if she had a reason to be mad. Eva was the one who should be angry. Annette had verbally assaulted *her*.

Eva rolled her eyes. "You don't have to play bodyguard anymore. I know my way around."

"Fine," Annette said, picking up her pace. "See you later."

There was no way Eva could move as quickly, and Annette soon disappeared into the crowd ahead. Eva was glad they didn't have the next class together. She held on to her book bag, carefully navigating the distance with her cane. The other students bumped her on their way by and Eva struggled with her frustration at being slow and lame. She was flustered when she made it to class just barely on time. She stood in the doorway and scanned the tables for an empty seat. Her eyes landed on Xavier. Right, he was in this class. She smiled at him, and he waved her over to the empty chair beside him. *He'd saved her a seat.*

"Hi," she said slightly breathless as she laid her book bag on the table.

"Hi." Xavier pulled the chair out for her. She sat and hooked her cane on the back. She gave him a sideways glance and noted with a certain satisfaction that his eyes were still on her. He didn't mask his interest in her. The way he stared made her shiver.

The professor started his lecture, and Eva found it almost impossible to focus. Xavier shifted his chair over, and his leg brushed against hers. She stiffened and felt a blush fill her cheeks. She rested her chin on her hand and let her hair fall like a veil between them. She risked a glance in his direction. His dark-like-Lindt-chocolate eyes stared straight ahead, but there was a mischievous grin on his chiseled face.

The lecture ended, and the room erupted as students stood and pushed chairs across the floor. Eva carefully packed up her books, unsure how to deal with Xavier's blatant attention. He was the only one left sitting, and he stood when she grabbed her cane to go.

"Can I walk you to your next class?" he asked.

Eva's heart stuttered. "Sure."

He took to her left side, opposite of her cane, and kept a slow stride. "So, Eva Baumann, do you have a boyfriend?" He knocked her shoulder gently with his elbow.

"Not anymore," she said boldly.

Xavier huffed. "Right, the rock star. Let's not talk about *him*."

"Let's not."

"If you're boyfriend-less, would you like to go out with me sometime? Dinner maybe?"

Eva blinked hard. She wasn't imagining it. Xavier *was* coming on to her. They'd reached her next class, and she paused near the door.

Xavier closed the distance and leaned one hand against the wall over her shoulder. Everything—all the passing students, the hallway, the rest of the campus—it all blurred away into nothing. Eva's pulse hammered in her throat.

Xavier leaned over until she felt his hot breath in her ear. "I know this is really forward, but I've been wanting to kiss you for days. Would it be terrible if I kissed you right now?"

Volcanic heat exploded in Eva's chest. Xavier ducked down to gauge the expression on her face. She stared at his lips as his mouth parted slightly. The only person she'd ever kissed was Sebastian. Here was her chance to change that. What would it feel like to kiss someone else? Different? Better? Worse?

There was only one way to find out. "Yes, you can kiss me."

She closed her eyes and waited. Her heart stopped when she felt his lips on hers. He moved his mouth expertly, like he'd done it a million times before. He probably had, and why wouldn't he have? He was handsome and charismatic and a lot of girls liked him.

Annette liked him.

A cool thread of unease worked its way through her belly. She pulled back.

"Is something wrong?" Xavier asked.

"No, it was nice." She smiled at him and then froze. From the corner of her eye she spotted red hair. She turned in time to see shock and hurt flash across Annette's face as she stared at Eva leaning against the wall with Xavier pressed against her.

Eva pushed back on Xavier's chest. "Annette?"

Annette shook her head and turned on her heels.

"Annette!"

Her friend didn't turn around, and Eva knew there was no way she could run and catch her.

IT'S OVER

Sebastian didn't think he could wait around for God to make a move. Instead he bought a gyro across the street and ate it in the cold, shivering while he waited for Eva to get home from her classes. She had a different schedule each day but he'd made it his objective over the last couple weeks to remember them. She wouldn't come into the soup kitchen until she knew he was gone, but she would call down to her mama to let her know she was home. Frau Baumann had a ringtone reserved for her daughters and Sebastian had overheard her talking to Eva on more than one occasion.

She got home at five-thirty on Tuesdays. It was five twenty-five. Sebastian tossed his garbage into a nearby bin and popped a stick of gum in his mouth. He tugged on his cap and then shoved his gloved hands into his coat pockets.

Finally, he spotted her walking toward him, her eyes trained on the icy patches on the sidewalk. Herr Baumann walked beside her and Eva gripped his arm.

"Eva!" Sebastian called. Herr Baumann's eyes reflected a hint of surprise but his expression remained friendly, giving Sebastian the courage to continue his pursuit. Eva's eyes darkened. He heard her tell Herr Baumann she didn't want to see him.

"*Schatz*," he started. "Give him a moment. Make peace."

He pulled himself free, taking Eva's book bag with

him, and sped up until he reached the door of their building.

"Papa!" Eva's voice was laced with exasperation.

"Just five minutes," he said to her. "You'll be fine."

Sebastian expected her to ream him out with hot, angry words, but she remained silent. Her tough demeanor had thinned considerably. She looked almost fragile.

"Are you all right?" Sebastian asked.

"Is that what you wanted to say to me?"

"No, I just wanted to talk. You've been avoiding me."

She rolled her eyes. "I don't want to see you."

Stab, twist, bleed. Sebastian wasn't sure how he thought this impromptu guerrilla move was going to go. He should've thought it through more obviously. It was too late to back down now.

"Can we just get a coffee or something? I'm not asking you to be my friend. I just don't want you to be my enemy. Please? Just five minutes."

Eva let out a long breath, her face awash with fatigue. "Okay, fine."

They headed toward the nearest coffee shop, and Sebastian had flashbacks of the previous summer, walking this same road with Eva when she had admired him and thought him capable of no wrong.

Sebastian ushered Eva to a table and then hurried to get them coffees before she changed her mind and bolted. At least the café was warm, even if Eva's heart was ice cold.

He returned and sat across from her.

"You look good," he said.

She huffed. "You're lying again."

"Well, you look tired, it's true, but you don't look awful. That's not possible for you."

Eva sipped her coffee without responding. Clearly, Sebastian was to take the lead.

"How is university? Do you like it? I'm glad you decided to go." He was babbling. She made him nervous..

"Is that why you sidelined me? For small talk?"

"I just want to make sure you're okay."

"Why wouldn't I be okay?"

Sebastian pushed back from the table. She wasn't bending. This was a waste of time. He became aware of a growing din of chatter from a nearby table.

"It's him."

"No, he's in jail."

"No. He's not anymore. It's him."

"Is that the girl? Are they back together?"

Eva stood. "I have to go."

Sebastian stepped ahead to open the door for her and followed her out. "I'm sorry about that."

"Yeah," she muttered. "Occupational hazard, I guess."

Sebastian let out a breath of frustration. He'd hoped to soften Eva up a little, but instead she just proved her immunity to him.

His phone buzzed in his pocket. He read the message and stopped short.

"Is everything okay?" Eva asked.

"It's my sister. My dad's had a setback. They've taken him to the hospital."

Eva's face softened a little. "I hope he's all right."

"No. He's dying."

"I'm sorry."

"Yeah. Me too." Sebastian took a reluctant step back. "I have to go."

"Of course."

"Good-bye, Eva."

"Good-bye."

ANNETTE REFUSED to answer her phone or respond to Eva's texts. Eva lay on her bed feeling sick with remorse. She'd done a terrible thing. Annette had been a steadfast friend when so many others had fallen away and Eva never even hesitated to trample on her friend's feelings. Just for a stupid kiss. She wiped at her mouth with the memory of it.

The daylight in her room turned to gray and then black as the winter night pushed away the late afternoon. Eva didn't bother to turn on her lamp. She lay still as the dimness shrouded her wishing she could disappear with the light. Self-loathing cloaked her as she stared at the outline on the wall where the poster of Sebastian used to hang. She wished she could turn the clock back to the days before she'd known what it was like to fall deeply in love— only to be torn violently away. Crushing on Sebastian Weiss was child's play in comparison to the burden of love and the hate she now bore.

Sebastian was forever gone from her life, but she couldn't stand to lose Annette's friendship, too. How could she be so stupid and so selfish?

The next day Eva arrived on campus with a bouquet of flowers in her hand. She needed something to get Annette's attention, and she knew her friend like blossoms.

"Annette!" she called when she spotted her mane of red hair. Annette stopped and narrowed her eyes. "Did Xavier give those to you?"

"*No.* No, *I* bought them. For you." She handed them with an outstretched hand. "Please. Let me apologize."

Annette took the flowers, then folded her arms over her chest. She peered down her nose at Eva. "You knew I liked him."

"I'm sorry. It was a terrible thing for me to do." Eva pleaded, "Annette, your friendship means more to me than any guy. I'm so, so sorry I hurt you. I really didn't believe I was capable of something like that."

Annette tilted her head. "Capable of inflicting pain on someone else?"

Eva heard what Annette was saying under the question. For so long she had been the afflicted one. "Just say you'll forgive me."

"You're asking me to give you something you're refusing to give away yourself."

Eva swallowed. "I know."

A nearby door burst open, and a rush of students flooded the hallway. Eva and Annette spotted the back of Xavier's dark head at the same time and stared long and hard as he strolled down the hall away from them, shoulder to shoulder with a tall, slender girl whose long, blond hair draped down her back. He bumped into her gently and whatever he said made her laugh.

"He's a player," Annette said with a frown.

Eva choked back bile. She couldn't believe she'd fallen for his act. She couldn't believe she'd let him kiss her. "I'm such an idiot."

"Yeah," Annette agreed. "So am I." She took a hesitant step toward Eva and slowly wrapped her arms around her. "Boys suck."

Tears of relief erupted from Eva's eyes. "Yes, they do."

FORGIVENESS

SEBASTIAN FINALLY ADMITTED to himself that working at the soup kitchen in an effort to get close to Eva had been a bad idea. Not only was he not able to restore any level of friendship, but his presence had also created a wedge between her and her family. The last thing he wanted to do was to make life harder for her.

After visiting his father in the hospital, Sebastian made a couple calls, and his lawyer was able to arrange a change in venue for his community service. Starting tomorrow he'd be mopping halls at the hospital. At least he'd be able to see his papa each time. The elder Herr Weiss wasn't doing well. His skin was gray and veiny and he had permanent tubes running from his nose and an IV in his arm.

Sebastian pulled Herr Baumann aside when he arrived to let him know about the change.

Herr Baumann's bushy eyebrows burrowed to a V. "I'm sorry to hear that you're leaving us. You're an excellent worker." The older man rested a hand on Sebastian's shoulder and smiled. "I've grown fond of you."

Sebastian laughed. "Likewise. But Eva is uncomfortable with my being here. For her sake I've decided to leave."

"I understand. Her heart… everyone deals with pain and loss in their own way. I'm sure she'll come around eventually."

Sebastian wasn't so sure. At any rate, the plan was in

motion and this was his last day at the soup kitchen. He'd miss hanging out with the folks who came in from the cold. He was surprised at how much he actually liked their company, and how good it felt to give back to the community in this way. He couldn't imagine that working as a janitor at the hospital would have the same rewards.

The time came to unlock the door, and Sebastian waved in the crowd that had formed outside. "Come in, come in. It's cold out there!" he said with a smile.

He was greeted in return with several choruses of "Hi, Bastian."

The folks settled into the empty chairs in the room. Some were regulars and claimed the same seats. There were a few new faces. The new ones usually gravitated to the back and avoided eye contact. Sebastian made an extra effort to make them feel comfortable. "Welcome," he said. "I'm Bastian." He never introduced himself as Sebastian because he didn't want to chance that people would make the connection. He heard a guitar strum and assumed it was Jörg getting ready to begin the pre-meal music. His jaw dropped when he turned and saw Eva sitting on the stool. She didn't look away when their gazes met, and he wondered how long she'd been there, How long she'd been watching him.

Eva hadn't played once since Sebastian started working there, and he felt more than a little confused as to why she showed up today—especially after their less than friendly meeting the day before.

He expected her to scowl and ignore him, but her eyes were soft and her lips actually hinted at a smile. His heart jerked in his chest as he tried to process.

Herr Baumann opened in prayer and Eva sang a short list of songs he'd recognized from when Jörg played, though Eva's versions were drastic improvements. Sebastian was mesmerized by her presence on stage and lassoed by her voice. It was customary to applaud after each song and Sebastian didn't hold back. He felt his lips tug up as he drank her in. She caught him grinning and smiled in return. A real, bona fide smile!

What was going on?

When she finished singing, he approached her tentatively. He clearly remembered her telling him that she didn't want to see him, but he couldn't let this opportunity pass.

"Hi," he said

"Hi."

"Nice set. I miss hearing you sing."

She buckled the guitar case shut and looked up at him from under her dark lashes, a move that made his knees quiver. "Thanks. I've missed playing."

She didn't tell him to shove off, so that was a good sign.

"I'm surprised to see you here," he added.

"I'm surprised myself."

Her demeanor was completely altered from the day before. Her eyes were kinder and her lips relaxed.

Sebastian snapped himself back to attention. He had to stop looking at her lips!

"Well, good to see you again," he said, taking backward steps toward the kitchen.

"Sebastian?"

Sebastian stopped. Eva waved him back and he took the three steps needed to return to her side. "Yeah?"

"I want to apologize for how I treated you yesterday. It was uncalled for and I'm sorry."

Sebastian scratched his head and gazed back at her, questioningly. "Accepted, though no apology is necessary. I'm the one in need of forgiveness."

Eva's eyelids fluttered, and her knuckles whitened as

she gripped her cane. "Yes, I'm aware of the situation. You are in need of forgiveness and I am in need of the ability to forgive. It's not easy, but I want to do it."

"Thank you, Eva. You can't know how much that means to me."

She nodded and grabbed her coat. Sebastian stepped up quickly to help her put it on. He inhaled deeply the scent of her shampoo, thankful that he had one last chance to stand this close to her.

She stiffened slightly at his touch but didn't pull away. He stepped back, not wanting to push his luck.

"Maybe I'll see you tomorrow?" she said politely.

Sebastian shook his head. "It's my last day."

Eva's eyes widened with surprise. "I thought you had another six weeks."

"I do, but I'm serving them at the hospital. That way I can be closer to my father."

"Oh. Of course. How is he?"

"Not well, but he's still with us."

Sebastian sensed her awkwardness. "I should get back to work. Don't want to slack off on my last day." He saluted her. "Maybe I'll see you around."

STRAIGHT TO MY HEART

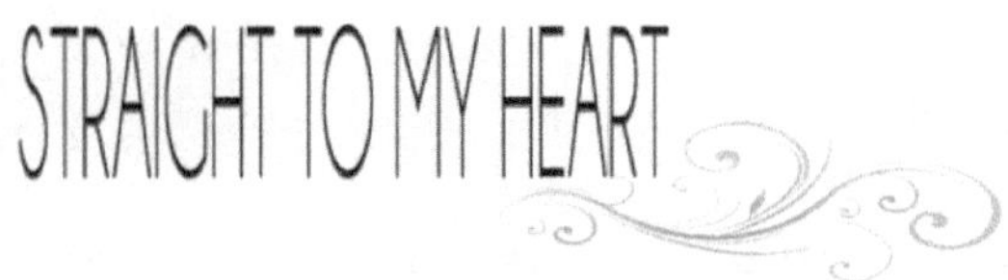

FORGIVING SOMEONE DIDN'T MEAN that what they did was okay. When Annette said she forgave Eva, she wasn't saying what Eva did was okay. Dismissing Annette's feelings by kissing Xavier wasn't okay. Just like what Sebastian did by fleeing the scene of an accident would never be okay.

So what did forgiveness mean? Why did Eva care if Annette forgave her or not? Why did Annette extend it? A lot of girls wouldn't have.

These were things that Eva pondered as she played for the homeless people in the street church. She'd been coming regularly over the last few weeks when her school schedule allowed, and it felt good. She missed singing and performing. She missed playing her guitar.

And she found that she missed Sebastian. Though her time with him at the street church only overlapped once, she could still imagine him standing in the corner, watching her with such intensity it made her feel like gelatin.

For the first time in months, reflecting on Sebastian Weiss didn't cause a boulder-size lump to swell in her chest. It didn't make the muscles in her neck tighten until the base of her skull throbbed. It didn't make her feel like she'd been bound by wire and hung from a line.

Today, when she thought about Sebastian, she felt... light, serene.

Was this what forgiveness did? All this time she thought Sebastian would be the only one to benefit from an offer of forgiveness, but Eva was starting to see that she was the primary benefactor.

She was just about to start her set when the door opened with a blast of cold and Sebastian walked in. Her heart stammered to a stop when he smiled at her with a shy nod. She couldn't bring herself to smile back.

Some of the regulars recognized him and called him over. "Bastian, we missed you!"

Sebastian shook the hands of each person at the table. "Missed you guys, too."

Eva wondered why he came. Not to work, obviously. To see the people he'd come to know. To see her?

The feelings swirling through her heart and mind were too complicated to assess in the moment. She closed her eyes and let herself hide in the music. Between songs, she'd peek out, and every single time Sebastian caught her looking at him. The corner of his mouth pulled up to one side and when she finished her last song he winked.

Her papa approached him, and they shook hands and smiled in a relaxed manner Eva never thought she'd see between them in a million years. Sebastian said something that made her papa laugh, and he patted Sebastian on the back.

Eva's stomach turned to goo. She felt like the world had turned upside down in a day and it made her dizzy. Sebastian stood in line with the homeless and accepted a bowl of soup and a bun. Eva did the same, choosing a seat two tables away. Far enough to not look like she wanted to be near him, but close enough that she could hear what he was saying.

The truth slammed into her. She did want to be near him.

She made polite small talk with a woman at her table who was continually interrupted by two young children. It gave Eva opportunity to eavesdrop on Sebastian. He was listening to a middle-aged man with salt-and-pepper hair tell his life story. Sebastian paid attention like he really cared. Eva believed he did.

Because, she realized, Sebastian was a good person. In many ways, a better one than she.

 YOUR LOVE IS SWEET

THERE WAS no mistaking that petite form with the stilted gait. Sebastian watched her through the dim light of his flat, standing back far enough from the window that, should she glance up and look, she wouldn't see him staring down at her.

He wondered where she was going and couldn't think of any place nearby that would account for her having to take his road to get there. He was more than a little surprised when she stopped in front of his building. She stood there staring at the door and finally reached up and pressed the buzzer.

Though Sebastian knew she had to be there for him, he still jumped at the sound. He sprinted to the button by his door and pressed it.

"Who is it?" he asked, though he knew it was Eva. He didn't want her to know he'd been watching.

"It's Eva."

Sebastian opened the door to his flat and waited for her. He felt pensive yet intrigued. "This is a surprise," he said. "Come in."

Eva smiled at him weakly. Her hair was tucked under a cap, and she had a purple scarf around her neck. Her cheeks and nose were rosy red from the early spring chill, and Sebastian had to bite his cheek to keep from grinning at how cute she was.

"Can I take your coat?"

"No, that's okay. I won't be staying long."

Disappointing. And ominous.

"Something to drink?"

Eva's hands went to her narrow throat and she swallowed dryly. "Water would be nice."

She took a seat in the chair she usually sat in when she used to come to write with him, in what felt like another lifetime. Sebastian sat across from her and placed two glasses of water on the coffee table. Eva's hand trembled slightly as she sipped hers, and Sebastian wondered what he could do to ease her nerves.

"Is everything all right?" he asked.

"Yes. Fine."

Sebastian waited, and the quiet between them felt like a cement wall, one he had to wait for Eva to climb.

"I'm always glad to see you," he said, hoping to prod her a little. "But I'm unsure of my role here. Is there something you need from me?"

She inhaled deeply. "I just need you to listen."

"I'm all ears."

Eva stared down at her hands clasped in her lap. "I have something to say and it's long and I just ask that you don't say anything until I'm finished. Agreed?"

Sebastian's own nerves were soaring. Whatever she came here to say, he wanted to hear it. "Agreed."

"I used to be outgoing, carefree," Eva began timidly. "A little reckless even. I had friends. We'd go hiking and biking, swimming. Hang out at the mall. Talk about boys and music and boys and school gossip. And boys." She paused and her lips pulled up in amusement.

"There was one I really liked a lot, Benni, and I thought he liked me. I used to entertain myself with long daydreams about our fairytale wedding." She scrunched her face, feeling embarrassed. "I was fifteen. It was what girls did.

"All that changed after the accident."

Sebastian stiffened at the word, *accident*, but remained still.

Eva continued, "I spent so much time in the hospital, I fell behind in school, my friends had moved on. Benni got a serious girlfriend.

"I felt weak and unattractive. I was embarrassed by my leg and preoccupied with my pain. Not just the physical pain in my body, but also the emotional pain of being left behind and forgotten.

"Except by Annette. She was the only one who went out of her way to stay my friend, and I didn't make it easy for her. I teetered on the edge of a dark, emotional pit, but she wouldn't let go. She wouldn't let me fall."

Eva paused, and Sebastian witnessed a myriad of emotions pass over her face.

"And a little while ago, I did something awful to her," Eva said. "I was thoughtless and selfish, and I hurt her." Eva bit down on her trembling lower lip, and Sebastian held back from reaching out for her. He didn't know if that was what she wanted—if she wanted him to touch her.

"Annette is everything good, and I don't deserve her friendship. But she forgave me. So easily. She's the one who challenged me to forgive you."

Sebastian cleared his throat, but Eva held up her hand before he could speak. "You said you'd wait."

Sebastian shifted back and kept his mouth shut. Eva took a moment to remove her jacket. Good, she was staying for a little while, at least. Sebastian watched her carefully, listening.

"I wanted to forgive you, I really did, but there was this mountain of pain in my heart and grief over what I felt I'd lost. But I had a revelation recently. I don't think I would've liked the person I would have become if it hadn't been for the accident. I saw what I was capable of, Sebastian, and I didn't like it. For the first time I'm starting to recognize that maybe the accident didn't just rob me of things, but maybe… maybe it gave me something, too.

"Without the accident I wouldn't have written "The Water Song." I wouldn't have had to battle anything, or known what it was like to conquer. I wouldn't have met you."

Tears were flowing freely at this point, and Sebastian couldn't stand it anymore. He ran to the bathroom and returned with a roll of toilet paper. "Sorry. I don't have any tissues."

Eva laughed through her sobbing and blew in a very unladylike manner. "I must look a mess."

Sebastian shook his head slowly. "No. You're more beautiful than ever."

"*Shh*," she said lightly. "I'm not finished. Where was I?"

"You wouldn't have met me."

"Sebastian, I wouldn't have met you. That night at the Blue Note, everything that led up to my being there and singing that song, it wouldn't have happened. I would've been this mean girl and I wouldn't have fallen in love with you."

Sebastian's heart stopped. Did she just say what he thought she said? Every fiber of his being was tense and heated as he waited for the rest.

"For the first time since the accident, I'm actually *thankful* for it."

Sebastian let out a breath. "Eva."

"Wait." She smiled. "There's more. I'm here to ask you to forgive me. I was unkind and thoughtless. I treated you horribly."

"I committed a crime. I left you," Sebastian said. "I'll never forgive myself for that."

"You must. It's the only way I will forgive you. And you want my forgiveness, don't you?"

His lips twitched. "More than anything."

"I love you, Sebastian."

He was on his knees in front of her, gripping her hands. "Can I speak now? Please?"

She smirked and nodded.

"I love you, too, Eva. So much." He kissed her knuckles and the palm of her hands, overwhelmed with gratitude and something close to shock at this unexpected turn of events. He reached for her face, tracing her jaw until his hand wove through her hair to the back of her neck. His lips gently touched hers, and she responded eagerly, desperate and thirsty. She ran her soft cheek along his rough one, her tears blending with his as they both wept. They were survivors. They were in love. Sebastian scooped her up like she weighed nothing and carried her to the sofa.

He held her beside him, careful of her leg. He pressed his lips into her hair. "I just want to hold you. Is that okay?"

She wrapped her arms around his neck in response.

He whispered in her ear, "I can't believe you came back to me."

"I can't believe you want me back."

He squeezed her tighter. "I so want you back. You're mine now. Deal?"

She giggled into his chest. "Deal."

WHERE I'D NEVER BEEN BEFORE

EVA HATED HOSPITALS. The bright lights, the squishy sounds the nurses' shoes made, the antiseptic cleaner that didn't quite mask the scent of sickness that permeated the halls. All of it triggered bad memories, and she stuttered to a stop in the lobby.

Sebastian squeezed her hand. "Are you okay?"

She forced a smile. She knew it would be tough on her when he asked her to come, and she'd said yes. No way would she back out now. "I'm fine."

The off-white paint on the elevator doors was scratched in places where stretchers and wheelchairs had banged into it—janitors with their overstocked carts, kitchen staff with food trolleys.

"My mother and sister are coming," Sebastian said, breaking the silence between them. He'd mentioned this already, but Eva didn't point it out. Obviously, he was nervous.

Which just made her more nervous.

They exited the elevator and moved down the hallway until they came to a private room, number 36B and Sebastian gave her another uneasy grin.

"We don't have to do this," Eva said.

"I want to. I want him… I want them to meet you."

Eva thought coffee and cake at Sebastian's flat would've been a more relaxed setting, but his father wasn't well enough to leave the hospital. Sebastian had told her he probably wouldn't be coming home again.

When Eva stepped into the room, her eyes skipped over the strangers to the IV pole and the monitor equipment. For an instant, she was the one with the tubes running from her arms and her nose. Her blood plummeted to her feet, and she gripped Sebastian's arm to keep from fainting.

"Eva?"

Get a grip!

"I'm fine."

A well-dressed middle-aged woman with greying brunette hair stood next to a younger version of herself.

"Mama, Leah," Sebastian started, "This is Eva. Eva, my mother and sister."

"Pleased to meet you," Frau Weiss said. Her handshake was dry and firm.

"Hello," his sister added.

"Nice to meet you both," Eva said.

There was a moment of awkwardness when they took in her cane and registered that she was the girl Sebastian had hit and the reason he had been arrested.

Herr Weiss grunted from his position on the bed. "I'm not dead yet," he muttered gruffly. "Let me see the girl."

Eva's eyes widened with trepidation, but Sebastian grinned and shook his head. "His bark is worse than his bite."

Herr Weiss smiled when his eyes landed on Eva. "So you're the reason my son's been in such a good mood these last few days."

"I hope so."

The four of them stood around Sebastian's father's prostrate form, quiet like they were at a wake and not a hospital with the man still quite alive. Eva wondered if she should say something but her mind was completely blank.

Finally, Frau Weiss broke the quiet. "Sebastian tells us you're a student?"

"Yes. I'm in my first year."

"What are you going to major in?"

"Art History and Music."

Eva felt the stares of Sebastian's mother and sister on her. When she glanced at them, their gazes darted away. *These are the people who ostracized Sebastian for pursuing music.*

"Eva's an excellent musician and singer-songwriter," Sebastian added.

"How nice," Frau Weiss responded politely.

Leah was more straightforward. "I'm surprised you're with Sebastian again, after, you know."

Frau Weiss reprimanded, "Leah!"

"It's true," Leah continued, undaunted. "Not many girls would. I have to commend you."

Eva wasn't sure how to respond to that.

"No one knows the truth to that more than me," Sebastian said, draping an arm over Eva's shoulder protectively.

Herr Weiss coughed and all eyes turned apprehensively to him. "I'm on my death bed so you need to pay attention to me."

"There's no danger in that not happening," Frau Weiss said without smiling.

Herr Weiss ignored her jab. "It's time I owned my faults. I was wrong, son. If music makes you happy, if this little girl makes you happy, then I bless you to pursue both. You only live once."

Frau Weiss's frown deepened but she didn't challenge

or contradict her husband. Eva wondered if the elder Weiss had wished he'd done things differently.

Sebastian rubbed his chin and cleared his throat. "We have to go now, Papa, but I'll come again soon." He patted his father's hand, then walked around the bed to give his mother a quick hug.

He nodded to Leah. "See you later."

"Bye, lovebirds."

"That was awkward," Sebastian said once out of earshot.

"Your sister's nice," Eva said.

Sebastian chuckled. "My mother's a tough nut to crack. It'll take time to warm up to her. But my papa… has changed." He slowed to catch her eye. "It means a lot to me that you got to meet him."

"I'm glad I came." She was. Another fear—hospitals— faced and conquered.

They rode a taxi back into the *Neustadt*. "Do you want to do something tonight?" Sebastian asked. He gazed down on her like he was afraid he was asking too much. Eva had made it clear that they needed to take things slow and already in just a few short days, she'd met the family.

But she wanted to see him again. She wasn't ready to say good-bye for the day. "Okay."

Sebastian let out a breath like he was surprised, but he didn't want to scare her by showing it. "What do you feel like doing?"

"Let's go to the Blue Note."

"Really?"

"Really."

Now he stood in their living room conversing comfortably with her parents and Eva had to shake her head and grin. She never thought she'd see the day when her mama and papa would approve of her dating Sebastian Weiss.

He was still on house arrest, which meant they couldn't go far, but the Blue Note was within range and in walking distance. She hadn't been there in forever. Plus, she had a surprise.

Sebastian rested his arm over her shoulder and opened an umbrella over their heads. Eva leaned into him, carefully navigating the damp sidewalk with her cane.

Sebastian shook the rain off the umbrella before collapsing it as they entered the pub. Maurice greeted them with a hearty hello.

"Thanks again for letting Hollow Fellows rehearse here," Sebastian said as he shook his hand.

"Hey, it's not being used in the mornings anyway, so why not."

He pointed to an empty table in the corner and winked at Eva as she walked by. "So good to see you smiling again, *ma Cherie.*"

They ordered beer and appetizers and watched as the house band played.

"They're not bad," Sebastian said.

"They'd probably die if they could see that you were in the house."

"Best if I keep in the shadows. It's been nice being out of the spotlight for a while. I hope to make that last as long as possible."

The band ended their song and Eva and Sebastian looked up to see Maurice at the mic.

"It's not open mic night, but the band has agreed to do me a personal favor and allow a friend of mind to come up to do one song. Please welcome Eva Baumann."

Sebastian gave Eva a confused look.

"Just wait," is all she said.

The crowd applauded politely as she made her way to the front. She had planned ahead and had her papa deliver her Duncan Africa for her earlier that evening.

"Hello, everyone," she said as she strapped on her guitar. "Thanks to the band for letting me hi-jack their set. Yes, give it up for the band." She waved her arm and the audience erupted in appreciative applause.

"This is a new song," Eva continued. "I hope you like it."

She stared at the dark corner where she knew Sebastian sat. "This is for you."

You went out of your way
I went out of my head
I shut you out
You pursued me instead
It took some time
But you knew from the start
I'd open the door
And you'd go straight into my heart

She was tempted to close her eyes, but she kept them steadied on the corner shadow. Pressing through her nerves, she sang out:

Your love is sweet
Just what I need

You have won me over
To my surprise
I realized
You had won me over
You have won me over

Heart to heart
A good head start
And it flew from there
You took me where I'd never been before
Truth for truth
That's when I fell for you
Love came down
And took me higher
Than I'd been before

Your love is sweet
Just what I need
You have won me over
To my surprise
I realized
You had won me over
You have won me over

The song ended, and a surprised crowd watched Sebastian Weiss jump on stage, carefully remove Eva's guitar and spin her around.

Eva squealed. "Does that mean you like it?"

He smiled. "I love it. And I love you." He kissed her, and the room around her disappeared into the brightness of the lights. Somewhere in the peripheral, the audience cheered.

"That's Sebastian Weiss! Hey, Sebastian!"

She pulled back and laughed. "Your cover's blown."

"This…" He kissed her again. "Is worth it."

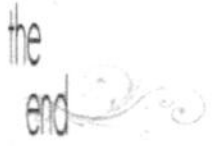

If you enjoyed reading *Your Love is Sweet*, please help others enjoy it too.

Lend it: This ebook is lending-enabled, so please share with a friend.

Recommend it: Help others find the book by recommending it to friends, readers' groups, discussion boards and by suggesting it to your local library.

Review it: Please tell other readers why you liked this book by reviewing it at Amazon.

Want more A Light & Love Sweet Romance?

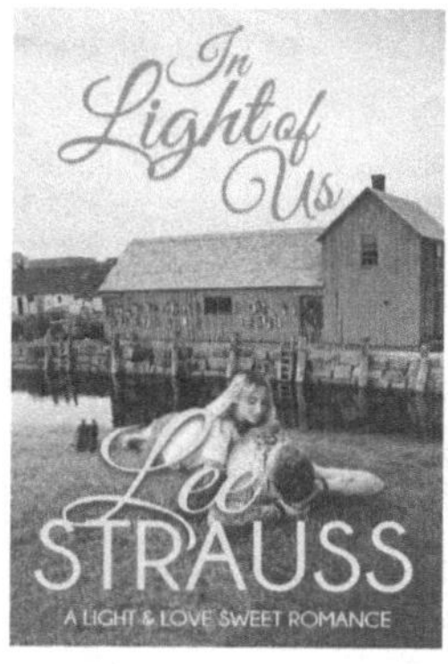

In Light of Us
Book 3 in A Light & Love Romance

Read on for chapter 1 of IN LIGHT OF US!

MEET GINGER GOLD

If you like your sweet romance mixed with a light-hearted mystery, I invite you to give my new cozy mystery series a try.

The Ginger Gold Mystery series is a fun, 1920s era romp featuring thirty-year-old fashionista war widow Ginger Gold.

To make sure you don't miss the next new release, be sure to sign up for Lee's readers' list and get 4 FREE short stories!

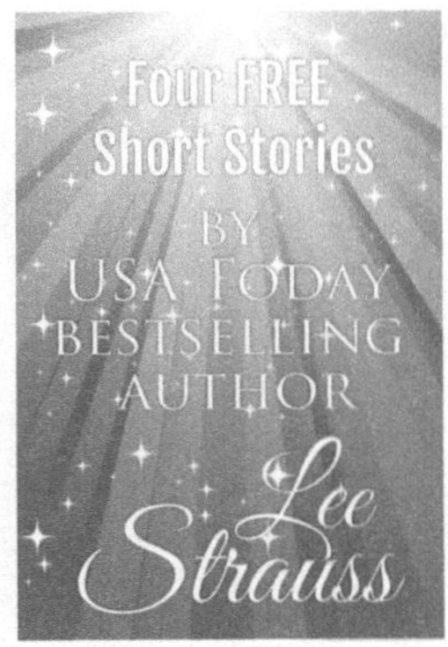

https://www.leestraussbooks.com/subscribe-four-free/

ABOUT THE AUTHOR

Lee Strauss is the bestselling author of the Ginger Gold Mysteries series and the Higgins & Hawke Mystery series (cozy historical mysteries), a Nursery Rhyme Mystery series (mystery, sci-fi, young adult), the Perception Trilogy (YA dystopian mystery), the Light & Love series (sweet romance) and young adult historical fiction. When she's not writing or reading, she likes to cycle, hike, and kayak. She loves to drink caffè lattes and red wines in exotic places, and eat dark chocolate anywhere.

Lee also writes younger YA fantasy as Elle Lee Strauss.

For more info on books by Lee Strauss and her social media links, visit leestraussbooks.com. To make sure you don't miss the next new release, be sure to sign up for her readers' list!

Did you know you can follow your favourite authors on Bookbub? If you subscribe to Bookbub — (and if you don't, why don't you? - They'll send you daily emails alerting you to sales and new releases on just the kind of books you like to read!) — follow me to make sure you don't miss the next Ginger Gold Mystery!

www.leestraussbooks.com
leestraussbooks@gmail.com

BOOKS BY LEE STRAUSS

On AMAZON

Ginger Gold Mysteries (cozy 1920s historical)

Cozy. Charming. Filled with Bright Young Things. This Jazz Age murder mystery will entertain and delight you with its 1920s flair and pizzazz!

Murder on the SS *Rosa*

Murder at Hartigan House

Murder at Bray Manor

Murder at Feathers & Flair

Murder at the Mortuary

Murder at Kensington Gardens

Murder at St. Georges Church

Murder Aboard the Flying Scotsman

Murder at the Boat Club

Murder on Eaton Square

Murder by Plum Pudding

Murder at Fleet Street

Lady Gold Investigates (Ginger Gold companion short stories)

Volume 1

Volume 2

Volume 3

Higgins & Hawke Mysteries (cozy 1930s historical)

The 1930s meets Rizzoli & Isles in this friendship depression era cozy mystery series.

Death at the Tavern

Death on the Tower

Death on Hanover

A Nursery Rhyme Mystery (mystery/sci fi)

Marlow finds himself teamed up with intelligent and savvy Sage Farrell, a girl so far out of his league he feels blinded in her presence - literally - damned glasses! Together they work to find the identity of @gingerbreadman. Can they stop the killer before he strikes again?

Gingerbread Man

Life Is but a Dream

Hickory Dickory Dock

Twinkle Little Star

The Perception Trilogy (YA dystopian mystery)

Zoe Vanderveen is a GAP—a genetically altered person. She lives in the security of a walled city on prime water-front property along side other equally beautiful people with extended life spans. Her brother Liam is missing. Noah Brody, a boy on the outside, is the only one who can help ~ but can she trust him?

Perception

Volition

Contrition

Light & Love (sweet romance)

*Set in the dazzling charm of Europe, follow Katja, Gabriella, Eva, Anna
and Belle as they find strength, hope and love.*

Sing me a Love Song

Your Love is Sweet

In Light of Us

Lying in Starlight

Playing with Matches (WW2 history/romance)

*A sobering but hopeful journey about how one young Germany boy copes with
the war and propaganda. Based on true events.*

As Elle Lee Strauss

The Clockwise Collection (YA time travel romance)

*Casey Donovan has issues: hair, height and uncontrollable trips to the 19th
century! And now this ~ she's accidentally taken Nate Mackenzie, the cutest
boy in the school, back in time. Awkward.*

Clockwise

Clockwiser

Like Clockwork

Counter Clockwise

Clockwork Crazy

Standalones

Seaweed

Love, Tink

IN LIGHT OF US
CHAPTER 1

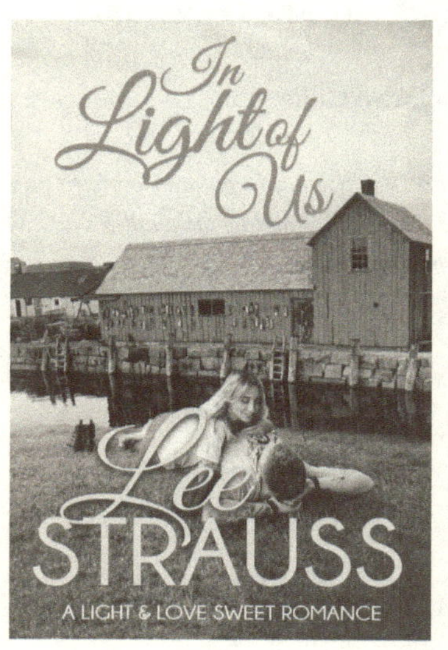

GABRIELE BAUMANN-SMITH IS DELIRIOUSLY *in love with her young husband, Lennon.*

Except, as it turns out, Lennon Smith isn't his real name. In fact, he's full of secrets: a cottage in a southern coastal town of England, an old girlfriend… an identical twin brother.

Callum Jones—not his real name—can't believe his brother's widow came to England. He'd warned Mick—Lennon—that an inheritance could put the girl's life in danger, and he was right.

"Mrs. Smith" is the last thing he needs to worry about right now. She's beautiful, sure, takes his breath away at times. But when she looks at him who does she see?

Gabriele's heart is battered and bruised. Can one brother fix what the other left behind? And will they live long enough to find out?

THE HAPPY COUPLE

GABRIELE BAUMANN-SMITH.

Frau Smith.

Lennon and Gabriele Smith.

Mr. and Mrs. Smith.

She was a married woman!

Gabriele grinned down at her super gorgeous husband as he lay bare-chested under a white sheet on a warm late September evening. He threaded his fingers together and wrapped them behind his head exposing nicely-toned arms, and unabashedly watched her through messy, almost black hair that fell across dark eyes. Wearing pink boy-cut panties and a grey cotton tank-top, Gabriele hopped on the bed, her laptop in hand, and sat cross-legged beside him.

"The photographer finally sent us our pictures," she said with a happy lilt to her voice, and flipped the laptop open. Its base warmed her bare legs as it whirled to life.

Lennon closed his eyes. "Don't be too disappointed. Pictures are never as good as the real thing."

"But this photographer came highly recommended." Gabriele clicked on the appropriate links and downloaded the files. "And I paid her good money." She held in a squeal. She was so excited to see these. Their wedding day had been perfect. Well, if she conveniently forgot about the tiny black mark put there by her drama causing sister, Eva, and her famous boyfriend.

The laptop screen filled with thumbprint-sized icons and Gabriele clicked on the slideshow. She snuggled in close to Lennon. "Here we go!"

The first few shots were of the gathering crowds in the park on Drie König Strasse. Some captured the black clock tower of Three Kings Church that poked the sunny, late August blue sky. Gabriele recognized almost everyone. She zoomed in on the faces of her childhood friends, family friends, and distant relatives.

"There's Onkel Alphonse and Tante Ruth. They came all the way from Freiberg. It was so good to see them again." A wave of sadness filled her when she recalled that Lennon wouldn't be able to pick out a familiar face. The whole ceremony had been for her sake since Lennon hadn't any family, something Gabriele found hard to imagine. He was an only child of only children. She almost burst into tears when he told her about the car wreck his parents died in. No wonder he didn't want to go back to England.

Lennon would've been happy to have had a simple civil ceremony with just the Baumann family present. "The honeymoon is the part I'm looking forward to," he'd said with a mischievous grin, but he gave in, somewhat begrudgingly, so she could have her own fairytale wedding.

The next several shots were of her in the upper room. Pre-service close-ups— her hair had been expertly styled with a fat rod curling iron, and decorated with diamond-like zirconia pins that reflected the lighting. Her chiffon gown draped beautifully along her body landing delicately on the grey tiled floor.

The next collection of photos was of her friends fussing over her. Julia looked like a movie star with her short-dark hair pinned and curled, and with all that make-up on, Gabriele barely recognized her. There were a couple of Eva standing demurely nearby. She wore a lovely sage-green satin dress with daring, spaghetti strap sleeves. Daring for her anyway. Her long, straight, milk chocolate brown hair was curled and pulled into an up-do. She looked beautiful, yet pensive as she leaned on the white cane Gabriele had purchased for her for the occasion.

There were several more of Gabriele as she approached Lennon at the back of the church. The focus was on her, the shots taken from Lennon's perspective, but he wasn't in the frames.

He squeezed her. "What a gorgeous bride!"

Gabriele smiled. "But where are you? I can't even tell you were there."

Lennon nibbled on her arm. "I only remember what came after."

She laughed, but her eyes never left the screen. Finally, a photo with Lennon in it. It was a profile shot of them standing together gazing lovingly at each other. Lennon looked spectacular in his shiny grey suit.

"So handsome," she said. "But your hair is hanging in your face." She had asked him more than once to get a haircut, but he insisted that he liked the longer look.

Shot after shot of the happy couple. A view from behind as they sat in the two chairs in the front of the sanctuary facing her papa as he conducted the ceremony. Many of them kissing.

"Oh, I like those ones," Lennon teased.

Gabriele felt a growing unease. So far she hadn't seen one good shot of both of them. None of Lennon at all.

The slideshow continued. In every single picture Lennon was looking down or behind or had hair in his eyes.

Gabriele huffed. "I don't believe this." She slumped against the pillow and bit her bottom lip. Disappointment was a black balloon in her chest. "Not even one picture of us worthy to hang on the wall!"

Lennon gently lifted the laptop and placed it on the floor beside him. "It's okay, Gabi. We can get more taken later."

Gabriele whimpered and tugged on her short bleach-blond hair. "It's not the same. I just don't understand how this happened. I know she took hundreds of pictures." She stared at Lennon. "How is it possible she missed getting one solid shot of your face?"

A dark look flashed behind Lennon's eyes. It only lasted a split second, but Gabriele hadn't mistaken it. She'd seen it before. Not often, only a few times. So seldom, she'd always pushed her concern away. It didn't mean anything.

It didn't.

Lennon reached over and turned out the light. "Get under the covers, love," he said. "Everything will look better in the morning."

On Amazon!

ACKNOWLEDGEMENTS

So much gratitude and cheer goes to the team! My beta readers, Angelika and Juanita; my online writing community without whom I'd be toast in a major way including The Indelibles, Dauntless Authors, Club Indie; the musical artists who so graciously jumped on board for this project, Trisha Robins, Andrew Smith, Bryan Steeksma and Joel Strauss; my husband and musician/music producer, Norm Strauss whose talent and proximity to me make this series possible; to the Noble Girls for your ongoing support, to my parents for holding down the Canadian fort, my kids for being just plain awesome, and to God who carries me through all things.

SONGS

The Water Song by Andrew Smith

Beyond My Flesh & Bone by Joel Strauss

Sun & Moon (remake) by Bryan Steeksma
Sun & Moon by Joel Strauss

Won Me Over (original) by Trisha Robins

Listen to all the songs from A Light & Love Sweet
Romance on Bandcamp at
songsfromtheminstrel.bandcamp.com

Trisha Robins
www.cdbaby.com/cd/trisharobins

Andrew Smith
www.andrewsmithmusic.com

Bryan Steeksma
www.cdbaby.com/artist/bryansteeksma
www.Facebook.com/pages/bryan-steeksma-fans

Joel Strauss
www.joelstrauss.com
www.joelstrauss.bandcamp.com

FLESH & BONE

Words and music by Joel Strauss. Copyright Joel Strauss. Remake recorded by Trisha Robins. All rights reserved. Used by permission.

THE WATER SONG

Words and music by Andrew and Tami Smith. Copyright Andrew and Tami Smith. Remake recorded by Trisha Robins. All rights reserved. Used by permission.

WON ME OVER

Words and music by Trisha Robins. Copyright Trisha Robins. Remake recorded by Trisha Robins. All rights reserved. Used by permission.

SUN & MOON (remake by Bryan Steeksma)

Words and music by Joel Strauss and Bryan Steeksma. Copyright Joel Strauss and Bryan Steeksma. All rights reserved. Used by permission.